BLAIR M.

Crystal IRIS

I

LEBLON PUBLISHING

Edited by Kristen Hamilton, Kristen Corrects, Inc.
Published in the United States
First Edition

ISBN Ebook: 979-8-9918004-1-9
ISBN Print: 979-8-9918004-0-2

LEBLON PUBLISHING

BlairShadows.com

The content warning can be found at the back of the book to avoid spoilers.

To Edward.
Thank you for never giving up on me.

To artists, historians, and writers.
You make the world a better place.

CRYSTAL IRIS

A WICKED SPICY ROMANTASY SERIES

CRYSTAL IRIS
BOOK ONE

BLAIR M. SHADOWS

LP

LEBLON PUBLISHING

ONE

"THE JOB OF THE ARTIST IS ALWAYS TO DEEPEN
THE MYSTERY." – FRANCIS BACON

Of course, I can't sleep—it's too much. My eyes have been closed for what seems like an eternity now, just waiting for him. How is he still moving? Is he still awake? I have to get up. The day keeps replaying in my head like a broken movie. I have to get up *now*.

I take a deep breath and decide it's time. It's worth the risk; the bed is suffocating.

I make sure to lock the door behind me after grabbing a drink. The bathroom—the only place in this house where I can get some privacy. I can't believe I'll be calling it home. I hate this place. It's like living in an office—no personality, no warmth. I guess I could change things. After all, *I'm going to be living here*.

I step into the scalding hot water and instantly feel better. This giant bathtub isn't so bad. What am I going to do if Aaron knocks on the door right now? I reassure myself that after that many drinks, I could be holding a baby unicorn, and he wouldn't notice or care.

I take another deep breath. Breathing— isn't that what I'm supposed to excel at after a decade of yoga? Why is it so challenging to control the most basic human function? I smile at the only

1

thing that could calm my nerves right now: *whiskey*. Another perk of this place—always a stocked bar. With everyone getting drunk at the party, I'm happy I saved enough space for this. There's a difference between drinking with people and drinking alone. Like everything else, I prefer doing it alone.

As I let the liquid gold work its magic, my mind dives into my past, searching for answers—some insight to explain why my dad decided to show up after all these years. *Seventeen fucking years.* Of course, there's nothing. My fingers toy with the necklace he gave me, turning it over and over. I've never seen anything like it. Obviously, I know it can't be the real thing—there's no way. A diamond this size, almost an inch long, on a delicate gold chain? My parents struggled to make ends meet for as long as I can remember. My mind goes back to all the hand-me-down clothes and toys. Mom stayed home with me while Dad worked in sales. He had good and bad seasons; unfortunately, the bad ones always seemed to last a lot longer. At least we always made rent. I shrug at the memories.

Tears spill down my face, disappearing into the bathwater. Crying on my birthday—classic me. *Then again, it's probably past midnight by now, no longer my birthday at all.*

I reach for my phone to check the time, and my glass slips from my hand and shatters on the floor.

"Shit."

Blood stains the water, and I suck on my finger, sighing heavily. *I want this day to end.* I dunk my head underwater, letting the silence wrap around me. When I resurface, my new necklace catches my eye. It's glowing. Not shining exactly, but there's a light trapped inside the diamond—a soft, pulsing purple. Or violet, as Akira would correct me. I lift it closer, turning it in my hands, searching for an explanation. Nothing. My mouth hangs open as I stare. The spilled drink on the floor is the only proof I'm not drunk.

What kind of diamond does this? What did Akira call it when I sent her the picture earlier? *A prism?* I'm not even sure I know what that is. Math has never been my thing. I count the edges. Five edges—but seven sides? Is there even a name for that shape? Probably something I would know if my parents had been around to help with my homework. I roll my eyes. Anger churns beneath the surface, anger I thought I'd worked through in therapy. Apparently not. Not enough therapy in a lifetime to fix all my bullshit.

My dad's voice slices through me. "You look...beautiful," he said, walking toward me just hours ago. How did he know to be there? Where did he even come from? Did someone invite him to my party? Amid all the questions swirling in my head, all I managed to say was, "Dad?"

To say I was shocked is an understatement. I barely remember the man. My idea of a father is split between hazy memories of a great dad playing with his little girl and the bitter truth that he walked out on his teenage daughter.

"Get out," I said.

And that was it. He nodded, murmuring, "I'm so sorry." He handed me his gift—or rather, my mother's gift—and left. Again.

It took me a while to process that my dad was actually standing in front of me, just like I used to dream about for years. But now, it's too late. *Way too late.* The music from the party pulled me out of my spiraling thoughts, along with the hollow wishes for happiness from people who barely knew me. Most of them were Aaron's friends. We were never going to be friends. It took one look at them to know that. Aside from Akira, Lara, and Ted, you wouldn't even know it was my birthday.

By the time I get out of the water, it's cold. I carefully dry myself, avoiding the broken glass on the floor. The prism's light vanished minutes after it appeared. I stayed in the bath, hoping to see it again. I didn't.

Now, staring at my reflection in the mirror, at my perfectly matching pajamas, one thought claws at my mind: *I'm so tired of being a good girl.*

* * *

The sunlight filters through the trees, bringing the colors to life. Yellow leaves are starting to pile up at my feet, and the brick buildings on campus feel perfectly in tune with the season. October always has a way of lifting my mood—my birthday is simply another perk of the month. Honestly, I've yet to meet anyone who doesn't love autumn. Soon enough, this place will be full of tourists who'll agree with me: Harvard in the fall is as good as it gets.

"Hey! How did it go last night? I mean, after the party," Akira asks, falling into step beside me.

I smile, noticing the coffee cart line is unusually short today. "Oh, you know, nothing too crazy," I reply, eyeing her outfit. "What are you wearing?" Between her tattoos, colorful hair, and chaotic style, I'm surprised she's even allowed on campus.

"Because I'm the best at my shit," she replies, like she read my mind. And she's right. Akira is some kind of astrophysics genius. We met during my first week here and bonded over coffee—always running into each other in this very line. Eventually, we said hello. Now, our friendship revolves around a shared love of Friday-night drinking, dancing at Spiral, and, occasionally, fantasizing about murdering our students.

"Don't change the subject!" she snaps, waving a hand at me. "Nothing crazy, huh? Not even in bed?" She tries to wink, and I can't help but laugh.

"Yeah, I got my birthday dessert," I shoot back with a playful wink, even though I told Aaron I had a massive headache and needed to sleep. He bought it after I blamed it on my father.

"I mean, who wouldn't, with that delicious boyfriend of yours? Shit! Fiancé!" she teases.

I stare at the new ring on my finger, opulent yet so simple compared to the other gift I received yesterday. I swear I can almost feel the prism warming up as I think about it. I lift my gaze in

Akira's direction, but she's already walking away, calling over her shoulder, "Gotta get to class!"

Nothing like the first sip of coffee. I ran out the door this morning, barely exchanging words with Aaron, even though I don't have to be in the classroom until eleven today. I can still see his face when he proposed last night. I knew it would happen eventually. It was the obvious next step. We've been together since we were teens. *The boy next door,* as my grandma used to call him. I wonder if she really thought he lived that close. Aaron lived on the West Side, where all the homes had been remodeled, and I lived on the East Side, where all the homes had been forgotten. Even though we lived on opposite sides of the park, it was an easy cross if you knew the shortcuts. He was there for me when no one else was.

After my mom died, Dad had a rough few years. Then, we had some good months before he left me for good. My grandparents moved in right away, trying to keep some semblance of normalcy in my life by keeping us local. Nothing has been normal since.

Aaron would sneak in after school on most days. We'd watch TV, do our homework, and, of course, make out until it was dinner time and we both had to show our faces to our families. My grandparents were too old to go upstairs; they mostly stayed on the first floor until bedtime, giving me almost full rein of the upper level of the house during the day. That, along with the constant sound of their loud TV, allowed me to grow up faster than most kids my age. Mostly, though, Aaron was there for me—when the anxiety attacks would creep in, when my breathing would get stuck. He was there to rub my back, guiding each inhale and exhale for as long as I needed. He was there when I cried on my birthdays, on Christmas, even at prom. He was the first one I showed my college admission letter to, and even though we went to different schools, we stayed tight.

Turns out, it's very easy to date your best friend. And then keep dating him, *because he loves you.*

I plan to do my research right away since I don't have any papers to grade this morning. After such busy weeks, I welcome the break. If any place has abundant information on prisms, it has to be Harvard's library. I understood nothing from the descriptions I found online. Words like "polyhedron," "base," "second base," and "faces" kept popping up. Although I got the gist—a glass geometric object used to spread out light—what I need to know is: *what the heck was that violet light I saw yesterday in the tub?* I haven't seen it again since. I stared at it in the mirror this morning, hoping it would happen again, like somehow I could turn it on. Now it's merely a beautiful piece of jewelry. I'm starting to wonder if I made the whole thing up.

The library is framed by beautiful large windows on both sides, with a dome ceiling that mimics classical temples. I'm used to getting lost in the maze, but I don't think I've ever made it to this section before—rows and rows of books I have no idea how anyone understands.

I don't ask for help; I don't want to draw attention to myself. I want to avoid the noisy students and the faculty who love to gossip. Does anyone have hobbies anymore? Like, the only reason to be researching anything should be because you're writing a damn paper. What happened to learning for enjoyment?

I fell in love with art history when I was a little girl. Mom, Dad, and I would spend our Sunday mornings at the art museum, like a religious appointment. Dad came because we loved it; I knew it wasn't his passion that brought him there. I remember how my mom could simply stare at something for hours, not realizing that Dad and I were waiting for her to keep moving along. She had an apologetic smile when she'd break the trance and find us looking at her.

After she got sick, Dad kept bringing me. I told him he didn't have to, but he reassured me that he liked it. I knew he did it for her. And after he left me—I was thirteen—I kept the habit. I would find myself there, even when I lied and pretended I was only going to the park. It was my home away from home, a place where I could still feel my parents nearby, happy. Dad and I would make up stories about who the people in the paintings were; sometimes, I imagined I was part of their life too. Especially when everything fell apart. I wanted to escape to those meadows, talk to those people, ask them to take me away.

When senior year came around, I knew the only thing I could imagine myself doing was studying those paintings. Aaron had asked me a few times if I wanted to paint, but I never had the desire. I wanted to understand the hand that created those paintings. I wanted to know what made someone take their time—often a long time—to create such things. What drove them, what pushed them, what fed them. I wanted to know the story behind each artwork, the real story. I became obsessed in college. I didn't have the ambition to become a professor; it was pure passion that led me to rise to the top of my classes.

"Professor De Loughery?" A voice breaks my blank stare.

"Hey, Darion, remember, Iris is just fine."

He's staring at his foot, a little uncomfortable with my directness. Darion is a little taller than me, with dark eyes that hide behind his glasses.

"What are you doing on this side of the building? I hope you're not thinking about changing majors," I ask.

"Just helping a friend."

If I didn't know better, I would say he was probably getting paid to do someone else's work.

"How nice of you," I say.

"What about you?" he asks, giving me an odd look.

"Personal project." Before he can say anything else, I start to walk away. "See you in class."

I gather more books about math than anyone could read in a lifetime. I scan the pages, but nothing explains what I saw in the bathtub last night. I do end up learning an interesting fact: apparently, prisms have been used as early as the thirteenth century to *generate rainbows*. Sunlight looks white to our eyes, although it's actually a mixture of many colors. A prism can be used to refract or disperse a beam of light, separating those colors. Still, you are supposed to see all seven of them, not just one. I'm startled by my phone buzzing—the alarm reminding me that I'm needed in the classroom.

* * *

"Is she pregnant?" Stella asks, a young blonde with a huge canvas bag who always sits in the corner. An artist herself, judging by the spilling contents.

I glance back at Jan van Eyck's iconic portrait of *Giovanni Arnolfini and His Wife*, one of my favorite pieces of art.

"That's a common question, Stella," I say. "Most historians agree she isn't. She's simply holding her large skirts. Young Renaissance women were also encouraged to clasp their hands like that. It was a sign of modesty. The subject of pregnancy is still debatable. Take a look here, at the bed's headboard... This is a wooden statue of Saint Margaret, the patron saint of childbirth. And let's look over here as well, at the window: another symbol, ripened fruit. Everything signals that, if she isn't pregnant—which artists typically avoided depicting, as it was considered improper—she is expected to be soon. What else is her gown telling us?"

"That she is wealthy," Ava says, typing quickly on her laptop.

"Correct. Her ermine-lined gown is proof of her husband's wealth. What else indicates that?"

"The brass chandelier and the oriental carpet," Darion says, still giving me a weird look.

"And the mirror," Stella adds, writing something down.

"Let's take a closer look at the mirror," I say, zooming in on the painting. "We see someone else there, wearing red—that is the artist himself. This mirror has enough details to warrant an entire lecture. I'll be brief now, but we'll discuss it in more depth next week. Around the mirror's wooden frame, we see scenes from the Passion of Christ—it might represent the premise of salvation, or God observing the vows of the wedding. Some believe this painting represents that: matrimony."

"What's with the dog?" Isaac asks.

"The little terrier could symbolize either fidelity or lust, or perhaps a desire for children. It might also be a gift from the husband to his wife. It also reflects the couple's wealth and their position in court. We'll revisit this painting next week. Now, let's hear how the assignment went," I say, closing the image.

"I thought I was going to lose my mind. The time did not pass," Stella says.

"I thought it was relaxing," says Paul, trying a little too hard to be agreeable. I see most of the students roll their eyes.

"I thought it was torture," says Mila, her voice dripping with sarcasm. She's the confident one who doesn't think she needs to be here.

After a few more similar comments, I explain, "The experiment wasn't meant to torture your souls, waste your time, or even put you into a trance—though I'm glad it did some of those things too. The idea was solely to teach you that you do have the time. The time to take your time. I can see the stress in your faces, the fidgeting in your seats. This goes beyond your addiction to screens; it's about the constant pressure to impress others by the sheer volume of things you do. You are now more than ever pressured to take more classes, write more papers, all while opening your own business and becoming millionaires by the age of twenty-five. The artists who created the works you sat in front of for two hours last week took their time, and that's how they achieved mastery. If you learn anything from this assignment, I hope it's the skill to slow down. Appreciate things. *The simple things.* Make room to truly wonder, to sit by a painting for as long as you want. The concept that we all have twenty-four hours is often debatable, yet time disappears when you are truly enjoying yourself." I pause, letting my words settle. Perhaps I needed to hear them more than they did.

I finished the lesson and lingered on campus for a while. There was one thing I was dreading more than facing Aaron when I got home at night: the *letter* that came with the prism.

Two

"LIFE BEATS DOWN AND CRUSHES THE SOUL AND
ART REMINDS YOU THAT YOU HAVE ONE." –
STELLA ADLER

I waited until I was home from the party to open my dad's gift. I wanted to throw the box against the wall, I wanted to yell at it, to tell it to go to hell. Instead, I tugged on the gold ribbon that enclosed the box, and it slid off like silk. My hands shook as I lifted the lid. The note inside read: *For Iris on her thirtieth birthday, not a day earlier, from Mom.* Relief flooded me knowing I didn't just throw it away. *This wasn't from him.* I would treasure whatever it was inside, just like I did with everything I kept from her. We didn't have much, so there wasn't much to keep. I have her favorite coffee mug, a pair of earrings she got from Grandma on her wedding day, and a handful of her favorite novels.

I found the necklace inside a black velvet bag, but it was what lay underneath that took my breath away: *a letter.* If the letter was also from Mom, I couldn't open it. I could barely remember her voice. My childhood videotapes would soon have to be packed up —where were they? It had been a while since I watched them. Only a letter... that was something else. New words from her—my skin tingled at the thought. I had never been more curious in my life. The expectation matched the intensity. Did I want to know what she had to say? What if the letter was actually from Dad? I didn't want to give him the chance to explain himself. For all I knew, it could be a damn receipt inside. Whatever it was, it was best unread.

* * *

A couple of weeks went by, and I let myself forget about the letter, only to be reminded as soon as my head hit the pillow. Dreams and nightmares about all the things the envelope could contain filled my nights.

Aaron cannot stop talking about the wedding. Every day, he adds something new or someone else to the guest list. If it were up to me, we'd simply elope. Only he's always had this need to prove himself to everyone. I cringe at the thought of what's becoming a massive event.

"You should invite George and the department chair lady," he suggests as we order food.

"I don't know them that well," I reply from the couch.

"What about your aunt?"

"Maybe. I'll call her."

Despite the wedding plans, we were having a nice time. Aaron had picked up sushi, and we laughed as we reminisced about our childhoods.

One of my favorite memories was when Aaron bought me a dog for Christmas. I named him Benny; he was a mutt, and I loved him the moment I saw him. He was a little shabby, a little dirty. Turns out, Aaron had just brought a stray dog into my house. I didn't care. Benny was mine. All he wanted was to cuddle in bed, which made it very easy to persuade my grandparents to let me keep him. "As long as nobody claims him, he can stay," Grandpa said that day. And so, Benny did.

Sometimes, like any untrained dog, Benny would get into trouble—chewing on furniture or a shoe. My grandma would blame Aaron and even demanded he pay for the damage once or twice. We never took him to the vet. He never seemed sick. He didn't look like a young dog, but my grandparents assured me he was fine. We couldn't afford a vet anyway. He lived with us for three years and died months before I left for college. I was determined to bring him along, even if I had to hide him in my dorm. Benny took care of me, not the other way around. I grieved him the most. I think my heart was still numb from the loss.

Those are my favorite moments with Aaron—casual nights, just the two of us, talking about the past. *They're rare.* He's turned into a full-blown businessman, constantly attending social events. He followed in his dad's footsteps, taking over the firm, and making it much bigger than his dad ever thought possible. He's always busy, angry, and tired from all the parties. Yet, he says yes to even more events the following week. He's addicted to the lifestyle. He has more friends than I can count, and I can't stomach them for long. I'm always coming up with excuses to avoid the dinners. If Aaron knows they're lies, he doesn't say.

I tell myself there are nice times between us. There could be more. Still, nice doesn't scream marriage, I know that. Even the sex with him has always been...nice. He was my first, but not the only guy I've slept with. We split during our first couple of years in college, only to reconnect after coming home for the holidays. My grandparents moved to a home for the elderly that year. I couldn't believe it when they told me my father had sent a check for that. *What kind of person leaves their family and still pays for things?* I almost asked Aaron to help me track the money, but then again, what could my father say that would matter? He hadn't even shown up for their funeral. Aaron and I have been together since. And the sex has always been that, nice. Much better than with the guys I dated in college. Even so, sometimes I wonder if 'nice' is all that's in the cards for me.

"I love knowing you'll be living here. We can do this every night," he says, pulling out the duvet.

"Tonight, it was nice, staying in," I say, knowing well this won't happen again anytime soon.

"Do you need help packing?" he asks again.

"I don't think so. I like taking my time, going through my stuff. A lot needs to be donated," I say, lying through my teeth.

"Okay. Let me know if you do."

"I will."

"I have to show my face at Arnold's tomorrow. You can join me if you want, but don't feel obligated; the plus-ones weren't exactly invited."

"Okay. I think Akira wanted to do something anyway." Another lie. They roll off my tongue easily these days.

* * *

I struggle to get out of bed—at least it's Friday. I bribe myself with coffee twice just to get going. I never sleep well; my anxiety always finds a way to creep in at night. But I can feel myself extra tense lately. I'm not sure if it's due to the wedding or the prism; both things are constantly on my mind. It's especially during moments like this that I wish I had my mom around to talk to.

I put on the simplest outfit and head to work.

"Remember, you're not being graded today. This is an exercise. I'll pull a different art piece for each of you randomly, and I want you to try to describe it. Let's talk about the time period, the material used. You can talk about the artist if you know it. You can mention the style, describe the subject matter, the symbols you recognize. If time allows, you can bring up meaning; however, let's leave that for last, as it tends to get complicated."

I have to work extra hard to pay attention to what the students are saying; my mind is scattered by the time they're done. I'm in desperate need of a break.

No sign of Akira at the coffee cart.

Coffee? I text her.

Can't right now, Spiral tonight? she replies.

Aaron has plans. Anything to avoid his stupid dinner. Still, there's a hint of guilt as I text her back, *Sure*. I know it would make him look better if I went to those events, especially now that we're engaged. I won't be able to avoid them forever, and a part of me thinks he deserves better.

* * *

It's a crisp night, and I wish I had waited a little longer before getting out of the cab. I'm meeting Akira at the corner of Melrose and Fayette. As I wait, I eye the long line of people waiting to get in. Spiral isn't a large club, yet somehow, all of those people will fit inside. We know the guys at the door by now, so we don't have to wait. Still, I always feel weird skipping the lines. I can hear the usual words shouted from strangers watching us enter: "slut," "whore," and "bitch" among them.

Akira is wearing leather pants and a shirt that leaves her stomach exposed. With her body, I would too. From behind, you can see a couple of her tattoos. Her hair is loose, strands of different colors catching the light. She's hot. And all the guys around notice. I envy her confidence—she doesn't hide behind any masks—not the professor one, not even the genius one. She owns herself with such ease, it's hard not to compare.

I opted for my usual combo of jeans and a tank top. My inherited red hair is in a top bun, mostly for lack of time. It took me an hour to do my makeup with the new eyeliner I decided to try out. I broke a sweat getting both eyes even.

"Can you believe that guy?" she asks, gesturing to a young man blowing her a kiss.

"Just ignore it," I say, as we wait to make eye contact with the bartender.

"Thanks for dragging me out here tonight. I think I really needed this," I tell her.

15

"Yeah, it usually takes another round of begging," she replies, still bothered by the guy across the bar. She raises her glass. "To us," she says, as we click our champagne glasses. Our habitual toast.

The first time I came here, Aaron was with me. Turns out, dancing wasn't his thing. He just stayed in the corner, on his phone, drinking. I managed to drag him onto the dance floor a couple of times, but he was ready to go soon after. It was also an important night for my career—my first praise in the papers—and we were out to celebrate. I puked on the way home. Aaron said something about us being too old to be clubbing, and I never insisted he come again. So now, whenever I find myself either free of plans or hating the ones he has for us, I come here. Akira started coming soon after we met, and it's been our thing for the past three years. We both agree it's the music, the lights, the letting loose we crave. Some nights, I don't even drink. My body moving with the beat is enough to set me free. Other nights, I drink more than I should. I made a point to stop doing the latter.

We have a great time dancing, and after a couple of drinks, I start to finally feel at ease. The music's doing it for me... *Who's the DJ in the house tonight?* I glance up at the top of the iconic spiraling steps. I find him with his eyes closed, his body moving perfectly synced to his own beat. DJ Jaxx is always a treat.

I'm on my way to the bathroom when I overhear bits and pieces of a conversation that make me feel relieved I'm not single. With everything that's happened lately, I really need this night to help me release some stress. I hear someone snorting something in the next stall. Drugs are not my thing, but who the hell am I to judge?

Back on the dance floor, the song changes and I recognize it. One of my favorites. I'm not sure where Akira is, but I know she's around. We have one rule: If either of us wants to leave, the other has to go too—unless we have other friends here. Not that I've kept in touch with many. I was the kind of teen who liked being left alone. *Not much has changed.* Our number-one rule is: never stay by yourself in the club. We both know that's a recipe for disaster.

I close my eyes, letting the music move me. I let go of everything—the wedding, my family issues, my job... all of it.

Minutes later, Akira's hands are on my shoulder, shaking me. "Iris!" she yells.

I open my eyes and realize that a lot of people have moved out of the way and are staring at me. I see the violet light reflected in her eyes, and I look down. My prism is floating in the air, like an invisible hand is holding it up. As I reach for it, it falls back down.

"What the fuck!" Akira says, her voice sharp with disbelief. She's looking at me for answers, but I don't have any to give.

People start to move closer again, quickly forgetting what they just witnessed. That's the allure of the club: The harder you try to stand out, the more invisible you become. I don't need to impress anyone here; I can just be myself.

"You should take that off!" Akira almost yanks it off me as we head for the door.

I can't. Not only because it was a gift from my mother, but because there's this strange, instinctive urge to protect it. "It was my mother's," I plead.

"Iris, this thing is possessed. I saw it. Everyone saw it."

How many people had seen it? From now on, I have to keep it concealed.

"You're telling me that you, Ms. Science Girl, believe in that stuff?" I ask her, surprised.

"Hell yeah," she says, her voice shaky. She looks genuinely freaked out.

"Akira, relax. It's just a necklace. I'm not sure what you think you saw—maybe they put something in your drink."

She shakes her head, unconvinced. I finally manage to get her into a cab, reassuring her that everything is fine.

I think about going to sleep at Aaron's, but the guilt of having bailed on him again weighs on me. I text him, saying I need clothes —I'm sleeping at my own place tonight.

But sleep is the last thing I get. I toss and turn, restless and hungover. At least now I know—wicked or not—*something* is going on with my necklace.

THREE

"ART IS NOT WHAT YOU SEE, BUT WHAT YOU
MAKE OTHERS SEE." – EDGAR DEGAS

I *should be packing*, I think, as I look around my apartment. Aaron has been asking me to move in for years, but I've always loved having my own space. Of course, things will have to change now with the wedding.

I run my fingers through the floral bedding on my bed, knowing it won't match his apartment. I survey the room— nothing here will fit there. Not the paintings, not my green antique lamp, and definitely not that wooden statue. My love for art goes beyond just paintings; the objects in my home have stories. I consider keeping this place. I honestly don't want to hurt Aaron's feelings, but he would never understand. He buys his home décor from a catalog; I buy mine from antique stores. Everything here, I've slowly curated, like my own personal collection. Many things were purchased needing repair, and I paid to fix them. I've brought them back to life. It's not so much the attachment to each piece, but the feeling that I'm about to move into somewhere without a soul. His furniture is modern, sleek, cold. I like my things a little broken, a little odd, a little complicated—like me.

As I'm clicking to purchase the boxes I need, I get a message from Akira. Another one. She's been texting me all weekend since our... incident at the club. *I know someone we can talk to, someone who can clean it.* She was going on and on about the prism needing to be...baptized, for lack of a better word. Not only do I not believe in whatever she's trying to convince me of, but I also like my prism the way it is. It's not like it's hurting me. I can't help but wonder... What if it's Mom who is still... around? Not that I believe in those things. Whatever it is, it's not evil—that I can feel for sure.

I text the only thing I know will calm her down: *I'll think about it.*

I put my phone away and start searching for one of my childhood tapes. *"They have to be here somewhere,"* I say to myself as I pull another photo album from the closet. Good thing I'm moving soon; this place needs some serious organization.

I get distracted twice during my search. First when I find an old sketch of me, lecturing; a student from last year gave it to me. He was a much better artist than historian, if his grades were any indication, and I haven't seen him since. The second distraction is almost laughable: my attempt at writing a novel. The manuscript is covered in dust. A few years ago, I tried to write my life's story on the recommendation of my therapist. I never finished it, though— I didn't want to add an end to my story. Somehow, I always felt like my life hadn't really even begun.

I almost fall off the step stool when I pull down the cardboard box that holds the four tapes. I just need to hook up the old VCR. If only I could find the cables. *How did I let this place get so messy?*

I sit on the couch, replaying the scene over and over, of my mom dancing. She was beautiful, her hair very much like mine. I have my father's hazel eyes; the rest—it's all her. The footage is shaky, but I love seeing her smile. I always want to picture her like this... joyful. She was spinning around, and when I got closer, she took me by the hands and twirled me. I looked just as happy.

I watch until I finally fall asleep on the couch.

* * *

I've had a constant headache for weeks now. I'm more than ready for the holiday break. November flies by in the blink of an eye—between packing my old apartment, grading the final papers, enduring wedding plans, and dodging Akira's questions. I'm craving solitude, and a visit to my favorite museum is long overdue.

The MFA museum is home to more than five hundred thousand works, and no matter how many times I've been here, I'm always surprised. There are prints by Dürer, Degas, and Rembrandt, drawings by Goya and Gauguin, Peruvian and Roman textiles, paintings and more paintings. A few of my favorites are by Van Gogh and Monet... enough to keep someone like me in a dreamlike state. I remember the words I gave to my students this season: *Take your time.*

I find myself standing in front of an artwork by Eugène Cicéri, from 1852. It's a painting of a forest, where its uneven terrain and massive trees surround a man with a walking stick. The heavy bag on his back is filled with sketching supplies, as I learn from my phone. It's a depiction of an artist's journey, I imagine. The painting shows a beautiful golden light filtering through the trees. I can almost hear the silence of the woods; only the man's heavy breathing breaks it. I crave that kind of peace.

I'm moving toward the next painting when a little girl's voice draws my eyes across the room. The sign above her directs to the jewelry collection. That's probably the section of the museum that I visit the least. I'm less drawn to the riches of the aristocracy, though they're as beautiful as one could imagine.

I follow the sign, my eyes blinking as they adjust to the dimmed lights. I pass a Roman cameo, worn to advertise the wearer's taste and profess devotion to gods or political forces. I'm amazed by all the details as I stop to look at an Italian medallion set into a silver-gilt case.

The next row holds a French beaded ring, along with brooches and a gold wreath of oak leaves and acorns. I let myself daydream about what it would have been like to live in a time when such accessories were worn.

I'm looking around when my eye catches the next object—a British tiara. The hair ornament, created by Cartier in the early twentieth century, is lit by focused light, setting the crystals to dance. It's not the tiara itself that delights me, but the idea that it sparks. *I should be looking into jewelry making, not math books.* It's not the shape itself that matters, but perhaps who created my necklace, or if other jewelry pieces were made with prisms. My specialization is in Renaissance paintings; I don't know much about the history of accessories. Though, I do know someone who does.

I pull out my phone right there to check if I still have Elena's email. She's a costume historian whom I helped with a research project a year ago. She had come to Harvard to finish a paper, and my colleague George introduced us. She was writing about certain costumes and accessories worn by Henry VIII and wanted help with viewing books in the private section of the school's library. George knew I had access, so he introduced us at lunch. Elena was quiet, kept mostly to herself during our visits, and was an expert in the subject. It won't startle her if I ask about this.

I can't even wait to get home. I stop at a coffee shop, order my usual latte, and sit down to write the email. It turns out to be harder than I thought. I have to be detailed enough to get the information I need, while also vague enough to avoid hinting that I'm in possession of such a thing.

Hi Elena,

I hope you're doing well. I've found myself a bit lost in my research for a project and was wondering if you could point me in the right direction. Have you ever encountered any jewelry myths in your past research? Perhaps folklore mentioning magical jewelry? Something involving diamonds? I figured if anyone would have insight, it would be you.

Thanks in advance! Let me know if I can return the favor.
Iris De Loughery

* * *

Harvard is bustling with a conference—too many egos per square foot. The students are beyond distracted today.

"What is the difference between balance and symmetry?" I ask, only to receive blank stares.

"Symmetry is a way to achieve balance," I continue. "It's when a portion of an image is mirrored. Many cultures have associated it with beauty. Let's take a look at this Greek temple—both sides are completely symmetrical. And here's another example in architecture."

"What about in a painting? You don't mean when artists just copy and paste half of a painting, right?" Isaac asks, his attention more on what's happening outside the window.

Influential names are supposed to be here today; everyone wants to shake hands with everyone.

"There are different types of symmetry. Let's take a look at this plate. What we have here is called radial symmetry. It's when an image is created around a central point. All around the plate, we see rows and rows of flowers."

"Can you show us an example... in a painting?" asks Paul.

"Sure." I pull up an image of *Christ Giving the Keys of the Kingdom to St. Peter* by Perugino. "Here, this is a fresco from the Sistine Chapel. There is a building in the center, and two more on each side. The symmetry in this case not only gives us a sense of balance but also a sense of formality. Now, we don't always need symmetry to achieve balance."

"Symmetry looks boring," says Mila.

"Perhaps. Asymmetrical balance can feel more natural or more interesting. In this case, we are talking about balancing with the same visual attention—maybe the same colors or amount of detail, keeping the eye at rest."

I'm about to bring up the concept of eye direction when someone mentions that Robert Fletcher is outside. Everyone stands up to look; even I, who don't care about technology, make my way to the window. I dismiss them. Whatever I say next won't be able to compete with this.

The positive side of all the commotion: the library is empty. I sit down to read about jewelry design when something in the book grips my curiosity: *Diamonds are better at dispersing light than glass due to their higher reflective index.*

I make sure I'm completely alone before pulling my prism out from underneath my shirt. Could this actually be a diamond, or is it a crystal? I recently learned the difference between the two—diamonds are harder and have more facets and cuts. I put it away quickly as I hear someone walking by. I glance at my phone. I have to be dolled up in two hours.

* * *

"So, you're the future Mrs. Dawson?" an elegant, middle-aged woman named Carmen asks me.

"Yes, lucky me," I say with a faint smile.

"Lucky indeed. The deal with FundsForge Aaron closed today... Well, let's just say blood could be spilled for it," she adds, eyeing Aaron.

He looks handsome in his suit, his dirty blond hair perfectly styled. Yet he's different from the boy I used to hang out with in my bedroom. He's obviously taller, stronger... but even the way he stands, he holds himself differently now. The only reminder of that boy is the grayish-blue of his eyes. Every time he looks at me, I try to catch a glimpse of our past; I hold on to that as tightly as I can.

I know very little about his business these days; I stopped being interested long ago. There was a time when we told each other everything, but it started to weigh us down. I'd hear him complain all day about his deals, and he'd listen to my stories from the classroom all night. We'd argue, and our relationship would suffer. We eventually decided to keep work out of the bedroom, then out of the dining room, and before I knew it, work was out of all our conversations. And with work being the main thing in our lives, once we stopped sharing it, we grew apart, too.

Carmen is still standing next to me, now talking to another executive, when a familiar voice catches my attention.

"How are you holding up?" Lara asks. She's wearing a gray suit like most of the men, except her heels and jewelry make her stand out. She could easily pass for a model.

I shake my head, a little confused.

"These events can be a little... toxic," she explains.

I laugh. I like Lara; she's not like the others. I remember Aaron's words: "Lara can be different; she doesn't have to work to be rich. She doesn't take anything seriously because she can afford to." Whatever her reasons are, I don't care. She's the only one I can talk to at events like this. She orders me another drink, even though the one in my hand is still full. I know better than to drink in a place like this, but Lara's husband, Ted, on the other hand, didn't get the memo.

"You seem very comfortable among them," I tell her.

"Well... I am," she says with a smile before someone comes to pull her away.

I'm looking for the balcony when Aaron comes to find me.

"Already in need of fresh air?" He knows I breathe better outdoors. I'm about to apologize when he says, "I hate how they all look at you, like you're a piece of meat to be devoured." He gestures toward a group of men.

"What are you talking about?"

"You're telling me you haven't noticed them looking at you?" His face can't hide his feelings.

I roll my eyes. "You must be out of your mind... If they're looking, it's because they know I'm your fiancée, and I heard the deal you made today is worth a bit of gossip."

I can feel his anger—not at me, never at me, but at any other man near me. The jealousy has always been a problem, even if I didn't want to admit it.

* * *

"Thanks for coming," he says on our way home.

"Of course. I guess I have to get used to these things now," I say more to myself than to him.

"I will never force you to go, Iris." Is it love I see in his eyes? Or pity?

"I know, I mean... I'm going to be your wife; it will be my... duty?" I try to smile, hoping my words don't sound as bitter as they feel.

He grabs my hand and caresses the ring. "No duty. But I can't wait to call you my wife."

I know he means it. And that hurts even more.

* * *

I want to stop Aaron but I hold the urge. I have been avoiding him for a while now. I decide to embrace the distraction. I move closer and kiss him back. I let him feel my body, his light fingers brushing my arm, drawing circles on my back. He touches me with muscle memory. I feel him ready against me and I kiss him harder. We move like a pair of dancers in bed, knowing exactly when to turn, with which pace to proceed. That's how long we have been together. There is nothing rough about the way he loves me; he's always the perfect gentleman. Always making sure I climax before releasing himself, never knowing the difference when I actually do or when I fake it.

FOUR

"CREATIVITY TAKES COURAGE." – HENRI
MATISSE

M y headache is now insufferable; no pill seem to ease it. It's woken me up again. It isn't even six o'clock, and Aaron is already gone. I check my phone and see his text about an early meeting. I find myself with nowhere to be for hours and in need of fresh air.

Days have passed since I emailed Elena, still no reply. I'm starting to get restless with the wait. I have no plan B. Nothing else to research. The more I search the internet, the more I realize it's pointless. Wherever I go, whatever I do, I always find myself wondering: *What is this necklace my mother gave me? Did she know something? Why did she give it to me?* The answers are probably at my fingertips... if only I could bring myself to open it.

I scan the calm water of the Charles River during the chilly morning. The sun has only recently risen, and a few runners jog by, completely lost in their exhaustion. I've always admired the discipline of those who run in December. If the cold isn't enough to fight against, they've got the holidays to deal with, too. They breeze past me and soon vanish from view.

So much to do, yet I want nothing to do with any of it. Aaron wants to decorate his place—our place—for Christmas.

Akira is still acting weird. My old apartment is a hot mess with boxes scattered everywhere. I still haven't come up with a plan for the final assignment I'm supposed to be giving. Despite the long list of things to do, all I want is to curl up with a cup of hot chocolate under the covers and let a good book help me forget it all.

As I shift my gaze to the water, I feel a pull to bring out the prism. Since the club, I've kept it hidden underneath my clothes—easy enough with all the winter layers. Even when it's dormant, I swear I can feel its presence. I debated telling Aaron about it. Although after seeing Akira's reaction, I knew this wasn't something I could share with anyone. I could almost hear Aaron's words if I did: *"There's no such thing as the supernatural. Everything has an explanation. Maybe you created this to satisfy a certain subconscious need."* He'd say anything except the word *pathetic*, and that's exactly how he would make me feel. Consequently, I have been keeping it all to myself.

I'm lost in thought, twisting the prism in my palm, when something cold hits my nose. I look up to see the first snowflakes of the season. I close my eyes, letting myself simply feel for a moment. A surprise welcomes me when I reopen them—the violet hue is exactly as I remember it. Alluring and trapped. The sight of it makes my heart race. I get closer and whisper, *"What are you?"* Only it begins to fade. I let out a soft laugh at the absurdity of talking to it. I keep staring, silently begging for it to stay longer, but it doesn't. When I look around again, I find that I'm no longer alone.

Staring at me from only a few feet away is Darion. Did he see...?

"What are you doing here?" I ask, a little too defensively. He startled me with his proximity. I quickly let the prism fall back to my chest, swinging gently, caught by the chain. I don't wait for him to respond. "I was... It's snowing," I add, gesturing to the air.

Darion looks at me strangely, his black-framed glasses perched on his nose and his hair—just a shade darker than mine—greasy and unkempt.

Before I can say anything else, he asks, "What is that?"

Of course, he saw it.

"What?" I'm not sure how to answer. "The necklace?" I realize he's staring at it. "Oh, it's... a family heirloom. I think it's broken though. The light goes on and off..." There is something about him that freaks me out. "I'm late for a meeting, but nice seeing you."

I'm almost out of breath by the time I catch a cab. The encounter was weird—he was so close, *too close*. My heart is pounding at a speed I can only associate with the runners going by. I feel dizzy. I loosen my scarf and practice my breaths in the car, completely aware that I probably look and sound disturbed. In and out, in and out. By the time I get home, I've managed to calm myself down.

I decide grocery shopping can wait. Laundry can wait. I grab my novel and head to bed, pressing the buttons of Aaron's automatic shades. I'm done with the world for the day.

* * *

I have another nightmare. This time, it's Darion hunting me. I really don't want to see him today. Still, I know it will be impossible to avoid him since he's my student.

The campus is covered in snow, and walking requires concentration. I'm focusing on my footing when I hear a ping from my phone. All notifications are silenced except one. Elena has sent a reply. If I could run without risking breaking my neck, I would. By the time I'm inside and no longer freezing my ass off, I read:

Hi Iris,

Sorry for the delay. I'm still on maternity leave and have been slowly catching up with my inbox. My guess is that you've already explored the classic tales like The Great Ring. If you need to go deeper, I recommend the book Accessories & Their Lost Fables by Phaedrus. (It's out of print, but the library should have a copy.) If you could give me more details, perhaps I might be more helpful. Best, Elena

I'm on my way to my office when I hear a student calling my name.

"Professor De Loughery?"

I turn toward her. "Hi, Mila." I don't know her friend.

"I was wondering if you could tell me what the final paper will be on. I wanted to get a head start."

"You'll be asked to write about what made art valuable in the Renaissance and what makes it valuable now." I'm not sure I should've answered her. I didn't mean to give Mila an advantage on the assignment; I just needed her to move along. When Mila wants something, she can be persistent.

"Oh, shouldn't we be focusing on critiques by now?" she says, her voice laced with attitude.

"You guys haven't proven you're ready for them yet." I try to stay calm. She doesn't like my answer. I'm already sorry for whoever Mila ends up critiquing.

With the girls gone, I look up The Great Ring tale. I remember it vaguely—every historian has come across it at some point. It's nothing more than a children's bedtime story. According to the Russian legend, there was once a diamond ring capable of making its owner live longer; however, there was a price for the longevity. When death finally came to claim the body, the wearer had to give his soul in return. It was the previous owner's soul that powered the ring and extended the new user's life. Classic myth.

Now I have to think about how to reply to Elena. I'm not sure if I should mention a prism. With Darion and Akira already knowing about it, I need to be more careful. My stomach turns at the thought of seeing Darion again, and I wish I had skipped breakfast. To my relief, he's nowhere to be seen.

"We're covering a Baroque painting today, *Las Meninas* by Velázquez. Remember what we talked about last week? About the highly ornate and dramatic style of the Baroque? This is a great example. Does anyone know who the main little girl in the center is?"

"The king's daughter," Becky answers proudly.

"Correct. Why is this artwork greatly known and discussed?"

"Because it's a painting about a painting," says Stella.

"That's right. Velázquez was able to create different illusions, playing with the perspective. We are left unsure if the portrait subject is Margaret, her parents, or the painter himself. He uses light and dark to define the focal points. It's often said that Velázquez meant this work to suggest that art, and life, are an illusion."

* * *

I heat up my leftovers and carry them back to bed. My eyes feel like they might bleed after staring at the thick volume for hours. The only copy I could find of the book Elena mentioned was in Italian. With enough drawings and charts to fuss over, I brought it home anyway. Depictions of *incantate—enchanted*—necklaces, rings, and crowns fill the pages. There are also grotesque sketches of body parts, including organs. Nothing looks like my prism. I'm back to square one.

With Aaron gone on a business trip, I'm relieved to have the place to myself. I know I need to go back to my apartment soon; I'm running out of clothes again. *I need to get my life together.* I think to myself before deciding to actually do something about it.

It's been ages since I've done a proper meditation session. They kept me steady in college, and later in grad school; I pretty much owe those practices my degrees. There isn't a yoga mat here; I simply push the coffee table aside and sit on the rug. I place a lit candle in front of me and begin the process.

A combination of inhales and exhales, and a focused stare at the flame. I was to acknowledge my body and the sounds around me and let them go.

I scan my feet, then an itch on my back lifts my attention, which I tell myself to let it go. I continue going through my entire body, from the bottom up, noticing the headache at bay.

I turn my focus to the sounds around me. There's nothing besides my breathing and the hum of the apartment's heat.

Before I can focus entirely on the flame, my tears start to fall. It requires no effort on my part. They wash away my makeup; I know my mirrored reflection would likely resemble a scary clown. But there's no one here. No one I need to look pretty for. It's a great feeling—being oneself, truly free.

And so I let myself cry. I cry for Dad, for my mom, for Aaron, for the wedding, for the prism... and then I cry for myself.

And then, once again, the prism lights up for me. This time, I understand. *Water.* The prism requires moisture to light up. First, the water from the bathtub, then the snow, now my tears, and the time at the club? My sweat. *At last, some answers.* However, something is still missing, something I don't understand. The prism didn't do anything when I showered. There's more to it than just getting it wet.

I bring the candle closer to the violet light. The reflection of the flame enhances the prism's inner glow, and the more I decrease the distance, the weirder I feel. But I'm done waiting. I need to know more. I push it closer and closer to the flame, defying what feels like nature's law. The prism begins to spin uncontrollably, suddenly alive and agitated. I blink—and everything goes black.

I can't see anything. Panic starts creeping in. I can't control my eyes. I open and shut them—still nothing. I reach for my phone, but the darkness doesn't relent.

Then, suddenly, the blackness gives way.

Somehow, I'm in another place. I can almost feel the ground beneath my feet. My brain fights the concept, knowing I'm still sitting in my living room. *I'm not actually here*, I tell myself. I scan the room, afraid that I'm losing my mind. *I'm not dreaming*. I'm stuck, imprisoned in my own eyes. I have no choice but to look around.

A fireplace casts a warm glow over the rustic room. Animal heads are mounted on the walls—far larger than I imagined they'd be in real life. My eyes dart around, frantically searching for a way out. Through the windows, I see mountains. It's snowing here too. I'm still looking for a door when I see... *him*.

A handsome, dark-haired man sits on a leather chair by the fire. By the look on his face, he sees me too. I step back, though something inside me tells me I have nothing to fear. I try to open my mouth, but no sound comes out. His green eyes are wide with shock as they scan me.

Am I shaking? I look down at my hands and realize... I have none. I'm... invisible—at least to myself. Before I can glance back at him, it all goes dark again.

FIVE

"I SAW THE ANGEL IN THE MARBLE AND CARVED
UNTIL I SET HIM FREE." – MICHELANGELO

My head was pounding. I lift my hands to my forehead and feel a bandage. "Easy..." I hear Aaron's voice, soothing but firm.

"What happened?" I struggle to ask, my voice a little weak.

I try to make sense of my surroundings. I'm in a bed—someone else's bed.

Akira's voice cuts through the haze.

"Oh my God! I'm so glad to see you're awake!"

I try to sit up, but Aaron gently urges me back down. "Easy. Just stay put."

"Why am I here?" I manage to ask both of them. The room is unfamiliar, but the clothes strewn across the chair tell me I must be in Akira's room. She always moved a lot. I hadn't made it to this place yet. I was still studying the space when Aaron spoke again.

"I have to leave for Toronto tonight," he says, his tone unreadable. "I'll be gone a couple of days. I didn't want to leave you alone. You need rest, and—"

"What happened?" I interrupt, my voice sharp despite the fog in my brain.

"There was a fire in the apartment," he says, his eyes shadowed with concern. "Luckily, the building was built to handle it. The sprinklers must've kicked in fast, so nothing really burned—just a corner of the couch. I think you passed out from the smoke, though. Probably hit your head on the way down."

Akira jumps in. "They found a candle."

Memories flood back in fragments. I start to shake my head, denying it.

"No, no, it's okay," Aaron says quickly. "I know you wouldn't burn the place down, Iris."

He had no idea. Was all that real? I reach up to touch my head. Of course not. I had hit my head—it explains everything. It had to.

"Akira has been telling me all kinds of things about this necklace of yours. Should I be worried?"

I instinctively reach for my neck, panicked, searching for the necklace. I feel my fingers graze the chain. It's still there.

They're both watching me, waiting for something—waiting for me to say something.

"What?" I ask, my voice tight.

"I told you she can't take it off," Akira says, speaking to Aaron like I'm not even in the room. *Were they talking about me behind my back?*

"Of course I can," I snap, my voice rising. "I just don't want to. My mother gave it to me. You both have no idea what it's like to not have a mother!" I'm yelling now, my frustration bubbling over.

Aaron's expression softens, regret flashing in his eyes. "You're right," he says quietly. "I'm sorry. I was so worried when they called me, Iris."

I pull my hand away from his, my chest tight. "I want to go home."

"They're still going over the insurance policy," Aaron says, his voice steady but concerned. "We can go back in a couple of days."

"That place is not my home!" I don't know why I said it, but the words sting. I can see the hurt in his eyes, and it makes my stomach churn. But I don't take them back.

* * *

I'm alone in my half-packed apartment, surrounded by boxes, trying to figure out what to do next when my phone rings. Aaron again. My heart sinks. I didn't handle things well yesterday. He left for Canada right after dropping me off here, and now I know I owe him an apology.

I've taken a sick day from work, though I definitely need more than just one day to sort through everything. I left Akira's place without even saying thank you. I'm a mess.

I pick up my phone and text Akira: *I'm sorry. You might be right. Is your offer to help with the necklace still standing?*

* * *

We are on our way to Salem. I laughed out loud when Akira mentioned the healer she knew lived there. Shockingly, she wasn't kidding. Apparently, the whole town was in need of "healing." Whatever that meant.

I can't help but think this is some kind of joke. I don't really care because I'm not actually doing this to get rid of an evil spirit like Akira is making my case out to be—I'm doing it because I want my friend back, and if this is what it takes, fine. I'm not afraid; whatever the prism is, nothing or no one can stop it.

We arrived at the hotel with plans to meet the healer at seven. The drive here gave us a chance to catch up a little—talking about the wedding, work, but in the back of my mind, I know I'm hiding too much. I hate lying to Akira, but I have no idea how to explain everything. Whatever happened with the fire, whatever I saw that night, and whoever that man was—it's still haunting me. Perhaps I do need the healer after all.

When Akira stepped out of the car to fill the tank, I pulled out my phone and texted Aaron: *Decided to go on a girl's trip with*

Akira; I think it will be good for me. Sorry for everything, we'll talk when I get back.

We dropped our bags off at the hotel and headed out to grab a bite before our appointment. The quaint town is exactly how I imagined: cute little shops selling trinkets and souvenirs, begging tourists to buy into what they are known for: witches. Although the locals don't seem to remember their own history. They all look too busy with their mundane lives to act any differently. I would have liked the town if something otherworldly wasn't actually happening to me. It feels like the entire place is mocking me.

"So, how do you actually know this person?" I ask, squirting ketchup onto my fries, trying to distract myself from the unease creeping up my spine.

"I don't," Akira replies, her mouth full.

I stare at her. "You don't? Then how...?"

"I found him online," she says with a grin.

I choke on my food. "You what?!"

"Relax, he came highly recommended." Akira continues eating as though she hasn't just shocked me to the core.

"By who? Online lunatics?" I can't believe what I'm hearing.

"Look, I did my research," she says nonchalantly. "He seemed legit." She took a sip of her beer.

I shake my head, still stunned. "I can't believe I let you drag me all the way here to see, at best, a charlatan." I scan the restaurant for the waitress. I need something stronger than fries and ketchup right now.

* * *

The cab drops us off in front of a house that's clearly old, but not in a haunted way—just the kind of building that looks like it has stories to tell. Akira and I both stare at it for a moment, and the driver, sensing our hesitation, asks if we're getting out.

I'm still taking in the place, trying to decide if I'm really ready to go through with this. We have no idea who's inside. *This was such a bad idea.*

"We should go back to the hotel," I say, looking at her.

Akira is already getting out of the cab, giving me a reassuring nod. "Whatever the necklace is, it's worse than anything that could be inside," she says. She's out of her mind.

"You know, we're asking for trouble here," I say, following her.

We stand there for a moment, the cold air of Salem brushing against my skin, making me feel more alive and alert than I've felt in days. I'm not sure if it's the cold or the anxiety of what's about to happen, but I'm ready for answers—or at least something to make sense of all this chaos.

She rings the bell. I eye the street, making mental notes of the neighbors in case... well, in case it's needed.

The person who opens the door is not who we expect. Not that I know exactly what to expect, but I definitely didn't expect her. The teenage girl looks us up and down, from head to toe. She's wearing a T-shirt with a band I don't recognize. She looks completely... ordinary. She opens the door wider and motions for us to come in.

"My dad's in the kitchen."

Lloyd is a short man in his sixties. He's bald, wearing glasses far too large for his bony face, and dressed in jeans and a button-down shirt. Again, ordinary. The inside of the house? Ditto.

"Please, take a seat," he says, pouring all of us a cup of tea. *There's no way I'm going to drink anything here.* Akira, though, seems completely at ease, which makes it harder to read what she's thinking.

"Thank you for seeing us," she says, blowing on the tea. She better not be thinking about—

And she does. She actually takes a sip.

I jump toward her, trying to stop her, almost spilling the whole thing on us.

"Trust issues?" Lloyd asks calmly.

I glance at Akira. Is she losing it?

"How does this work?" she changes the subject, unfazed.

"You've got nothing to fear," Lloyd continues. "That's why I let my daughter open the door. As you can see, I'm just a father."

I listen carefully, trying to hear if the girl is still around. It helps to know there's someone else in the house.

"Where did you guys come from?" Lloyd asks, clearly curious.

"None of your business," Akira replies coolly, taking another sip of her tea. I tense, watching her. She looks... okay.

"I grew up in Salem," he says, his voice turning wistful. "It's a shame what they've done to this town. Dismissing our heritage. People's greed turned what was once something sacred into a gift shop. There's a clear divide here: those who think witches were just misjudged women and that the occult is all myths, even though they're fine profiting from it. Then there are those who know the truth."

He's about to keep going when I cut him off.

"Right. So what does that have to do with my necklace?"

Lloyd smiles, his eyes glinting with something I can't place. "May I see it?" He gestures toward the necklace with his hand.

"I'm not taking it off," I say, placing my hand protectively over it.

"Iris!" Akira gestures for me to hand it over.

"You don't have to take it off, but I need to touch it. To know." he says, extending his hand.

I hesitate. I lean over the table, and just as his hand gets an inch away, a sharp pain shoots through my head. I gasp, and Akira quickly helps me sit back down.

"I see," Lloyd says, taking another sip of his tea, his gaze never leaving the prism. "How did you come across it?"

"It was a gift," I answer, still feeling the lingering pain.

"So, how do we fix it?" Akira asks, concern edging her voice.

"There's nothing I can do," he tells us.

"What?" Akira stands up, her voice rising.

"I'll give your money back," he offers.

"I don't want my money back," Akira snaps. "I want you to fix it." She shoves her chair backward in frustration.

"Some energies are best left... undisturbed," he says softly.

Akira slumps back into her chair, exhaling a frustrated breath.

"I recommend you get rid of it and never look back, while you still can." He looks directly at me now.

"What do you mean, 'while she still can'?" Akira grabs my arm, her voice urgent.

"When I sense a lingering entity or energy," he continues, "I can often convince it to go elsewhere. Sometimes they just need a nudge, a reminder to let go. Other times, I need to offer something to incentivize the transfer. Whatever is in that necklace, though—it has no intention of leaving. In fact, it's the opposite."

I swallow hard.

"Do you hear him?" Akira practically pleads. "You have to get rid of it."

"And what if I don't?" I turn to Lloyd, challenging him.

"Then I suggest you learn to control it. Or else." His voice hardens.

"Is it possible? To control it?" I ask, my voice quieter now, my mind racing.

"All in the universe is energy," Lloyd replies. "Some believe controlling it is our original and only purpose. But to do so, you'll have to fight your senses. Go against everything you've ever known to be true. If you're willing to go that far, to lose your sanity for the sake of something greater, then yes, everything is possible. Including mastering the mystique of life."

* * *

I sit in bed, watching my friend drink.

"This isn't a movie, Iris," Akira says, her tone sharp. "This won't end well." She's leaning back against the pillows, sipping from a mini vodka bottle. I feel too queasy to partake.

"I can do this," I say, my voice steadier than I feel. "You heard the guy, it's possible to control it." But... *is it?*

"Oh, now you trust him?" Akira raises an eyebrow. "The online charlatan? Isn't that what you called him?"

"I said that before I met him."

"I'm pretty sure he said you would lose your mind before learning to... manage this thing. Shit, this conversation is making me lose mine already."

"Figure of speech."

"Was it?" She stops looking at me.

"It's worth trying," I say, lying down on the bed.

"Is it? Because you could have died in the fire."

"That fire had nothing to do with my necklace," I lie, both to her and to myself.

"Right." She takes another long sip. "It hurts to know that you don't trust me."

I feel the sting of her words. Aside from Aaron, she's my closest friend.

"Of course I trust you." I move to sit next to her on her bed.

"Then why don't you tell me the truth? Why can't you get rid of this thing?"

I take two deep breaths. I brace myself, and then I tell her everything. I tell her about the letter, the times I've seen it light up, about Darion, the night of the fire, and even the guy. I expect her to be shocked, but surprisingly, her response is gentle.

"And all that doesn't freak you out?" she asks, her voice soft.

"No, maybe it should, but it doesn't. I know it sounds completely nuts, but I feel like the energy in it is... good."

She grabs my hand. "Okay, then."

"Okay? That's it? You're not going to keep asking me to burn it?"

"This whole thing scares the shit out of me, but I'm not going to let you do this alone. I'm here if you need me."

"Crazy or not?"

"Crazy or not."

"Thank you."

I finally sleep through the night.

* * *

I wait for him to open the door when I ring the bell.

"Why are you ringing the bell?" Aaron asks, looking handsome. There's something about him in gym clothes, sweaty after a workout, that turns me on.

"I wasn't sure if I should use my keys."

"Iris, this is your home." My hateful words hang between us.

"I know. I'm sorry for what I said; I didn't mean it."

He walks to the kitchen to pour himself a glass of water, and I follow him.

"Aaron, I'm sorry."

He comes closer and kisses me lightly. His lips taste salty. He pulls back and asks, "How was your trip? Where did you even go?"

"Salem."

He spits his water. "What the hell? That's your idea of fun?"

"Well, Akira's idea."

He laughs. "And did you? Have fun?"

"I did, actually."

"Then I'm glad you went."

There's so much left unsaid, but I can tell neither of us is ready to confront it. Instead, we fill the silence with casual dinner plans, pretending everything is fine.

SIX

"COLOR IS MY DAY-LONG OBSESSION, JOY, AND
TORMENT." – CLAUDE MONET

I t's the last week of school before the holiday break, and I have a mountain of tasks to tackle—grading papers, buying last-minute gifts, and picking out a dress for Aaron's party. At least this year, we're going to his family's place instead of hosting dinner ourselves. But before I do anything else, there's an email I need to send.

Hi Elena,

Congrats on the baby! And thank you for the book suggestion; I did find a copy in the library, though unfortunately, it didn't have what I'm looking for. I've narrowed my research down to necklaces, diamond pendants, geometric ones... anything along those lines. I was asked to write about European folklore, and I've found myself in a rabbit hole that's worth pursuing. So, I'm letting myself stray a bit from the original theory. You know how it goes—we have to scratch the itch sometimes. I know this doesn't give you much to work with, but any tips you can offer would be greatly appreciated.

Thanks again,
Iris.

I'm on my way to meet Akira. I've asked her to help me pick a dress; I knew she would say yes, even though our taste in clothes couldn't be more different.

"How are you doing?" she asks as we enter the store.

"If you're wondering if I've completely lost my mind yet, sorry to disappoint. Still sane."

She smiles, raising an eyebrow. "Sane, my friend, you never were."

I nudge her playfully.

"This store is so boring," she mutters, running her fingers along every single dress on the rack.

"It's a formal party, Akira. 'Boring' is the dress code."

"How about this one?" the sales lady asks, holding up a dress.

I shake my head. "No thanks." We keep searching.

I'm trying on the sixth dress when Akira asks, "You never told me—was the guy you saw with the candle hot?"

I cough. "What?"

"You never mentioned."

"I didn't think it mattered. He's not real."

"That hot then?"

I roll my eyes, my cheeks turning warm. "I'm getting married."

"I know. I'm your maid of honor."

I pause, eyeing her. "And have you decided who's going to be your plus one?"

She grins. "I've got options."

"You'll have to settle down one day, you know," I say, stepping out of the dressing room and eyeing myself in the mirror.

She gives me a knowing look. "And why's that?"

I roll my eyes again, knowing this conversation is going nowhere.

"This is the dress," she says as she zips me up.

I nod in agreement.

"I wish you could come to these parties with me."

"When hell freezes over."

I laugh. "Stranger things have happened recently."

* * *

I'm grading my last paper when I realize Darion hasn't handed his in. I haven't seen him on campus since the day of our encounter by the river. It's odd for him to be gone for this long. Did I have anything to do with it? He's not a straight-A student, but he could still probably still pass my class. I can't help but wonder what's happened, even though a part of me still hates the idea of seeing him again. I email him like the great professor I am:

> *Hi Darion,*
> *I haven't received your final paper. Just wanted to make sure it*
> *didn't get lost somehow.*
> *Hope to hear from you soon.*
> *Iris De Loughery*

It feels good to be done with work for a while. I've been extremely distracted this semester, and my job has fallen to the back burner. Hopefully, things are slowing down now. I'm looking forward to the break, despite having to stay with my future in-laws for several days. Aaron gave me my Christmas gift early—tickets to *The Nutcracker* in New York City. He knows I prefer experiences over material things. We're staying in a hotel until Christmas Eve, when we'll rent a car and drive upstate to his parents' house. I ask him why we're skipping a driver, and he says he doesn't want people to work on a holiday because of him.

I realize Akira's new place is only a few blocks from my old apartment when she texts me the address. I barely paid attention the last time I was there. She's catching a flight this evening, and Aaron and I leave in a couple of days. Her parents live in Chicago, and she has a new nephew to meet this year. I can see her excitement when she talks about the baby. She's already a proud aunt.

"How long are you staying?" I ask, eyeing her place.

"Five days," she replies.

"So, you aimed for... a bag a day?" I count her luggage.

"They're all gifts."

"Wow, you don't do anything... small, do you?"

"Not my style."

I laugh.

"Well, my gift now seems pretty pathetic." I hand over my gift bag.

"Oh, stop it." She's already pulling at the tissue paper.

I'm not very good at buying gifts; I know that. I always opt for the plain things anyone could use—candles, wine, sweaters. The people I care about already have everything they need.

"I didn't see you buying this; I love it." She holds up the mug that reads *Bewitched Bitch*.

"I snuck out when I left to get us coffee." The Salem sales lady smiled when she rang me up, asking if I was interested in any of their scented candles. I ended up picking two for myself—one that smells like fresh pine trees and another that reminds me of an apple pie.

"And this will be handy when I'm supposed to look like an adult on Christmas Eve." She holds up the sweater I got her to go along with the mug.

"Red is festive," I say, almost apologizing for my plain gifts.

"Crimson," she corrects me.

She had explained, what seems like forever ago, about her deal with color names.

My parents wanted more for me than they had. They knew we had to move to America; it had been their plan since, well, forever. They spent all their extra money hiring me an English tutor. It wasn't cheap for a low-income family in Japan to hire tutors, especially for a foreign language. Sadly, they only had enough money for one child; they picked me over my sister. I was younger, and they believed I had

*a better chance of assimilating than her. I had to make sure I
absorbed enough for both of us. I would try to teach her everything I
was learning, but she hated it all. It affected her, not being chosen.
She rebelled against studying; she was always out, hanging with
friends my parents didn't like. They worked too hard, long days, and
couldn't restrain her. I had after-school classes every day for years.
They said I needed to be prepared; we were moving soon. Yet, it took
them years to save enough. I was fluent by the time we finally left. I
don't know if I would've made it to college if it hadn't been for those
classes. Mrs. Turner was strict, but she drilled her lectures into me. I
was learning way more than the kids my age. I was studying
advanced geometry, calculus, and even physics—all in English.
Before the end of each lesson, Mrs. Turner would quiz me with a few
interesting questions, some of them for fun, like riddles. And the last
question of the quiz was always a color. "You must learn to notice all
the hues if you want to learn to really see," she would often say. So I
learned the names, and I still see them this way—each color hue for
what they are, unique.*

"Let me help you bring those bags down," I offer.

"There's an elevator here."

"You still only have two hands." We haul all the suitcases down, and I give her a kiss goodbye.

"Try not to burn anything down while I'm gone," she says, half-joking.

I smile at her. "I'll do my best."

I've promised not to do any experiments again—at least, not alone. I leave holding Akira's gift, a rare first edition of an art history book I love. Unlike me, she gives great gifts.

* * *

One last chore, I tell myself as I put on my lipstick. Aaron's already waiting for me by the front door.

"It's freezing," I tell him as I pull my coat tighter.

"The driver should be here any minute." There are lots of positives to having the kind of money Aaron has; never having to drive, find parking, or catch a cab is one of my favorites. The black car pulls up in front of us moments later.

The entrance to the party is nothing short of elegant, with the expected red carpet and valets opening doors. The lights reflect in all the shiny shoes and sparkling diamonds. I'm still shivering when I hand my coat over to be stored away.

"You look beautiful," Aaron says as he touches my open back, moving us along the hall.

"Thank you."

I never quite feel like myself in dresses and heels, but despite that, I like how I look in his eyes. I'm wearing my new diamond earrings—the ones he surprised me with hours earlier. "Another gift?" I had asked. "This one is more for me than for you," he replied. I smiled as I put them on. "Thank you anyway."

He looks impeccable in a tuxedo. He belongs in those clothes.

"Try to have some fun," he says as we enter the main room.

I look for a familiar face when we reach our table, but Lara is nowhere to be seen. Aaron is already doing his rounds when a waiter passes by with champagne flutes. I take a glass. *Just one sip*, I promise myself, breaking my "party-sober" vow. Enduring the conversations is extra painful without a drink in hand. Even when I pretend to be busy with my phone, people know Aaron, and I'm an easy target for anyone trying to impress him. It's hard to be left alone in a sea of sharks.

As soon as the alcohol touches my lips, I know I won't stop at one sip. *Just one glass*, I change the promise to myself.

McKenzie's wife looks like she needs a drink even more than I do as we both listen to her husband talk.

"I hear you teach at Harvard," he says, sipping his whiskey. I want to trade glasses with him.

"Yes, I'm an art history professor."

"You like art? Miranda here likes to spend a good chunk of my salary on those things. Don't you, hun?" He's a large man with a solid mustache. She gives me a thin, embarrassed smile.

"No better way to invest your money, in my opinion." I give her my condolences look.

The champagne helps as I talk to three other couples. Jack and Cindy are like two hungry dogs, biting anything that comes their way. New money, I make a mental note. Then there's the power couple, Camilla and Paola. They mean business; I could close deals myself if I wanted to. And finally, Omar and Christy—both too drunk or high to make much sense, but I listen to them anyway. None of them can hide their true intentions: They're only interested in getting access to my fiancé.

I move on to playing arm candy, standing next to Aaron while he talks to his business partners.

An hour later, I excuse myself and make my way to the balcony.

I don't care how cold it is; I need space from those people. The champagne is starting to get to my head, and I have to concentrate to keep my senses from becoming overwhelmed. I beg the prism to stay hidden, feeling it pulse under my bra. Only a few people occupy the balcony, and I let the crisp air cool my nerves. Through the windows, I can see people enjoying themselves, even if it's all a mask. They're dancing, smiling, all in their beautiful fancy attire.

I'm so distracted by people-watching that I don't notice the man standing next to me until he says, "They can be a little... suffocating." I hold my breath at the surprise of the stranger so close to me. *I know those green eyes.* He's staring at me with such intensity that I wonder if he's recognized me too.

"Aren't you cold?" he asks, his voice cutting through me.

I shake my head no. I'm still searching for words.

"I needed some... air," I manage to say, my voice weak.

"First time?" he asks.

"It feels like it, but no. Yours?" I ask, trying to keep myself together.

"I have to do this sort of thing frequently."

How could this be happening?

"I'm sorry to hear that." I try to continue the conversation.

He snorts, letting out a laugh.

Waiters are coming our way, and I shorten the distance and pick up another glass. I don't know how to handle my feelings. There he is, so... *real.*

"I'm Hoyt," he introduces himself, and I shake his hand. As soon as our hands touch, we both pull back immediately, gasping. The heat almost burns our hands. I'm still holding my fingers when I look up and see that he, too, has felt it.

"What was... that?" he asks me.

"I don't... know." I can feel my prism pulsing, and I start to wonder if it's going to light up even without water.

I need to walk away before I make a scene. I'm looking for somewhere else to go when Aaron finds me. I could swear he knows when another man is near me.

"There you are," he says, glancing over at the guy.

Hoyt looks at me, winks, and says, "Good luck in there," before walking away.

I can see Aaron's hand curl into a fist. "Was he... bothering you?"

I take a deep breath. "Nothing I couldn't handle."

To my surprise, he says, "Let's get out of here."

"Oh... Don't you have more... negotiating to do?"

"Everyone's drunk. They don't really want to do business. It's already the second part of the evening, when people are only thinking about their drugs in the bathroom."

For the first time, I'm the one who wants to *stay longer.*

SEVEN

"ART WASHES AWAY FROM THE SOUL THE DUST
OF EVERYDAY LIFE." – PABLO PICASSO

How am I supposed to sleep after last night? I toss and turn until the clock tells me it's reasonable to get up. I want to text Akira, but I don't want to distract her from her family. She would only worry about my mental state. To her, I'm a fragile creature, just moments away from breaking.

I pack my bags, well aware that I'm not bringing enough. I'm probably forgetting something, yet my brain isn't cooperating. I zip the bag up after checking that I have at least enough underwear, my phone charger, and my wallet.

The flight is busy with families, and I let myself doze off and on. Aaron is still replying to emails. There are bags under his eyes. I worry that he's working too much. He needs this break more than I do.

New York is buzzing with all the holiday lights. Aaron has picked a beautiful hotel for us to stay at, right across from the Rockefeller tree. It's hard to remember our childhood. It feels like a different life compared to all of this. The room is large, with a separate living area. A beautiful view of the city stretches across the glass walls.

I'm lost watching the people below when he walks over.

"Do you like it?" he asks, holding my hand.

"I do."

"Who would have thought we'd ever stand together in a place like this?" His words describe exactly what I feel.

"Definitely not me." I wonder if he knows how little it all means to me—the money, the extravagance. At the same time, I know it means a lot to him, so I try to enjoy it.

"Do these people ever take a day off?" I ask when he tells me he's going to be right back.

"I'm sorry. Why don't you use the huge bathtub to relax? I promise, this is the last work thing for a while."

I'm left alone in the hotel room. It's either take a bath or venture into the shops the day before Christmas Eve.

I drop the robe and step into the giant footed tub, big enough for two. I change the music a few times, searching for the perfect vibe. I want more than just to relax. *I want to escape.* If I can't make it to the club, I'll bring the dance floor to me.

I'm tired of holding back. I've been practicing my breathing and concentration since Salem. I guessed the prism was aligned to my feelings—if I can stay calm, steady, perhaps I can keep the energy in it calm too. I'm determined. *I need to be in control.*

I'm absorbed in the beat, letting my body move in the water when Hoyt comes to mind. I'm about to push the thought away, as I've been doing for a while now. But after seeing him yesterday, it's almost impossible—he's real, *too real.* I'm not sure what scares me most: what I felt when I touched him, or the realization that the prism has led me to him before.

It's a disaster. I'm getting married in a few months, and all I want to do is see him again. I have the urge to try again with the prism, but I hold back. I promised Akira I wouldn't do such things alone. Though circumstances have changed—she doesn't know that I've met him... She would understand.

"No!" I say it out loud.

He was more beautiful than I remembered: his eyes, the

jawline, the messy hair. He looked sharp in the tux, yet so rough. I felt his callused hands in the brief moments we touched, and I ache for it.

I close my eyes, imagining what I wish he would do to me if he ever touches me again. I move my hands and pretend they are his. My prism glows with intensity as I let myself orgasm. Only to be consumed by guilt seconds later.

* * *

"Are you ready? We gotta go," Aaron asks, returning an hour later than promised.

"Yeah, almost," I say, tying up my hair.

"You don't seem as excited as I hoped you would be." He can tell—of course, he can.

"I am. I'm just a little... tired. But I am."

"I'm sorry I was gone for so long. No more business until after the holidays." He kisses my cheek.

"That sounds lovely." I make sure to smile.

The ballet is one of those places I don't mind dressing up for. I never mind getting ready for art. It deserves to be appreciated. Aaron is ordering us something while I watch the joyful people around us. I'm not sure if it's the holiday cheer or the event that gives them their glow. Whatever it is, I wish I could bottle up that feeling.

I love everything about the performance. My eyes tear up when I think about how much Mom would've liked it too. I think of her twirling me around in the living room, wearing one of her home-made tutus. She was a natural dancer, without training, yet so graceful. There's something about dance that will always hold a special place in my heart.

On the way out, I beg Aaron to stop for a slice of New York pizza, but he insists on eating at a proper restaurant.

"It's been a while since we've talked. Let's sit down," he says.

Nothing would taste better than the cheap, greasy pizza from the corner joint, but I do want to spend time with him. We walk into an Italian place, and my stomach growls at the smell. I want everything on the menu.

"How does it feel to be done with work for a bit?" I ask, munching on the breadsticks.

"I don't think I'm going to know what to do with myself, honestly. It's been a while since I took any time off." He looks extremely tired.

"It really has, probably since... Mexico."

"No, or maybe... Wow, it has been a while."

"Two years, Aaron."

"I'm sorry, work has been crazy... but I didn't realize it bothered you."

"I'm okay with it if that's what you want to do. You just look worn out."

"Ouch."

"You know what I mean. What do you want to do for your birthday this year?"

"I wouldn't mind repeating Mexico... I just need to close a couple of deals before clearing a few days."

"Cancun was fun."

The waiter brings our food. I'm eating my pasta dish when Aaron suddenly blurts out, "I didn't get anything for my parents."

"Are you serious?"

He nods.

"We can't show up empty-handed, not on Christmas. They already don't like me as it is."

"Iris, we're getting married. You have to let all that go. My parents are happy about us."

"Accepting it isn't the same as being happy."

"You've changed. You're a Harvard professor now. They'd be crazy not to be happy about it."

"I didn't change, I just... grew up. Do you think we can find a store open this late?"

"It's New York City. Let's enjoy our dinner, and we can get them something afterward."

"I think this is the best dinner I've ever had," he says with a grin as we leave.

"You say that after every meal."

"Only when you aren't cooking."

I stick my tongue out at him, but it's true. I can't cook to save myself.

We walk out of a shop with expensive wine bottles, a card, and some hope that it'll be enough.

"It's not like I didn't buy them a boat six months ago," he says, taking the bags from my hands.

"It's because you did that for their anniversary that they'll expect more than... wine."

"Whatever. It should be enough that we'll be there."

It should be, yet I know it won't be.

* * *

With the city glowing outside, I lie awake, staring at the ceiling, watching the shadows. I can still taste Aaron on my lips—guilty sex does that, it lingers. Even though I didn't do anything wrong, it was the fantasy of Hoyt that played in my mind as Aaron made love to me tonight. My wedding is months away—how long will it take to sort through my feelings? I love Aaron, I owe him so much, he's my best friend, since... always. Of course I love him for everything he's done for me; still, *is it enough?* Enough to say yes, until death do us part?

* * *

"When was the last time you drove?" I watch him fuss with the keys.

"It's not something you can forget, Iris."

I laugh at him, and that's when I finally hear the engine.

"Stupid modern cars," he mumbles as he puts on his seatbelt.

We're lucky the snow isn't sticking to the road. I make sure to remind Aaron to slow down enough times to hear him swear he's never driving again.

We pull into the driveway, and Don greets us.

"Iris, it's so good to see you, it's been a while," Aaron's dad says, taking our bags inside.

"How are you, Don?"

"Oh, you know, getting old, but can't complain."

The house looks impeccable, as always—beautifully decorated but completely impersonal. Exactly like their previous home in Massachusetts. I still don't understand why they had moved to New York, especially with their only son living in Boston. Aaron mentioned it had something to do with an identity crisis after Don's retirement.

Maria is wearing her signature outfit: a matching set of pants and sweater, pearls, and flats.

"How are you, sweetie? How was the drive? I hope the roads weren't icy." She eyes me from head to toe, and I immediately regret my choice of comfy leggings and sneakers.

Aaron responds before I can open my mouth. "No need to worry now, Mom. We're already here."

"I heard about Stanley and Rile. Everything under control?" His dad hands Aaron a beer before we even shut the front door.

"Please, Don, can I say hello to my son first?" Maria kisses him and immediately wipes the lipstick off his cheek.

"We'll talk later, Dad."

* * *

I'm making myself a plate from the table of appetizers when Aaron's cousin Steve asks, "How's Harvard treating you?" Steve is just a few years older than Aaron, though already going gray.

"As good as one can expect, I guess." I bite into a piece of cheese. "How's business?" I reciprocate the fake interest.

"Same old struggles. We can't all be as lucky as the golden boy, can we?"

"Steve! Can you get your sons to turn off their games? They need to eat something." Peyton waves at me from the living room, and I nod back.

I'm still snacking from my plate, glancing at the TV when Princess, the family Persian cat, brushes against my leg. I drop my hand to pet her, but she swiftly moves away.

I want to follow her, to disappear without having to excuse myself. I mumble, "Wait for me," and watch as she makes her way toward the yard. I pop another olive in my mouth.

To my left, sitting in a leather chair, Aaron is giving his dad a full report on his latest transaction. Next to his father, he still looks like a scared little boy.

On my other side, his grandparents are dozing off on the couch.

I envy Aaron sometimes—even with their issues, his family is still around. I'm all alone, have been for quite some time. My dad's parents stepped in to take care of me after he left. I know he asked them to. Growing up, I often wondered if they still talked to him, but they told me, many times, "We get his check every month; otherwise, we wouldn't even know if he's still alive." During the first year after he left, I begged them to bring him back, to apologize for whatever I had done to make him leave. No matter how much I cried, they only hugged me and said, "I'm so sorry, sweetheart."

I still talk to my aunt Sheila once in a while. Apparently, Dad disappeared from all their lives when he left, and now his sister lives somewhere in Atlanta.

And then there's my mom's side of the family. They could be tight-knit, but I wouldn't know. *I never met them.* Apparently, Mom left their abusive household when she was young and never looked back. My dad didn't like talking much about them. I know I have cousins, but I don't even know their names. I've searched my mom's maiden name enough times to accept that they could be anyone.

Maria and Peyton are discussing shoes, and I find myself bored on Christmas Eve. There's not a single thing to do. No food to prepare, no dishes to clean, no last-minute errands to run —not with the number of servants they have to handle everything. Judging by the perfectly crisp and neatly wrapped presents under the tree, they haven't bothered to wrap a single gift themselves.

I retire early to the bedroom, and no one seems to care. Aaron kisses me and says he'll be up soon. I unpack my suitcase and hang my clothes in the empty closet. The bedroom is comfortable, with a large television and a couch across from the bed. I slip off my shoes and massage my foot—I'm definitely tired.

I must have fallen asleep with the movie still on because I hear Aaron shutting it off when he comes to bed.

* * *

"Merry Christmas," I say for the tenth time as I pour myself coffee. I feel much happier after a full night of sleep.

"Can we open them yet?" I hear Rick ask Peyton again.

"Not until everybody is down," she tells him.

"But Mom..."

"No buts. Your great-grandparents want to see you open your gifts too." She's firm enough that he sits down.

The boys are too old for Santa, but too young to have much patience. I'm on my second cup when I hear footsteps.

"Here they are," says Tucker, the twin.

"All right, now, one at a time," Don says as he hands out the gifts to his kids.

"Lower your expectations," I say, handing Aaron my gift.

"You forget we've been exchanging gifts for over a decade. My expectations are as low as possible," he says with a smile.

"Asshole," I mutter, kicking him.

His mother glances at me, clearly disapproving of my foul language.

"I was looking into getting one of these," Aaron says, thanking me.

"Really?" I knew it; I had asked his secretary for recommendations. The espresso machine I picked has more functions than the car we drove here.

I come back from the bathroom to find three presents by my chair. The first one holds an expensive wallet from Maria. The second, an engraved pen from Don. The third, chocolates from his cousins. I'm just finishing my thanks when Aaron walks over with a box.

"Aaron, another gift?"

"This one's for both of us."

I open the lid to find our wedding invitations. I pick one up; the paper is incredibly delicate and beautiful. A pile of elegant pale blue envelopes sits on the side. I had given the wedding planner, Chiara, free rein to decide on these things after getting overwhelmed by the options and constant decisions.

"Do you like them?" Aaron asks, still waiting for my response.

"Of course. I didn't realize they were already here."

"They sent them here by mistake, actually."

"Oh, I see." Something tells me it's no accident that his mother received the box instead of us.

The twins scream with excitement when they open Aaron's gift to them. It turns out everyone gives better gifts than I do.

With nothing else to open, we move on to breakfast. The table is filled with a buffet of omelettes, pastries, yogurt, and fruit. His parents sit across from me, and from the looks on their faces, it's clear they're still waiting for a big surprise from their son—as if the wine bottles we gave them were just a tease. Despite of the delicious food, my mouth tastes sour at the thought. I didn't grow up that way. Even with my parents gone, I had enough time with them to understand how sad that kind of greed is.

"Are you done unpacking, Iris?" His mom sips her coffee.

"I haven't... moved yet." I search for Aaron.

"She's still packing, Mom."

"Oh, it's been months, no?" She acts surprised.

"I've been... busy. With work," I tell her.

"She is, after all, a Harvard professor, Maria," Don says, winking at me. For fuck's sake, I don't need his help. I am, after all, *a Harvard professor.*

Don and Maria were never on board with their son dating the poor, messed-up girl whose dad disappeared. To them, I was broke and broken, a headache that needed to go away. I was sixteen when his mom told me, "You're holding my son back. You'll never make him happy." She even offered me money to break up with Aaron. He had forgiven his parents, but those words still hurt. Even now, after all these years, I can tell they still look at me the same way—a liability.

* * *

A while later, Aaron finds me reading a book in bed and sits next to me.

"Can I hide in here with you?" he asks.

"I'm not... sure."

"I'm ready to leave whenever you are."

I put my book down. "That might break the record."

He gives me a tired smile. "Two more days. I don't know if I can make it."

"You can't make it? How do you think I feel? Thank goodness for Peyton and the kids. At least your mom has someone else to..."

"Terrorize?"

"Yeah, sounds about right."

* * *

Dinner is exactly what I expect: uncomfortable conversations that are better left unsaid, like this one:

"So... how much money did you make this year, Aaron? I saw your name in the papers last week," Steve asks.

"Steve!" Peyton makes a face.

"Like you don't want to know," Steve says, taking one too many sips of his beer.

"It's rude to talk money at the table, cousin," Aaron says, already used to the comments.

"How's school, Rick?" Aaron asks the boy closest to him.

"Fine. I'm going pro, so whatever."

"Rick can kick both of our asses on the field," Steve says, chewing with his mouth open.

"That, I have no doubt," Don replies.

They all laugh.

"Any plans for kids of your own?" Peyton asks. *Every. Single. Year.*

"Who knows? Let's get married first," Aaron says without a hint of stress. We've talked about kids, and both of us agreed we're not ready for them.

"We're close to finalizing the details. Let's hope we don't have a very hot summer," Maria says, talking about my wedding like it's hers.

"I didn't know you were helping Chiara," I say, pretending I didn't know.

"Of course. Chiara is great, but someone needs to... supervise."

When Aaron told me his mom had recommended Chiara, I

wanted to veto it, but in the end, it was probably good that someone cared about the infinite details I couldn't bring myself to focus on.

"Right." I can't find the words. Perhaps it was a mistake to ignore my bridal duties. Whatever his mom is planning, it's not out of love for the marriage.

* * *

I'm coming out of the shower when I hear a knock on the bedroom door.

"Just a second!" I call, wrapping a towel around my body.

"It's me."

Whatever she wants, it can't be good.

"Hi," I say, opening the door to my future mother-in-law, my hair still dripping wet.

She walks in, looking around the room, judging everything her eyes land on.

"Everything okay?" I ask.

"You tell me," she replies.

"I don't know what you mean."

"Well, it's pretty obvious you don't want to marry my son, so what do you want?"

"What?"

"Only a fool wouldn't see it, Iris. You don't love him. I'm not sure if you ever did."

"You should leave."

"Perhaps this has been your plan all along, waiting for Aaron to make the big bucks. You were smart to push me away then; Aaron is worth a lot more now."

"I... I signed the prenup, Maria. I'm not after his money. But I don't care if that's what you think." I start to move toward the door, my hand almost reaching the doorknob when Aaron opens it from the other side.

"Mom?"

His presence startles her.

"I was..."

"She was just asking me about my wedding dress."

She looks at me, surprised.

"Oh, good," Aaron says, sitting on the couch.

His mom leaves immediately, looking confused by my choice of words.

I take a seat and tell Aaron *the truth*. He asks if I want to leave. I can't move; I just sit there, still dripping wet. It's one thing to wonder if his parents still feel the same way about me, but it's another to hear the confirmation.

"Iris, come here." He hugs me, and my prism responds to my feelings, lighting up between us.

"What the fuck?" he says, backing away.

I realize Aaron hasn't seen my necklace act abnormally yet. I'm used to it by now.

"Yeah, it does that when it gets wet and... and when I'm feeling vulnerable."

"I didn't... know. Akira mentioned something about evil. I thought she was just being... Akira."

"You don't have to be afraid of it. It's only a light."

He lifts his index finger and starts to move closer to me. The light goes out before he reaches it.

"Why didn't you tell me before? About your necklace? I thought we told each other everything." He's hugging me again.

"I'm sorry." That's all I can say without crying. *What the hell am I doing?*

EIGHT

"TO BE AN ARTIST IS TO BELIEVE IN LIFE." –
HENRY MOORE

After the third time she asks, I start to wonder myself if it's a good idea.

"I have to know," I tell Akira as search for a candle.

"This is nuts. How? I just can't believe he's real."

"He was standing next to me, in a tuxedo. I don't even know why he was at the party." I open a recently packed box, searching for the gift I bought myself in Salem.

"Do you know his last name?" Akira's dressed unusually casually in jeans and a gray hoodie. Her colorful hair is tied up in a ponytail.

"I don't."

"And you think you'll be able to... see him again if you do this?"

"I don't know. That's what happened the first time, but..."

It has to work. The thought of not knowing is driving me insane. Aaron went back to work this week, and without him or work to distract me, I'm a basket case. I can't eat or sleep. My mind's on a loop.

"What if it takes you somewhere else?" she asks.

"I guess it could... But I think... It should be okay if it does. I'm invisible there."

"What do you mean? I thought you said he saw you."

"I'm not sure he did. When I looked at my hands, there was nothing."

She shakes her head, trying to understand. "What are you going to do if you find him?"

"I don't know. I didn't think that far. I just need to know why. There's got to be a reason the prism took me there, to him. It can't be random, not after knowing he's real," I say, fishing out my pine tree candle.

"And how do I get you to... come back?" She looks stressed.

"I have no idea. After I blacked out, I woke up at your place."

I roll out my yoga mat.

"Iris, I don't know about this... Maybe we should have someone else here, too."

"No, nobody can know," I say, filling up a glass of water.

Akira takes the longest breath.

"If I don't come back in ten minutes, start shaking me," I tell her.

I sit on the floor of my apartment, surrounded by boxes. I close my eyes to keep from being distracted by the mess. I take a few deep breaths. Akira sits across from me, phone in hand to track the time. I lift the glass of water and dunk my prism in it.

"Now," I say to Akira.

She lights the candle. "Ten minutes," she says. I nod.

I hold the prism in my hand and bring it closer to the fire. Just like the first time, I feel the urge to stop myself. I have to fight the feeling. I have to keep going. I have to get it closer to the flame. I close my eyes again and think of Hoyt—his green eyes winking at me before walking away at the party, his handshake, *and the heat from it.*

My pendant fights my hand as I force myself to keep imagining Hoyt, pushing my instincts aside, getting so close to the candle it almost burns my fingers. The prism starts to spin, and I watch it while focusing on my breathing, telling myself I'm safe, I'm not alone. My entire body tingles, and I black out.

When I can see again, I'm not home anymore. I'm not in the same place as before, either. I'm outdoors, in the snow. *I should be cold*, I note. Apparently, I have no physical sensations here. I look again, searching for my body, but I can't see myself. I look around —I'm alone. Tall trees, covered in white layers, surround me.

"Easy boy..." I hear the familiar voice and follow it to the barn. I don't know how I'm moving without legs. I hear a horse neigh. I keep moving until I spot... him.

Hoyt looks very different from the last time I saw him. He's messy, a little dirty, and dressed in heavy winter gear. The jacket is so thick I wonder how long he's been outdoors. Does he live here? I eye him from head to toe—his boots are covered in snow. There's something intrusive about being close to him without... permission.

In front of him, a horse struggles to stay still. I know nothing about horses, but this one doesn't seem ordinary. Its coat is black, not brown, not even a speck of another color—completely black. Beautiful.

Hoyt seems to be doing something with the animal's hoof, completely unaware that I'm here, watching them. Again, I try to speak, but no voice comes out. I move closer, but the horse goes still. Its brown eyes lock in my direction. *What is it seeing?*

Hoyt follows the horse's gaze, and when he sees it too, he stands up, his eyes wide open. What are they seeing? I look down and around until I spot, through the reflection in the window behind them... a violet light, hanging midair. *My prism's light.*

Hoyt steps closer, hand extended in front of him, as if he wants to touch me, only I realize I'm not me. He wants to touch the brightness. *I am the light.*

I don't move. I want to feel his touch. Will I be able to feel it if

I don't have a body? I prepare myself for his hand when someone else grabs my shoulders.

Akira is shaking me, almost violently. I have to yell for her to stop.

"I'm sorry, you were..." she walks to the kitchen.

I lift my hands to my face. She hands me a towel.

"It's only been eight minutes, but... your nose started to bleed."

I stare at the red-soaked dish towel.

She continues, "And your eyes... they were white, completely rolled up. I... It was terrifying."

"I didn't feel... anything," I tell her, realizing my head now hurts. "I saw him, and I wasn't me—I was the light, the violet light. I have to go back." I'm happy it worked. I'm excited, even. I wanted to stay longer.

"No way!" She's already putting out the candle and getting rid of the glass of water.

"I have to, he was about to—"

"I don't care if he was about to kiss you."

"No, that's not what I was going to say. I wasn't *me*."

She's no longer paying attention.

"Akira, nothing happened."

"Oh, really? Go look in the mirror." She gestures to my face.

"It's just a nosebleed, probably from the dry air."

"This wasn't a little nosebleed, Iris. Your face, you were..."

"What?"

"I don't know, different. Not... yourself."

"You don't understand. I have to go back. I need to know more."

"Not today." She's assertive.

"It's not up to you." I sound like a teenager.

"I'm not sticking around to see you get hurt, or worse."

"What's worse than getting hurt?"

"If you want to do this alone, go ahead, but I'm not helping you again."

I try to stand up and suddenly feel very dizzy. She holds me steady.

"Shit," I say, sitting back down on the couch.

"I shouldn't have helped you in the first place. Look at you."

"Yes, you should have, and I'm fine. I just need... to sit for a second."

"If you're not you there, then how can you even... communicate with him?"

"I tried to talk, but I had no voice."

"So what do you want to do? Watch him?"

"I was hoping I could... I don't know, find out who he is."

"There's gotta be another way."

"Like how? All I know is his first name. And that he has a horse."

"A horse? In Boston?"

"It wasn't Boston. Last time I saw mountains, and now, it was a barn."

"Okay, a barn. So we look that up." She's typing something on her phone. "What kind of horse?"

"I don't know, a black one."

"Black one?"

"Yeah."

"Hmm."

"What?"

"Black horses are not very common."

"How do you know?"

"I like to watch animal documentaries before bed." She's scrolling on her phone. "Why don't you ask Lara? She might know him." She puts her phone down. I introduced them at my birthday party.

"I guess I could... I don't want Aaron to know, for obvious reasons."

"Let's start there. No more psychic shit until then."

I smile at her. "Okay."

* * *

I decide to stay in my apartment for the night; I need to be alone. I text Aaron saying I'm going to work on packing things.

I'm waiting on Lara's reply when another notification catches my attention.

Hi Iris,

It took me a while, but I think I found something you might want to look at. It was a colleague of mine who brought it up when I mentioned your research. A few years ago, there was an exhibition of rare jewels at the Met. My friend remembered there was info on folklore myths in the catalog. He has a copy and promised to give it to me on Monday. I can send it to you if you don't find a copy first yourself. Hope this helps.

Happy New Year.

Elena

There are no copies of the catalog for sale on the website. Maybe Harvard has one. The library is open, even though classes haven't started yet. I make plans to check it out first thing in the morning.

Another notification startles me.

Hey Iris, I would love to grab a coffee. How about tomorrow at 10:30 a.m.? I'm leaving for Morocco on Friday.

I reply immediately: *Sounds good. Stanleys?*

Perfect, see you then, Lara replies seconds later.

With actual plans for the following day, I order a pizza and eat in peace while researching black horses. I realize I know nothing about the animal; I'm lost in details about breeds and genetics when I make myself get up to pee.

Does Hoyt live in the mountains? Or does he live in the city? Why was he at the gala? Was he someone's plus one? The thought stirs up the food in my stomach. I remind myself that I'm the one *engaged*. Still, whatever reason the prism had to introduce us, it has to mean something.

* * *

Aside from my anxiety, I sleep well; I miss my bed. It's lumpy and small, yet my body fits perfectly in the indentations.

Stanley's is only a block away from Lara and Aaron's office. I've been here a few times waiting for Aaron.

I order a vanilla latte and take a seat by the window. I hope Aaron is too busy to walk anywhere today. I don't want him catching me with his coworker.

"How are you?" Lara is wearing a tailored cream suit with a blue blouse underneath. Her silky long blonde hair falls over her shoulders.

"I'm good, how are you?"

"I'm good, a little stressed. I'm sure you know all about the stuff we're dealing with in the office. Everyone is going crazy."

I pretend I do.

I gesture for her to order something first before sitting down.

She comes back with an iced coffee and sits next to me. "I'm curious why you needed to meet in person. Everything okay?"

"Yes, yes, nothing serious... It's this friend of mine, Akira—she was at my birthday, not sure if you remember her."

"Colorful hair girl?"

"Yep, that's her."

"What about her?"

"Well, she met a guy at the office gala; you weren't there... Aaron doesn't know him, and I just wanted to know... if he is, you know, decent. She's my best friend and has a tendency of... making bad choices... if you know what I mean."

"What's his name?"

"Hoyt, I don't know his last name."

"Hoyt Locklear?" Her expression isn't what I expect. "Rugged, tall, strong, green eyes?"

"That's him," I say, butterflies in my stomach.

"Seems like your friend does have an eye for the lousy ones."

"Why is that?" I ask, not wanting to hear her next words.

"He's known for not... settling down. Every party, he brings a new girl. His dad got sick, and he took over the business a while back."

"I see. Do you know him?"

"I know of him. He lives in the country, I think; his dad was known to own a lot of land."

"Well, I'm glad I asked then. I would hate for her to... waste her time."

"Yeah, sure. I'd suggest she stay away, especially with so many good guys around here." She winks at me.

Did she think...? *She knows there's no friend.* I blush with embarrassment; she works with Aaron...

She reads my face. "Don't worry, your secret is safe with me."

"I wasn't planning on doing... anything."

"None of my business anyway. Perhaps I'm being a little selfish, but... I like having a friend at those parties." She takes another sip of her coffee.

"Thanks for coming, I don't even know..."

"Water under the bridge."

We talk a bit about business and Aaron, but her phone is ringing nonstop.

We're saying our goodbyes when she turns around and says, "If your friend does decide to... test the waters... I suggest she keeps her options open. In case she needs a safety net."

She walks away before I can say anything. Did she just imply I...? I shake my head. Lara is... Well, I can see why she's good at business.

NINE

"THE GREATER THE ARTIST, THE GREATER THE
DOUBT. PERFECT CONFIDENCE IS GRANTED TO
THE LESS TALENTED AS A CONSOLATION PRIZE."
– ROBERT HUGHES

Lara's words are still echo in my head as I arrive on campus. As expected, the buildings look haunted by the absence of people.

I pause my search for the catalog and pull my phone from my purse. I type: *Hoyt Locklear.* I don't want to know, yet I can't help myself. There are no social media accounts—though I wasn't expecting any. He doesn't seem like the type. My heart races when I spot his photo in an article. He looks younger, with a shorter haircut. The article briefly mentions that he took over his dad's business and lands. John Locklear died of heart failure six years ago. From what I can tell, the lands span several states, including North Dakota, Idaho, and Montana—the latter being where I guess the mountains I saw are located.

There are numerous reports about sales and purchases of estates, acres, and ranches, but nothing personal about him. *A different girl at every party.* I hate the thought of him with... anyone. I want to slap myself—it's ridiculous. I don't even know the guy. I shove the phone back into my purse.

I'm about to give up on my search in the library when I hear Darion's voice. I freeze. *The last thing I need is this.* I duck behind

72

the bookshelves and wait for him to move. All I can see is the top of his head.

"There has to be something you can do. I never missed a class, not until..." he says to someone hidden by the shelves.

"If they say there's nothing they can do, then I'm sorry," comes the second voice. George. The English professor. My colleague.

"I think it's time you pay the debt. I would hate for them to find out how you got this job," Darion says, his voice now cold, like a dog on a tight leash, just waiting to be freed.

"I don't know what I can do," George's voice trembles.

"Figure it out!" Darion snaps, walking away.

I exhale. Why hasn't Darion replied to my email?

I leave campus immediately. I have no desire to run into him, especially with no one else around.

* * *

On my way to update Akira on what Lara said, I check my phone and see three missed calls from Aaron, followed by a text: *Call me ASAP.*

"Hey, I was in the library..."

He cuts me off. "My parents are here."

"Here? As in Boston?"

"As in the apartment. I didn't want you to show up here unprepared."

"What are they doing here?"

"They want to... apologize?"

"What? I don't want—"

"Can you come home? They won't leave until they talk to you."

"Fine. Have a glass waiting for me."

This day quickly becomes one of my worst. I barely realize I'm home when the driver parks.

"Good afternoon, Ms. De Loughery," the doorman greets me.

"Hi, Nelson. How are you?"

"Doing well, ma'am."

"I heard I have visitors, huh?" I glance at the elevator, hesitating to press the button.

"Yes, ma'am."

"Wish me luck?"

"I'm sorry to hear you need it, ma'am."

Aaron is sitting on the armchair to the left, while his parents sit on the couch in front of him, each holding a glass. I don't know where things stand between them since we left their house. His mom tried to apologize right then, but I was too angry to listen. I knew we'd have to talk eventually, even when Aaron threatened to never see them again. It's enough that I don't have a family, but I don't wish the same fate on him, even if his parents are... these two.

Don speaks first, getting up to kiss me hello. I hold up my hand. He sits back down. I pour myself a double and take a seat in the second armchair.

"Let's hear it," Aaron says, looking at his mother.

Maria is wearing a black dress with a sweater draped over her shoulders.

"Iris, I'm sorry about... what I said during Christmas. I took a couple of pills, and with the drinks, I don't know what came over me. I didn't mean to..."

I look at both of them. "There's nothing you can say to make me forget."

Don starts to apologize again, but I interrupt him.

"I don't want to cause trouble in your relationship with your son—God knows I've tried with you two—but from now on, I hope we stick to... pleasantries. Leave me alone, and I'll do the same."

I'm still sipping my whiskey when Aaron finds me in the kitchen.

"That was a little harsh, don't you think?" he asks, opening the fridge and pulling out the cheese tray.

"Really? After everything they've done?"

"Well, they came to apologize..."

"Did you ask them to come?"

"No! Of course not, but they're still my parents, Iris. How are we going to—"

"I don't care who they are, not anymore. You need them in your life, not me."

"Iris, they're going to be your in-laws. How are you planning on keeping them away?"

"I don't know. I'll... manage." I rub my temples. *Shitty day, indeed.*

* * *

When Aaron tries fooling around later that night, I stop him with, "Sorry, not tonight. I'm just not in the mood." He turns around like the gentleman he is. Perfect little prince. I'm obviously still angry. Angry that I can't make myself love him the way he loves me. Angry that he's too perfect to walk away from. Not only does he adore me, he's kind, hardworking, good-looking, and even donates to charity. I can't come up with any good reason to leave him. Not a real one, at least.

I get out of bed and text Akira from the bathroom.

Are you up?

Hey, she texts back. *Everything okay?*

Yeah, no... Did I wake you?

Nah, just watching something with penguins. What's going on?

I talked to Lara, I write. *Hoyt is a douchebag, apparently.*

Sorry, Iris.

Whatever. It's not like I know him.

What are you going to do about it? she asks.

I don't even know what options I have, I write.

You could tell Aaron you aren't ready to get married yet.

Maybe... though we've been together for fifteen years. I don't think asking for time is going to fly.

He'll understand, she texts. *He loves you.*

Maybe. I feel so stressed.

You know what you need? Spiral.

I write back: *Tomorrow night?*

See you then.

Night x.

* * *

I spend the day searching online for any more information on Hoyt, but find little. I learn his brother died when he was seventeen, but the cause of death is vague. Besides obituaries and land deals, there's nothing else.

It's noon when I finally notice I smell and realize I haven't showered yet. I've spent the day in bed, on the computer. At least I've done something productive. I emailed Elena, asking her to send pictures of the catalog pages—waiting for the post office isn't an option. Maybe it's the PMS or yesterday's conversations, but whatever the reason, I'm in a grumpy mood. Getting ready helps a bit.

I'm not sure Spiral will fix me, but as soon as I step inside, I feel a little better. The music drowns out my thoughts, and it feels great to give myself a break from them.

"To us!" I say, clinking my glass against Akira's.

We're moving with the music when I feel my prism warm against my skin. I'm sweaty again, just like last time, and I don't want to put on a show. I walk to the bathroom to dry off my necklace. Akira follows me. She hands me another paper towel, and a few people glance at us for a second. Nobody cares.

"Why do you think the"—she gestures to the necklace with her eyes—"made you see him?"

"No clue. At first, I thought it meant something, but now I'm leaning toward it being a stupid coincidence."

"Seriously?"

"I don't know. Any ideas?"

"No, but..."

"I told you what Lara said."

"So?"

"So I don't have any desire to be just a number on his list," I say.

"Maybe you shouldn't go trusting Lara without double-checking yourself."

"You're the one who told me to ask her."

Akira scoffs. "I didn't say trust her over your intuition."

"More like common sense."

She's reapplying her lipstick, her movements deliberate as always.

"What would you have me do?" I ask. "Are you really saying you're going to help me again?"

"Well, I don't know about that," she says, glancing at me in the mirror. "Maybe you can get his phone number?"

I raise my eyebrows. "And say what? Hi, this is me, the girl who burned your hand at the party. Want to meet up?"

"Yeah, something like that."

"Very funny."

"Didn't you say Aaron has another event to attend next week? Maybe Hoyt will be there."

"I'm not planning on going."

"What if I go with you?"

"Seriously?"

"I'm curious too."

I smile at her. "It's a date, then."

* * *

Across the kitchen island, Aaron asks, "Want a piece of toast?"

"Just one slice, please."

He pours both of us a cup of coffee, his brow furrowed as he glances at me. "Any plans for today?"

"I have some paperwork to send. I can't believe classes start next week already."

"I thought you've been bored."

"Yeah, kind of."

"How many classes are you teaching this semester?"

"Four," I say, surprised by his interest.

"That'll keep you busy."

"Oh, and I need another ticket for the SMPS Awards."

"Are you going?"

"Akira too."

"Really?"

"Yeah, she's single again."

"Okay." He laughs, processing the information.

Minutes later, he's out the door, leaving me with the mountain of work I have to tackle.

The stack of papers to sign and submit seems endless—the same routine every year. At least it's giving me something to focus on other than Hoyt. I glance at my students' list, already feeling the familiar rush of anticipation. Though many names are familiar, one is conspicuously missing—Darion. Has he dropped out? Two of the classes I'm teaching this semester are mandatory for his major: HAA 310A – Methods and Theory of Art History and HAA 233G – The Body and Embodiment in Greek Art.

I can't stop thinking about the conversation I overheard in the library. How does Darion know how George got his job? Something feels off about it, and I can't shake the suspicion. I search for him online, hoping to find something—anything. His social media accounts are almost entirely pictures of books, art, and the occasional food diary—no friends, no people, actually.

I start to feel pathetic as I scroll through everyone's online lives, my own existence fading into the background. I've become obsessed with these searches, living through the online profiles of strangers. *I need a life of my own.* I shut my laptop with a heavy hand.

I grab my phone to text Akira, but before I can, I see that Elena has texted me—dozens of pictures. I feel guilty for giving her the task; it would've been easier for her to just mail me the book.

I reply, *THANK YOU VERY MUCH, sorry for the loaded favor.*

She replies immediately: *No worries, you are welcome.*

I start going through the pictures right away, zooming in and out. They're heavy on text, and I regret having to read on such a small screen. I decide to transfer the images to my computer. On the third page, I see a mention of alchemists. It describes the alteration of properties in an object, and something about the topic sparks my interest. I keep reading about the classic myths of turning matter into gold when I spot the fine print: *Physical alchemy relates to the transformation of physical matter, while spiritual alchemy is the art of freeing the spiritual self from inner fear, limiting beliefs, and lack of self-acceptance.* I make a note to research more.

There are also photos of the jewelry displayed in the exhibition —delicate and exuberant—but, of course, there aren't any necklaces that resemble my prism. I'm starting to think mine is a one-of-a-kind pendant. It has to be. Perhaps I hold the only information on it, tucked away on my bedside table, in an envelope.

TEN

"THE QUESTION IS NOT WHAT YOU LOOK AT,
BUT WHAT YOU SEE." – HENRY DAVID THOREAU

It's the first time I struggle to find something to wear for a formal party. Usually, I'm fine with any pretty dress. Tonight, I feel different—nervous. I'm not sure if Hoyt will be there, but the possibility that he might be is enough. At the same time, I can't contain my excitement. I'm equally nauseated by what I'm doing to Aaron. He deserves better.

I end up choosing a sparkly silver dress, one I've never worn. It has a slit that goes up higher than I'm comfortable with; however tonight, I need to go above average. I'm not sure if I'm the hunter or the prey, only that *it feels good to like what I see in the mirror.* I leave my hair down with curls and opt for no jewelry. Tonight, I'm letting my prism show.

"Wow," Aaron says, appearing at the door, looking charming himself.

"I figured Akira will take over the show if I don't... step it up," I tell him.

He smiles. "There isn't anything Akira can wear that could overshadow you. I need to prepare myself; all eyes will be on you tonight."

I think about Aaron's words as the driver pulls up to Akira's place to pick her up. She looks beautiful in a red dress with a neckline so low, I don't know how she looks comfortable.

"You look amazing," she says as we walk in.

"You too. Only you can pull off that kind of dress. I love that for you."

I'm overthinking my entire outfit. I feel naked when I drop off my coat.

"I'll see you ladies in a bit," Aaron says as a friend calls him over.

The building is old but carries its character well. Massive chandeliers illuminate the place. A jazz band plays, and the awards sit in glass cubes on stage. I don't even know what kind of awards they're giving out. I'm now aware I know nothing regarding the event.

"Let's get a drink," Akira says, eyeing the bartender.

"I don't normally drink..." I start. She looks at me like I'm speaking a different language. "At these events!" I finish, making a face.

"And why not?"

"Because I'm afraid I'll say something... I don't know... I don't want to embarrass Aaron."

"Oookay. Don't worry, I got your back tonight."

I take a deep breath, steadying myself. Perhaps leaving the prism out in the open was a bad idea.

The bartender is flirting with Akira when she shifts her gaze to me.

She lifts her glass. "To us."

I chuckle at her memorable words. "To us."

"Now what?" she asks after taking a sip.

"Now, we wait. If he is here, he'll come get a drink."

The band is great. I'm observing them when Lara walks over in a beautiful blue dress. Classier than mine, and way classier than the one Akira is wearing. We look... desperate next to her.

"So glad you guys came, I was starting to think this was going to be a dull event," she tells us.

"You remember Akira..." I reintroduce them. "Is Ted here?" I ask, not seeing her husband nearby.

"Yeah, somewhere with Aaron."

I sip my cocktail while Lara updates us on the latest gossip about the people around us when I feel my prism pulse. I look up and see Hoyt ordering a drink; he catches me staring. He nods and smiles at me.

His green eyes almost glow with the light above him.

My friends are staring too.

"Well, well, Mr. Locklear is looking hot as ever," Lara says, devouring him with her eyes.

"That's Hoyt?" Akira blurts out.

Lara has her *confirmation* that I lied. Akira hasn't even met the guy.

"Yes," I answer.

"Go talk to him!" Akira urges, pushing me.

"Are you crazy? Aaron could be anywhere." I look around.

"Then I will." She moves toward him.

I'm mortified by what she might say to him. I pull Lara into a conversation, but I can't help but stare at them.

"What's going on?" Lara asks.

I roll my eyes. "Akira is single, so..."

"Iris, we both know Akira isn't going over there for her."

"It's not like I can go there myself..."

Lara looks around. "There's no balcony." She glances at the stairs. "We can distract Aaron long enough for you guys to... talk," she says.

"I don't know... I'm not sure if it's a good idea."

"Better now than after the wedding." She sips her drink casually.

"Oh my god! This is crazy."

"Head upstairs. He'll meet you there," she affirms.

I walk upstairs, my heart throbbing stronger with each step. I hold on to the beautiful ornate railing to steady myself. I need to get my feelings under control, or this conversation will be about the light in my necklace. *Wait, it's not wet*, I remind myself. Still, I can feel something happening with the prism, like it's pulsing with my heartbeat.

I wait a couple of minutes when I hear his voice behind me.

"Iris?"

I turn around. "Hi. I didn't know you knew my name..."

His eyes lower from my face to my chest, straight to the necklace. "Your friend just told me... Where did you get that necklace?"

"Oh, this... My mother gave it to me."

He reaches for my hand, but then recoils, remembering what we felt last time we touched. "Follow me," he tells me.

I look around. "Follow you? Where? Why?"

We turn a corner, not exactly in private, when he starts undoing his shirt buttons.

"What are you doing?" I ask in a panic—someone's going to see this.

"Look!" He pulls out his own necklace—*his own prism*. It's different from mine, a triangular-shaped one held by a silver chain. Still, it's obvious that they're... similar.

"Is that..." I'm shocked.

"Does your prism light up?" he asks, buttoning his shirt again.

"Yes. A violet light."

"Mine does too, a dark blue." He seems rattled by our words.

"Where did you get yours?" I'm trying to understand what it all means.

"From my family."

"I didn't know... that there were... others," I tell him.

"My brother had one too." There's pain in his eyes as he says it.

I remember what I read about his brother online. "I'm sorry..." My phone starts to ring. It's Akira. "Hello?"

"Where are you?"

"Upstairs."

"I'm upstairs and I don't see you."

"Around the corner."

"What? Why? What are you doing?"

"Nothing, Hoyt was—"

She finds us. "You guys can't stay here. Aaron is looking for you. They're about to give the awards, and he's giving a speech and..."

"He is?"

"Yeah, come on."

I look back at Hoyt. I have a million questions. Akira pulls me away.

"I'll catch you later," he says, motioning for me to keep going.

Aaron is presenting an award, and I had no idea about it. I'm so caught up in my own little world that I didn't even ask him why we're here. Shame and sadness wash over me. I don't like the person I'm becoming—lying, hiding... it's not right. Aaron loves me; we're getting married. He makes eye contact with me from the stage and smiles. I listen to his words when I glance at Hoyt on the opposite side, watching the speech like everyone else. I keep my face forward. I barely make out the words Aaron is saying—something about donations for buildings and charity boards. It lasts an eternity.

I wait for Aaron to walk off the stage so I can excuse myself to the bathroom. *I need a minute.* I'm almost there when a hand touches me, and this time, it hurts him, but *only him.*

"I'm sorry," he says, shaking his hand.

"I didn't feel... It didn't hurt me."

"Really?"

"Not like the first time."

"Huh, why is this happening?"

"I don't know, it only happens with you."

"Something to do with the prisms, I guess."

"I'm not alone here." I'm trying to explain... I can't be seen with him.

"I know. Give me your number."

* * *

I drop Akira off at her place, wishing I could go with her. I need to talk about everything that happened. But I can't find a reason to leave Aaron.

"Brunch tomorrow?" she asks me.

I love her. She knows me well.

"Sure, text me where."

"Are you okay?" Aaron asks on the way home after she leaves.

"Too many drinks, I think."

"Between you, Lara, and Akira, I don't know how you guys are standing."

I laugh. "Yeah, I think they were doing shots at one point."

"I don't think people noticed, though; they were handing out drinks nonstop."

"I didn't know you were giving a speech. I'm sorry, Aaron, I should have known."

"Nonsense. I could have mentioned it... it was no big deal."

"Yes, it was. I'm your fiancée. I should know if you're giving a speech."

"We don't talk about work much."

"Maybe we need to change that."

I've had too many drinks. I take an aspirin and go to bed. I make sure to put my phone on silent in case... in case Hoyt messages me.

He has my phone number. He has a prism.

I don't know how I sleep. My alarm reminds me in the morning that I did, though. It sounds louder than normal. I shut it off quickly; Aaron is still sleeping.

There are two unread texts.

One from Akira: *Cafe Magnolia, 11 a.m.*
And one from an unknown number: *Hi.*

* * *

I dress quickly to meet Akira. I haven't replied to Hoyt yet. I don't know where to even begin. If it weren't for his prism, I'm not sure if I should keep up with whatever is going on between us. Only now that I know he has a prism, this changes everything. *I need to know everything he does.*

Too many people have the same idea to meet for brunch at the popular spot. "Downside of living in the city," I hear someone in line say.

"What are you getting?" I ask Akira while reading the menu.

"Benedict, bacon, butter."

"Sounds perfect," I agree with a smile.

"Start from the beginning," she says, pouring cream into her coffee.

I tell her about my... encounter with Hoyt in the corner, and the one by the bathroom. She almost chokes when I mention his own prism.

"That explains... I guess," she finally says when I finish.

"What does?"

"That your prism has a connection to his."

"You think the prisms are connected?"

"That would make sense."

"Nothing about any of this makes sense, but I see your point."

"Did you text him?"

"No, I don't even know what to say. I feel awful. I hate lying to Aaron."

"Well, you're not cheating on Aaron."

"At this point, it's just technicalities."

"Have you thought about asking to postpone the wedding?"

86

"Whatever I say, it will break his heart. I know it will. I just wish there was a way that didn't end up with me hurting him."

"Whatever you decide to do, you can't go wrong with being honest."

"Right. I'm just terrified I'm throwing away my..."

"Your what?"

I say, "The one. Aaron was supposed to be the one."

"If he was, we wouldn't be having this conversation."

My appetite is disappears.

"What did you talk to Hoyt about?" I ask her.

"I barely introduced myself when Lara came over. He asked your name."

"Do you think I should text him?"

"I think you need answers."

Akira can't stay long; she has an appointment at the hair salon.

"You sure you don't want to come along?" she asks as she heads out.

"Next time. I need to sort things out."

"Text me if you need anything."

"I will," I reply, making a mental note to repay all she's done for me. And in that line of thought, I text Lara to thank her for last night, too.

* * *

Half an hour later, I'm walking around the museum, having simply drifted here. I'm sitting in front of a favorite painting of mine—*Entrance to the Village of Vétheuil in Winter* by Claude Monet (French, 1840–1926)—when I decide to reply to the text.

I read his message again: *Hi.*

I reply, *Hello.*

I'm looking up at the painting when he responds, *Oh good, I thought you had given me the wrong number on purpose.*

I thought about it, I text back.

Why didn't you?

I scoff as I type, *I'm still wondering that myself.*

What did you want to talk about last night? he asks.

What do you mean?

Your friends told me to meet you upstairs. I figured there was a reason.

Oh right... I text. I pause, then add, *Perhaps I'll tell you another time. It's best said... in person.*

Let's meet, comes his reply.

Don't you live in the country? I ask.

How would you know that?

Lara, my friend. She knew.

Did she? And what else did she say about me?

I think about how to respond. *Apparently, you have a... reputation.*

You don't say.

Apparently so.

And what am I known to be?

I laugh as I type, *Manwhore.*

What!?

Well, you bring a new date to every party. People notice.

They are models or friends.

None of my business.

Your fiancé gave a nice speech last night.

He knew about Aaron? I don't know what to say.

I saw the ring. When is the wedding? he asks.

None of your business, I reply.

Okay.

This is going well.

What do you know about the prisms? I ask.

It's best said... in person.

Are you serious?

Very.

Okay, well... do you or do you not live in the country?

Yes, but I'm still in the city until tomorrow.
I can meet today.
All right, where?

I think about my apartment. I don't feel comfortable taking him there. There's Akira's place, but I want to talk to him alone. *I'm at the museum right now*, I text back.

Right now?
Too busy?
Which museum? he asks.
MFA—465 Huntington Ave, Boston, MA 02115.

Then comes his reply: *See you soon.*

Eleven

S omehow, I end up in the musical instruments section, my mind busy with all the questions I have for Hoyt. *I need information.* That's what I'm doing. My invite has a purpose. I have a reason. I tell myself.

The collection includes flutes, whistles, panpipes, and other instruments spanning from ancient times to the late twentieth century.

I stop to study a cane flute with six finger holes. Its surface is covered in engravings of a battle. I wish I could hear its sound. Moving on, I find another cane instrument—a nineteenth-century Spanish panpipe, held together by strings. Apparently, I'm drawn to music whenever I need an escape from my feelings.

When I reach the wooden drums, my heart begins to beat in rhythm. An English bass drum, adorned with white and blue ensigns, sits next to a mallet.

I check my phone—Hoyt will be here any minute. The rhythmic drumroll continues to beat in my chest until he arrives.

Hoyt seems a little out of place in the museum—he moves slowly, as if worried he might break something if he's not careful. He's dressed in jeans, a plaid button-down, and a corduroy jacket.

His hair is tied in a man bun. He looks a bit wild in this city environment.

"Have you been here before?" I ask when he finds me in the sculpture gallery. I'm eyeing a sarcophagus adorned with relief carvings from the Hellenistic period when he walks over.

"First time," he replies, slipping his hands into his pockets.

"Not an art fan?" I ask, trying not to let his... scent distract me. *Is that cologne?*

"Can't say that I am. I grew up in the country. You?"

"I grew up here." I gesture to the museum.

"Like your parents work here or something?"

"No, but we came here a lot."

I detect something citrusy mixed with musk. I shake my head to distract myself.

"And you still come often?" he asks.

"Yes, when I need to be alone or... when I'm missing them." I didn't plan to be so open, but the words fly out.

"I'm sorry, have they... passed away?"

"My mom died when I was young. My dad decided he didn't want to be a dad anymore and left."

He stops in front of a Greek bronze sculpture of Apollo.

"Iris, I'm sorry," he says, his green eyes locking onto mine.

"Thanks, I'm... I'm recovered, I think." I look away, feeling a tightness in my chest.

He gives me a faint smile.

"I'm sorry about your dad, too." *Shit*, that slipped out.

"And did your friend tell you that too?"

"No, I looked you up."

"Hmm."

"What?"

"Nothing."

"What?"

"I'm glad you did."

"Why?"

"I like that you were... curious about me."

My prism pulses, and my stomach turns.

We enter the painting gallery. Hoyt stops in front of Monet's *Fisherman's Cottage on the Cliffs at Varengeville.*

"Do you like it?" I ask, noticing he seems genuinely interested.

"I love the ocean. Living in the countryside, I don't get to see it much."

"My favorite part of this one is that there isn't a path to the house. We're left wondering..."

We move to the next wall.

"My mom loved this one," I say, eyeing *Portrait of a Dancer* by Nicolas Lancret. "See her turned foot? She's a dancer. My mom liked to dance. And this one," I add, walking over to the next painting. "My dad used to say it's about a father. The man is gently holding his daughter's hand while yelling at his son, who is playing with a sword. My dad used to joke that's why he loved having a daughter. I was sweet, like the fruit the girl's carrying in the basket, and I'd never try to fight him. I never looked up the true story. I like the one he made up."

"You do seem comfortable here."

"I come here a lot. I'm an art history professor."

"Oh, where do you teach?"

I can hear him breathing in the quiet room.

"Harvard."

His eyes lock onto mine. "That's impressive," he says.

"Not really..." I shrug. "I know you took over your dad's business. Do you like it?"

"I never had a choice. It was supposed to be my brother. He was the smart one... I always thought I'd just take care of the horses, but..."

I don't say anything. I can't say I know about the horses. I don't want to say I know about his brother.

"When my brother died, I knew I'd have to take over one day."

"I'm sorry about your brother. You said he had a prism too?"

"Yeah, a rectangular one."

The museum lights flicker. I glance up. It happens again.

"It must be the storm," Hoyt says, eyeing another painting.

"What storm?" I ask, looking around—there are no windows here.

"It's snowing," he says casually.

"Is it? I didn't know." I pull out my phone.

There's a text from Aaron: *Don't be stuck in the storm. Come home.*

"I heard they're expecting a foot of snow. That's why I'm leaving tomorrow," Hoyt says, glancing at my phone.

The realization that he's leaving makes me feel sad. *What am I doing?*

"You came here knowing a storm was coming?" I ask.

"I wanted to see you."

His words strike something deep inside me.

We walk in silence for a few minutes, observing Pacific wooden masks from the twentieth century.

"I should go home," I say, trying to make sense of my actions.

"Why? Is your fiancé calling?"

"As a matter of fact, yes."

He stops walking. "Are you going to tell me what you wanted to say at the party?"

"Can you tell me what you know about the prisms first?"

"Right. Let's go somewhere... else. Too many people here." There are only three other people nearby.

We turn a corner, where the tapestries hang on display, when the lights go out.

"The generator will kick in soon," a guard says.

I'm not sure how close I am to Hoyt. I move an inch, and his hand brushes mine. He curses in pain.

"Are you okay?" I ask.

"Fuck, this hurts."

"I'm sorry, I didn't mean to. I can't see."

"Why the fuck does it only hurt me now?" He sounds frustrated, and I wonder the same thing.

"I don't know... I'm stepping back."

The lights flicker back on. Hoyt is hunched over, and I see the red mark on his hand.

"Did I...?"

He nods.

"I'm sorry, Hoyt." I hate the thought of hurting him.

"I'm okay. Maybe we should keep our... distances for now."

"Of course."

"This sucks," he mutters, running a hand through his hair.

"Are you sure you're okay?"

He doesn't answer.

We take a seat by the window, and I watch the snow falling outside. *How am I going to get home?*

"What do you know about the prisms, Hoyt? Because I know nothing."

"Honestly, I don't know much either. Only that they can drive you crazy. It killed my brother."

"What? How?" I wasn't expecting this.

"It was my fault."

To my surprise, he doesn't shy away from my stare.

"What was?"

"That he died."

I want to reach out, hold his hand. The pain in his eyes is almost palpable.

"What happened?"

"I haven't told this to anyone."

"Because nobody knows about the prism?"

"And because I never felt... I feel like I can honestly talk to you."

I know what he means, but I say, "I'm a stranger."

"You don't feel like one."

He's looking at me, really looking.

"I'm getting married, Hoyt."

"We can be… friends."

"Friends?"

He continues, "We found the prisms together. I was sixteen, Luke was seventeen. We fought about some stupid shit, who was better with a bow. The fight took a turn, as it often did with us, and we ended up all bloodied. I said something about him being a coward, that he'd never stand up to Dad. An hour later, I was challenging him to open the safe. We knew the combination—we'd watched Dad open it for years. I thought we'd find money, maybe spend it on beer or something. But instead, we found the two prisms. Mine was a necklace, and his was a bracelet. I don't even know what happened. As soon as we put them on, their lights turned on. His emitted a green glow, and mine a dark blue. As you probably know, there was no taking them off after that."

"What did your dad say?"

"He went crazy, yelling at us to take them off, saying we didn't know what we'd done. But it was too late—he knew it, too."

"And how did your brother…?"

"The prism drove him mad. He started hearing voices, couldn't shut them out. He kept saying he couldn't take it anymore. He died months later. Suicide."

"I'm so sorry, Hoyt. It's not your fault. You didn't know."

"Luke was the responsible one. He never wanted to step out of line. I was always pushing him. Dad made sure I knew it was my fault."

"Hoyt." I move a little closer, but he jumps back.

"Oh my God, I forgot. I'm sorry."

"I hate this thing," he says, staring out the window. "Every time I try to take it off, though, I feel… wrong. But I hate it."

He looks outside again. "It's getting crazy out there."

"We should go before it gets worse," I say, standing up.

"Can I call you?" he asks.

"Let's keep it to text. Aaron can be…"

"Jealous?"

"Yes."

"Okay."

Hoyt puts me in the first cab, and I watch him close the door. *We needed more time*; there's so much I still need to ask him. I want to know if his prism can make him travel like mine. I want to know more about his brother—what did his dad know about the prisms? Why did he keep them in a safe?

Somehow, I have to push all of this to the back of my mind. Aaron is waiting for me when I open the door.

"Where have you been?" He helps me take off my wet clothes.

"The museum."

"I was worried."

"Sorry, you know I get distracted there."

"I ordered soup and a sandwich for you, but it's cold by now."

"Thank you. I'm hungry."

All I want to do is tell Aaron I'm sorry. The nicer he is to me, the worse I feel. I'm in a deep hole now. I have to dig my way out, and I know exactly what will happen once I do. Whatever I'm feeling for Hoyt, even if I barely know him, I've never felt with Aaron. I wish I did. And when it's time to tell him, I know I'm going to lose my best friend too.

I eat in front of the TV while Aaron watches the news.

I spend the evening checking my phone, hoping Hoyt has texted me. He hasn't. How can I be so drawn to a guy I barely know? Especially one who's known for dating someone new every week? I need to get my focus back. I'm going back to work in the morning.

TWELVE

"ONE CAN HAVE NO SMALLER OR GREATER
MASTERY THAN MASTERY OF ONESELF." –
LEONARDO DA VINCI

I t never really makes much sense to call it a spring semester in Boston. It will feel like winter until May. I daydream about a beach vacation as I put on my second layers.

The first day back to school always makes me feel more like a student than a professor—I still get a little nervous. I stayed up late going over my lectures. *I need more coffee.*

I spot Akira from a mile away. It's our little joke—our hair; we can find each other anywhere.

"Morning," she says, handing me a cup.

"Thanks. Next one's on me."

I pull her aside. "We have some catching up to do."

I tell her about the museum.

"You're talking too fast. Slow down, I can barely keep up," she says.

"Sorry, we have no time—we're going to be late for our first day."

"Whatever, we're the teachers."

I try to finish at a more normal pace.

"Has he texted you since?" she asks, drinking her coffee.

"No." I take a sip of mine.

"You should text him."

"You think?"

"Do it now."

~~safe travels?~~

~~good morning~~

~~hi~~

I erase everything I wrote. I have no idea what to say.

"We gotta go." I put my phone away, and we part ways.

* * *

"The *Madonna of the Carnation*, also known as *The Madonna with Child*, is a Renaissance oil painting by Leonardo da Vinci. It's permanently displayed in the Alte Pinakothek in Munich."

"Really? Another da Vinci?" one student asks.

"Excuse me?" I wasn't expecting an interruption.

"There are other artists out there who deserve more recognition," she explains.

"We will cover various artists this semester. What's your name?"

"Fran Kelly."

"We aren't skipping da Vinci, Fran. However, rest assured, you'll hear about many others in this class. Now, let's take a look at the carnation Mary is holding. What is the symbolism here?"

"Passion, blood," says a student in the back. It will take me weeks to learn their names.

"Correct. And baby Jesus is trying to reach for the flower."

"The baby looks too big," says a girl with a colorful scarf.

"He does look a little disproportioned. This is probably an early work of da Vinci. He would later master a few things, including the chiaroscuro technique." I go on about the painting for a while.

I feel better with my first class behind me. I check my phone. I made sure it was tucked away at the bottom of my bag during class so I could focus. No new messages.

I start typing again: *Back in the countryside yet?* I hit send, put my phone away, and head to the meeting.

Every year, the dean gives his annual talk, and each year, a little more of my soul dies with his hours-long speech.

George sits next to me. He's always friendly, often finding me at lunch to share his latest papers. He's a bit of a show-off, but I like him—he makes me laugh. Plus, he has great taste in clothes. Today, he's wearing a beautiful wool vest that I'm sure has to be vintage. A Scottish flat cap completes the look.

"How are you?" he asks me.

"I'm good. My first group seemed enthusiastic. Yours?"

"Yeah, but they all do on the first day. Then they slowly start to drop out."

I laugh. "True. How's the renovation going?"

"The contractor is out to get me, I swear. Every day, he comes up with something else that needs to be done. It's a money pit, but I can't help it—I love that house."

Bethany looks back at us. Our lack of respect for the dean is bothering her.

"Sorry," I whisper to her and wink at George.

We're on the hundredth slide when I excuse myself to the bathroom. I check my phone again.

Just arrived. The weather is not much better here.

We're talking about the weather now? I reply.

You are tough to please, aren't you, firecracker? he sends immediately.

Firecracker?

Seems appropriate.

You don't know me well enough to give me a nickname.

I just did.

I send an emoji: *eyes rolled.*

He sends one back: *smiley face.*

Do you ever come to the country? he asks.

I've been to California.

California doesn't count.

There was grass, and trees... and wine.

I live in Montana. California is a whole different beast.

Never been.

He sends a photo of his horse by the mountains.

Looks beautiful.

You should come visit sometime.

Maybe I will, I type. *Heading back to my meeting.*

Say hello to all the nerds for me.

There are too many.

He sends a laughing face.

My second class is upstairs. I prefer the classrooms on the first floor; they're older but bigger. The ones upstairs feel stuffy. My nose crinkles as I open the door that's been shut for too long; it smells moldy, and it's too cold to open the windows.

There are only ten students in my HAA 259G – Caravaggio: Light and Shadow, Life and Death class. I love teaching this one, mostly because it's an elective—only those who are truly passionate about art sign up. They're my kind of students, the ones who aren't just here to get a degree. I'm about to start referencing the Italian painter known for his dramatic use of chiaroscuro when a familiar student walks in.

"Hi Stella. Take a seat."

She's cut her hair.

"I'm sorry I'm late. I was in the wrong classroom."

"No worries, we just got started."

I realize, for the first time in a long time, I'm feeling... happy. Being back at work keeps me grounded. Nothing makes me smile more than talking about art, though I know the bubbly feeling has something to with something else, *someone else.*

* * *

Hoyt texts me that evening and every day since.

How was your day?
Okay, for a first day back. Yours?
Never thought I'd be missing Boston.

* * *

Good luck today.
Lawyers are the worst.
You'll be fine.

* * *

Did you find the book?
Someone got it first. You gotta be fast around here.
Nerds.

* * *

That sounds awful.
I've had worse. You get used to stitches when you grow up on a ranch.

* * *

Hangover?
We only went for the music.
Liar.
Even the light from my phone screen is too much.

* * *

That's beautiful.

You should come see it in person; there's nothing like the sunset over the mountains.
Tempting.

* * *

Again?
Stop judging me.
But it's so fun.

* * *

Shitty day... just swirling some poison in a cup.
Sorry, I'll have one too... in your honor.
Somehow, that makes me feel better.

* * *

Firecracker.
?
What's your favorite color?
White. Why?
Just trying to get to know you better.
Yours?
Blue.
Like the ocean?
You know me well already.

* * *

Favorite artist?
Jan van Eyck.
Animal?

Dogs. Yours? Horses?
Correct. You didn't ask me about my favorite artist.
I didn't think you had one. Sorry.
Just kidding, I don't. I barely know any.
We'll have to change that.
We?

* * *

Stupid city traffic. I'm gonna be late again.
You know where there isn't any traffic? Montana.

* * *

Are you serious?
No, yes.
Which is it?
You'll have to come and find out.

* * *

Don't you sleep?
Not well.
Why?
Life.
We'll have to change that.

* * *

What are you doing this weekend?
Reading. You?
Riding.

* * *

Wish you were here.

* * *

Sorry about last night's text, had one too many.
Sometimes I wish I was there too.
Are you drunk?
It's nine a.m.
Are you still drunk?
Funny.

* * *

Favorite drink?
Whiskey. Yours?
Same.

* * *

How was the movie?
Don't recommend.
They don't make good movies anymore.
Agree. It's the popcorn that keeps getting better.

* * *

Any cavities?
No, I even got a lollipop.
Good boy.

* * *

Why not?

Can't stop thinking about you.
Don't.
I'm sorry.

* * *

How was your day?
Okay, I'm tired. Stayed up late reading again. Can't wait for the break.
I know a great place to unwind during the break.
Let me guess...

* * *

What the hell!
I'm taking them down. Never been much of a fan of dead animals watching me. I kept one though; he seems peaceful.
I'm gonna have a nightmare now.

* * *

Did you?
What?
Have a nightmare?
No.
It's after midnight and you just replied.
Can't sleep. You?
I have friends over.
Party?
Just dinner, it's my birthday.
Happy birthday! Go be with them!
I prefer talking to you.
Enjoy your party, goodnight.

* * *

How was yoga?
Exactly what I needed.
Maybe I will try it sometime.
Seriously?
No. I can't even touch my toes.
It's all about practice.
Are you offering to teach me? Professor De Loughery.

* * *

Which one?
The one on the right.
Why?
Looks cozier.
It's a truck.
I've never bought a truck before.
But you've seen one before, right? Cozy is not a thing.
The back seat looks bigger, more space, cozier. The leather looks softer,
cozier. The lighting is dimmer, cozier...
Cozier it is.

* * *

"What's he saying that's so important you can't even talk to me?"
Akira asks, annoyed, glaring at me across the café table.

"Sorry." I put my phone down, only to pick it up again.

Akira's jealous of the texting.

Tell her I don't like to share you either.

I don't reply.

As your friend, he sends right after.

I send a sticking-tongue-out emoji.

She's still staring at me.

"Sorry!" I put the phone away for good this time.

"Iris, have you talked to Aaron yet?"

"I've been busy with my classes and all."

"Iris."

"I know! I will."

"Have you learned anything related to the prisms, or are you and Hoyt just... gossiping?" She's swirling her soup.

"We've been keeping it... casual."

"Casual? You're wasting time."

"What are you talking about? What's the rush?"

"I thought you were gathering facts."

"I am." I take a bite of my garden salad.

"What have you found out then?" she presses again.

"Well, I know his brother's prism made him... lose his mind. He was hearing voices."

"We already knew that. What else?"

"I don't know how to ask him questions without seeming..."

"Interested?"

"Invasive."

"You need to cut right to it. Does he even know you were at his place? Can his prism do this too?"

I glance around to see if anyone else can hear us, but we're alone at the corner table.

"I don't know. I can't just say, 'Hey, by the way, my prism can transport me to you.'"

"Why not? Maybe he's been spying on you this entire time too."

The thought had occurred to me. Many times.

"I don't think so."

"But you don't know for sure."

I try to keep eating. I have to be in the classroom in half an hour.

"Would you go with me to... Montana?" I ask between bites.

"What? Why? When?"

"Spring break."

* * *

February flies by with my lectures at Harvard and the yoga classes I've started attending again. Aaron's gone for days on business in Asia, and when he's home, he's jet-lagged. Akira's dating someone new, leaving me texting Hoyt during my free time. I decide to get back to the yoga studio, realizing the anticipation for his replies is becoming... unhealthy. We never talk about anything serious; it's like we're both afraid to ruin what we have going on.

It's spring break next week, I text him after breakfast.

Any plans? I see his reply before I leave the house.

Depends on what you say next.

? he replies seconds later.

Are you free next week?

As in... coming to Boston?

No, as in, me coming to Montana.

Seriously?

Akira would come with me.

I will be here, he says.

I was expecting a little more... emotion?

He sends a heart emoji.

I send my usual rolled eyes one.

Can you recommend a hotel? I ask.

You guys can stay here. Plenty of room.

I squirm in my seat. *I don't know...*

He sends a picture of the house.

That's your house?

Yep.

If I didn't know his family had that kind of money, I would have thought he'd sent a picture of a fancy lodge. The mountains I saw when I visited him with my prism are visible in the background.

Wow.

Plenty of room, he texts.

I'll ask her.

Let me know, firecracker.

THIRTEEN

"THE WORLD OF REALITY HAS ITS LIMITS; THE
WORLD OF IMAGINATION IS BOUNDLESS." –
JEAN-JACQUES ROUSSEAU

I'm struggling to find something to wear. I'm still in my yoga clothes when Aaron gets home. I completely forget about Lara and Ted's party until he brought it up this morning. My head is definitely not on straight lately.

I have an entire closet to myself here, but my clothes are still split between this place and my apartment. I also realize I need to do laundry. *When did I become such a mess?* Not that I've ever been great with domestic chores, but still—this is bad, even for me. I throw on a simple black dress, tie up my hair, and slip on the most basic pair of shoes. I look too... boring. I open my jewelry box and decide to wear my mom's pearls. Tomorrow would've been her birthday, and she's been on my mind all day. There's never a day I don't think of her, but on her birthdays, it's like she's right there with me. I've created a few rituals to celebrate her, like drinking my coffee from her favorite mug... which is still at my apartment. I make a mental note to stop and grab it tomorrow before work.

"Do you have their gift?" I ask as we head out.

"Yes, I got it. Let's go," Aaron replies.

I'm thankful for Tina, Aaron's secretary, who arranged a last-minute gift like it was the easiest task ever. She even seemed excited when I called her for help.

Lara and Ted are celebrating their fifth wedding anniversary with family and friends. I can't understand why anyone would want to do such a thing. Their home is beautiful—exactly what I imagine Lara's place would look like. Everything is light, classic, and neutral. Abstract paintings decorate the walls, along with sculptures that I know are mostly there because of their price tags. The living room opens to an outdoor pool, too cold to use in March.

"If you like this place, you should see their house in Martha's Vineyard," one of Aaron's friends says as we walk in.

"Your home is beautiful," I tell Lara, giving her a kiss on the cheek.

"Thank you! You guys need to come over for dinner sometime."

"I'd like that," I surprise myself with the honesty.

"Ted has to be here somewhere," she says, looking around. "Ted!" She calls when she spots him.

"Hey, you came!" Ted is wearing a navy sports coat, matching Lara's dress color.

"I like what you guys did with the... outfits," Aaron says, pointing out their matching look.

"Lara's idea that we match," Ted says, smiling at his wife and grabbing her hand. They seem happy.

"Congratulations, five years! Your wedding feels like it was yesterday," I say, remembering their beautiful celebration. The food was so exotic, I didn't recognize half of it. I remember someone mentioning an expensive Japanese melon; I had no idea fruit could be a luxury item. They chose to get married in Ibiza— nothing will ever compare to that place, that water. Our time there was spoiled when Aaron got food poisoning after the rehearsal dinner. Lara and Ted took it personally, even though no one else got sick. I told them it had to be something Aaron ate on the plane. They made sure we had the best room in the hotel after theirs, as if that would make him feel any better, but we were still grateful for the gesture.

"Anything I should avoid eating today?" Aaron jokes, and our thoughts sync.

"I made sure to test everything," Ted says, patting his belly.

We all laugh.

"Would you excuse us? I have something to show Iris," Lara says, pulling me toward her bedroom upstairs.

"What is it?" I ask when we're alone.

"I know it's none of my business, but I'm dying to know—any news between you and my favorite bad guy?"

My cheeks flush. "We are... talking."

"That's it?"

"Well, as you can see, I'm still engaged. Talking is all there can be."

"If you say so."

"You and Ted seem... happy together," I say, trying to change the subject. As I look around, I notice her bedroom is so clean and organized, it makes my home—both homes—look like disasters. Even with Aaron hiring cleaners, they just pile my things in corners. There are no piles anywhere in this room, in this house.

"We had our share of troubles, but we're happy now."

"What's it like to be married?" I genuinely want to know her opinion; I haven't met many happy married couples. With my family and Aaron's parents, we're doomed to rely on their examples.

"It's the best and hardest thing you'll ever do, if you marry the right person."

"And how did you know... Ted was the one?"

"When a lifetime together doesn't seem long enough."

She sees I'm thinking about my own life and says, "You'll know once you find him, if you haven't already."

I smile at her, and we make our way downstairs.

Lara's words swirl in my head when I find Aaron by the pool.

"It's usually me who needs fresh air," I tell him.

He attempts a smile.

"What's wrong?" I ask, noticing the worry on his face.

"Do you think this will be us one day? Celebrating five years of marriage and still looking as happy as they are?"

I sigh, not wanting to have this conversation here. "I don't know." It's all I can say.

He looks back at me. "Are you happy with me?"

I'm not ready for this talk. "Yes, of course." I kiss him lightly.

"Sometimes I get a feeling this is too good to be true, you and me."

"You deserve to be happy, Aaron." I mean it. *Even if it's not with me.*

We get distracted by someone yelling at us to come inside—they're giving a toast.

* * *

After the party, Aaron falls asleep in the living room. I leave him there, knowing the couch is as comfortable as the bed. I cover him with a blanket and am glad to be alone with my thoughts. I stare at the ceiling, pondering the day's conversation, when I check my phone—the habit stronger than ever.

What are you doing? I read Hoyt's text.

Just came back from a party, I reply.

Good time? he answers immediately.

I'm not a huge fan of them.

Of parties or people?

Both.

Me neither.

It was supposed to be a joke, but somehow, I can tell he also enjoys his solitude.

What did you do today? I ask.

Rode my horse to the river, then had some annoying business calls.

What's your horse like?

He's a black Irish, a little stubborn, like me.

I smile at the thought. *What's his name?*

Blackwater.

I'd like to meet him.

Are you guys really coming?

Yes, Akira is game.

Send me your flight info once you have it. I'll pick you guys up.

It's okay, we don't want to inconvenience you.

Nonsense, I'm happy to.

Okay, thank you. Anything I should know before arriving?

Bring boots.

Noted. Goodnight.

Goodnight, Iris.

* * *

I need to tell Aaron I'm leaving for spring break. I don't think he'll care, but I'm struggling to say it. Maybe because I know what I'm doing to him is wrong. If it were the other way around... it would be unforgivable.

He's not in the best mood. He got some bad news from his secretary. Someone wants to see him bright and early, and he's rushing out the door when I say, "Hey, I know you're late, but I just wanted to let you know Akira and I are going away on Saturday for spring break. Girls' trip."

"Where to?"

"Montana."

"Why... Montana?"

"I've never been to the countryside, and I thought it could be fun."

"There's nothing to do there."

"I'm craving some... peace."

He just looks at me. "Okay, I don't have time for this right now."

"There's nothing to do, I'm just letting you know."

"Fine."

"Bye," I say as he walks out the door.

* * *

I have no idea what to pack. I bought a pair of boots that seem fitting for mud and a few other accessories the sales guy insisted I couldn't live without, even though I told him I'm only staying for a few days. All my clothes are either too dressed up or too casual. I want to look decent without trying too hard. *I have no idea how to pull that off.*

I realize I've never had to impress Aaron. We met as teens, and we skipped a lot of the normal dating stuff. Akira and I are going for four days, although my bag screams otherwise. It's so stuffed that I have to sit on it to close it.

Aaron and I had another fight last night regarding the trip. I lost it when he said I should be spending my time off packing and finally moving in. I mentioned needing to relax, and he threw it in my face that my job wasn't that demanding. I hate it when he, or I, compare our jobs. It never ends well. Still, it was easier to leave after the argument, and I wonder if I picked the fight on purpose.

* * *

The airport is crowded with everyone who had the same idea as us —to leave for break. I can tell by their age that most are students going back home. For a second, I let myself wonder what it would have been like to have a family to visit—or a family at all. I shake the sadness away.

"What's the plan when we get there?" Akira asks as we eat dinner and wait for boarding.

"Absolutely no idea," I reply, stealing one of her fries.

"It'll be good for you. Us. Nature is... healthy."

"What kind of animals do you think we'll see?"

"Horses, for sure." I take a sip of my wine.

"I hope we see a bear or an owl."

"For being such an animal lover, I can't believe you don't have a bunch of pets."

"I like the wild ones."

"To the wild ones," I say, lifting my glass.

And I think she knows I don't mean *just* the animals.

* * *

The flight would've been terribly long if Aaron hadn't switched our tickets to first class. I had no idea he'd done it until we were boarding. He texted: *I upgraded your seats. Enjoy your trip.* I swallowed hard after reading it. Why does he have to be so nice? It made me nauseous for the entire seven-hour trip. No matter what happens in Montana, I'll be telling him the wedding is off as soon as I get back. I can't stomach this any longer, quite literally.

"Are you feeling better?" Akira asks as we wait for our luggage.

"A little." I open my water bottle and take another sip.

I'm about to use my new yoga strength to haul our bags onto a cart when another hand grabs them.

"Welcome to Montana," Hoyt says, looking painfully hot in his casual jeans.

FOURTEEN

"GREAT ART PICKS UP WHERE NATURE ENDS." –
MARC CHAGALL

I'm not sure what I was expecting Montana to look like, but I didn't expect it to be this beautiful. Our late-night flight arrived just in time for us to witness a stunning sunrise during the drive to Hoyt's place. Mountains higher than the clouds surround the highway, making me feel both small and safe. I'm gawking at the nature outside my window when Hoyt says, "There's a road a few hours away called Going-to-the-Sun Road, which has the best view of the mountains around here."

"I can't imagine it getting better than this," I say, taking it all in.

"It is," he replies with a smile.

"It's all so... natural. Like civilization hasn't arrived here yet," I note, seeing no man-made structures besides the road in front of us.

"And hopefully, it'll stay that way. That's my only goal with my lands—to keep them safe from men and their destruction."

I glance at him.

"This sounds more like a mission than a business plan," Akira says from the backseat.

"Thanks," Hoyt replies.

He turns on the radio to a country station, and I let myself relax. I can see why people feel more at ease in places like this. The city feels like a different world from here.

"Do you guys want to stop and pick anything up?" Hoyt asks.

Akira and I exchange a look and say the same thing at the same time: "Coffee."

* * *

Country Brew is a local coffee shop in the resort town of Whitefish, and the barista behind the counter seems to know Hoyt.

"Good morning, Locklear," the young man as we walk in.

"How's it going, Tristan?" Hoyt replies.

"Doing well, thanks for the help with the fence. My family's in your debt."

"Don't worry about it. I'm glad Broc could fix it."

The man insists our coffees are on the house. A vanilla latte for me, an iced coffee for Akira, and a black coffee for Hoyt.

I want to take a look around, but Hoyt promises to bring us back another day.

"That's my kind of road trip," Akira says as we get back in the car.

"You mean, one where you don't have to drive?" I ask her.

"That, and coffee. I'll go anywhere."

Hoyt and I laugh.

Forty-five minutes later, we pass a tall sign that reads *Locklear Horse Ranch* in metal letters upheld by wooden posts.

"This is where your land starts?" I ask, stating the obvious.

"For now. The government's constantly trying to steal inch by inch from us. From me."

"You have to... manage all of this?" I ask, realizing how much greenery stretches out in front of me.

"A lot is left untouched—my father liked it that way, and I agree. The less we interfere, the better."

"Do you have cows?" Akira asks.

"No, we only breed and train horses here. My dad owned a few cattle ranches, but I sold them all after he died—too much of a headache. I kept only the land I know the government wants."

"Why not sell them all?" I ask.

"Because I feel like it's my responsibility... to preserve them. We've got enough cities already."

"Hoyt Locklear, a hero in disguise," Akira says, making us all laugh once more.

* * *

"Holy shit!" she exclaims before I can.

Those are the only words in my head as we step out of Hoyt's massive truck.

"It should be illegal for someone to live in a place like this. It should be... shared," she continues, stepping into the immense house.

"And I'm sure this is the part where you say it should be shared with... you?" I tease her.

"Us," she responds with a grin.

"I'm happy to share," Hoyt says behind us, dropping off our bags.

Glass windows are held by wooden beams, lining the entire place.

The glass windows, framed by wooden beams, line the entire house. It's rustic yet modernized, with an enormous TV and electric shades. I'm not sure how to take it all in, as the mountains and river outside capture most of my attention. Thick rugs line the floors near the giant couch by the fireplace—the same one I'd seen with my prism. I realize now that I was too nervous back then to fully appreciate the beauty in here. I would call his home perfect if it weren't for the enormous animal head staring down at me from the wall. Stuffed, repulsive, and *very dead*.

"Is that a...?" I begin, realizing I don't know the animal.

"It's a bighorn sheep," he answers.

"I thought sheep were fluffy and cute."

He laughs. "Not all of them."

I continue eyeing the place.

"The bathroom?" Akira asks.

"End of the hallway, to the right," he answers. "I'll take your bags upstairs," Hoyt says, leaving me alone in the living room.

I walk toward a table lined with photographs. I recognize Hoyt in the pictures, along with who I guess is his dad and maybe his brother. I see the boys with bows and arrows by a large tree. Right next to them, I spot a picture of a couple of horses and a young woman wearing fringes. I wonder if it could be their mom—Hoyt never mentioned her. I don't want to ask; I figure there's a reason for the privacy. *I don't know anything about this man, and yet here I am, in his house, all the way in Montana.*

"I put each bag in a room, both on this side," he says, gesturing upstairs. "My room is on the other side." He makes it clear.

I obviously wasn't expecting to share a room with him, though I thought I would be with Akira.

"Thank you. I didn't know we'd each get our own room."

"Scared of sleeping alone?" he asks with a grin.

"Should I have reasons to be?" I fake being nervous about being in a stranger's house.

"Shit. Sorry, I didn't mean to—"

"I'm kidding."

He runs his hand through his hair, seeing that I'm laughing at him.

He walks over to where I'm standing and points at one photo. "That's me, naked."

I giggle as I see a little baby in what I assume are his dad's arms.

"You need to check out the bathroom!" Akira says behind me.

"We have our own rooms," I tell her on my way to do as instructed.

The bathroom definitely doesn't disappoint. Between the ornamental marble sink and modern toilet, I'm pleased with our accommodation. This place is exquisite.

Akira excuses herself to take a nap, saying she's tired from the travel, although I know she's just giving us privacy.

I follow Hoyt to the large back porch that overlooks the river. The sun beats down strongly, and I close my eyes to feel it on my skin. The sweet scent overtakes my other senses.

"It smells like... cookies," I say, taking another whiff.

He looks at me, pleased. "It's the bark of the ponderosa pine. On warm days, it can smell like vanilla or butterscotch."

"Which one is it?"

"The one over there," he points. "With the deep grooves in the trunk, looking like a difficult yet fun puzzle."

I take a seat on the steps by the water. He sits next to me, making sure we have enough space between us.

"I don't know what I'm doing here," I say, looking out at the sun reflected in the water.

"I'm glad you came."

"I'm still engaged."

"I figured."

"I'm planning on... postponing my wedding... when I get back."

"Do you mean breaking off the engagement or just... delaying?"

"Breaking off, I guess."

"How long have you two been together?"

"My whole life, pretty much."

"Hmm... that's a lot of history."

"Yeah."

"Do you love him?" His raw question goes right through me.

"No. Not in that way."

"So why..."

"I... he was there for me when nobody else was. It happened... naturally."

I pull my prism out; it feels good to be able to do it in front of someone, *him*. I dip my hand in the water, put on the prism, and it lights up immediately.

"The day I figured out it needed water, I was caught in the rain. My dad had just told me Luke was having another episode, and he was blaming me for it. I stormed out of the house. I didn't even notice I was soaked until I reached the barn. I rode my horse, Boone, all day."

Hoyt leans down to the river and does the same with his prism.

"Not Blackwater?"

The indigo light from his necklace reminds me of the night sky. It's incredible to see the brightness from a different perspective.

"I got Blackwater after my dad passed. I realized I had no idea what to do with all the money. So I bought three horses on the same day. More money than I'd ever spent at once."

We're both looking at each other's light when we feel the prisms... they're attracting each other, like two magnets. We let go of our hands and allow the prisms to get closer. And closer. Until they're touching, the lights almost merging, and we're standing only inches away from each other. I look into his eyes, and I almost forget I can't touch him.

"It feels different," he says.

"What does?"

"My body."

"What do you mean?"

"When I'm around you, I feel... warm. Like I'm near a fireplace. But it stops when the prisms... touch. I wonder if I can..." He's about to touch my hand when I jump back, almost falling into the water myself.

"Don't. Please. I don't want to hurt you."

"I'm okay, Iris."

"It's not worth the risk."

"I'd have to disagree."

"I should go... change."

I walk upstairs, still trying to wrangle my feelings. I close the door behind me. The knowledge that he can't touch me made it easier for me to come to Montana. I need to know there's a physical force between us, making sure I don't cross the line. Even if I've already blurred it. If there's a way to touch or be touched by him, I don't want to know. I'm not sure I'd be able to control myself.

Akira knocks on my door half an hour later.

"What are you doing up here?" She finds me looking out the window.

"Resting, like you."

"Iris, I left so you guys could have a minute alone."

"I know, we did... It's just... I don't know what I'm doing."

"It's Aaron, isn't it?"

"I can't do this to him."

She grabs my hand. "You haven't done anything you can't walk away from."

"Yes, I have. I have... fallen for..."

She nods in understanding.

* * *

"Do you guys want to go out for lunch or...?" Hoyt asks casually, glancing away from the golf tournament on TV.

"I was hoping we could see the horses," I respond.

"I could eat first," Akira says, taking a seat next to Hoyt. I feel instantly jealous, not because she's sitting there, but because she can, if she wants, touch him. I felt it too when she gave him a hug hello at the airport.

"We could order something," I say, taking the chair on the right side.

"Nothing will arrive in less than an hour. We're kind of in the middle of nowhere," Hoyt replies.

"Right, I forgot." I pull out my phone. *How far from town exactly are we?*

"I can make you sandwiches," he says, standing up.

"You can?" I joke.

"Damn good ones," he says, heading to the kitchen.

"I can help," I offer.

One look at the kitchen, and I want to move in. The appliances look brand new against the hardwood floor. It's the same throughout the house—wooden planks that seem a hundred years old. I'm not sure why, but seeing the kitchen finally makes me realize Hoyt is beyond rich. Sure, I knew about the land, but now I'm seeing his... *lifestyle.*

"Who else lives here?" I blurt out.

"Just me."

"Just you?" Akira says, grabbing a tomato.

"It was just me, my brother, Dad, and... but now it's just me."

"You're telling me you take care of this place by yourself?" I ask, astonished.

"I have employees, but they have their own homes."

I watch as he pulls out ingredients I never would've thought to put on a sandwich.

"What is this?" I ask, turning the strange vegetable around.

"Fennel. When you said you'd help, did you mean...?"

"Spreading something onto bread?" I finish, reaching for the ingredients on the counter.

"Why don't you two take a seat?" He gestures toward the table by the window.

"Fine by me," Akira says, making herself comfortable. "Cowboy by day, businessman by night, and still has time to... cook?" Her directness makes me uncomfortable, but Hoyt laughs.

"We all need hobbies," he says. "Not all of us can be geniuses." He points his knife at both of us.

"How much is the rent?" Akira asks, taking a bite of her sandwich.

I agree—it's that good.

"What's in this?" I ask, trying to figure out the flavors.

"A bunch of stuff... and bacon," he answers.

"I could eat this every day," I say, wiping my mouth.

"Of course you can. You can't cook anything." Akira winks at me.

"True," I tell Hoyt. "I'm a horrible cook."

"I know," he says with a smile.

We both look at him.

"You didn't even know what fennel is," he says, explaining.

"Nobody does," Akira replies.

"I just... didn't think you could put it in sandwiches," I admit.

"Anything tastes good with bacon," he says, taking another bite.

FIFTEEN

"THE ARTIST'S WORLD IS LIMITLESS. IT CAN BE
FOUND ANYWHERE, FAR FROM WHERE HE LIVES
OR A FEW FEET AWAY. IT IS ALWAYS ON HIS
DOORSTEP." – PAUL STRAND

"Nice boots," Hoyt says when I come downstairs after changing. I'm wearing my new outfit, a perfect replica of the mannequin from the store where I bought it. I just hope my shoes don't need breaking in.

"I hope they're the right kind," I reply.

"They'll do," he says with a quick smile.

Akira somehow is wearing an old pair. "You had boots?" I ask her. I completely forgot to tell her to bring some.

"No, I borrowed them from the closet in my room," she says, like it's the most normal thing in the world.

"Your closet has... clothes?"

"Yeah, doesn't yours?"

"No, it was empty."

Hoyt is already waiting for us outside and doesn't hear our last exchange. I don't want to think about why there are *girl things* in a room in his house.

The barn is at least a mile away, and with the ground wet, I get mud all over me. My new clothes quickly blend in.

"Broc!" Hoyt yells at the guy brushing a brown horse. The tall, strong man is wearing a cowboy hat. He stops what he's doing and walks over to us. He's one of those people who smiles with their eyes.

"I'm Iris," I say.

His tan, muscled arms shake my hand. "Nice to meet you."

"This is my friend Akira," I introduce them. He looks down at his hands and removes his glove before shaking hers. I notice from the corner of my eye that their hands... linger.

I walk straight to pet Blackwater; he's the only black horse around.

"Can I?" I gesture to touch him.

"Yes, but first, let him smell you."

I move my hand closer to the horse's face.

The three of them laugh out loud.

"It's not a dog," Hoyt says, coming closer to pet the animal himself.

I make a face at him. "I've never..."

"I can tell." He's smiles.

I run my hands over the softest, smoothest, and shiniest coat. I could swear Blackwater's eyes can see right through me.

"What's this one's name?" Akira asks, petting the brown one with white spots.

"That's Lumberjack, our tobiano," says Broc. "And this one is Elmwood, his foal." He points to the smaller one.

"Can we ride them?" Akira asks.

"Broc, you take Iris. Akira, you come with me," Hoyt says, getting the saddles ready.

"I can ride my own horse," Akira says, already looking around.

"Not here you can't. I'm not going to have you two getting hurt while staying under my roof."

"How hard can it be?" I ask.

"I find it pretty easy," Broc says, offering me a hand.

No amount of yoga would strengthen the muscles I'm using. I'm holding so tightly to the reins that my hands are getting red marks.

"You can let go. I'm not going to let you fall." Broc is being respectful, though he's close enough that I know I'm safe in place.

Hoyt and Akira are far ahead, going much faster than us. I'm sure she's begging Hoyt to speed up.

"What if he starts... racing?" I ask Broc.

"He won't. Jet here is a fast one, but he knows not to take off when it isn't time." We're riding a brown horse with a white blaze —Broc mentions that's what the white streak on their head is called.

I try to let go a bit.

"How long have you worked with horses?" I ask him.

"I grew up here, with Hoyt. My dad worked for his dad, training the horses."

"So you live close by?"

"Yeah, in the west house."

"West house?"

"Yeah, Hoyt wouldn't take no for an answer. After his dad died, he made sure we moved in there—my brother and me."

"So you live here, on his land?"

"Yep, he's a good boss, but... he always treated Sawyer and me like brothers."

"And does Sawyer take care of the horses too?"

"Yes, you'll meet him tonight."

"Tonight?"

"Hoyt invited us for dinner. We never say no when he's cooking."

The land is vast and devastatingly beautiful. Miles and miles of grass stretch underneath us, as far as the eye can see. The tall trees sway gently with the breeze while the mountains watch us from afar. We ride to the river and back.

I have a hard time getting off the horse, and I could have done without Hoyt watching me dismount ungracefully. I thank Broc for his help.

"Anytime. See you both at dinner." He tips his hat to Akira before heading back to the barn.

"I need a shower," I tell Akira as we take off our boots in the mudroom before entering the house, copying Hoyt's habit.

"You ladies are free to roam around until seven."

"What's at seven?" Akira asks.

"Dinner," he replies.

My room has a private suite, and I almost want to cry when the extra powerful water jets start doing their thing. The bathroom is simple yet luxurious, like the rest of the house. Large, irregular brown stones cover the walls while tile lines the floor. There are plenty of fluffy towels, nicer than the ones in any hotel I've stayed at. I take my time drying every part of my body, letting myself enjoy their softness. I still have another hour before dinner. I offered to help with the food, but Hoyt dismissed me, telling me to relax. I'm not the best at doing nothing—my mind has a way of ruining those moments. Still, I'm trying to take my time, enjoying my shower and the view.

What am I supposed to wear? I look at my wide-open suitcase. It's probably a casual thing, even though Hoyt has invited his friends. I would hate to be overdressed and feel like I don't belong with them. I would also hate to look... unattractive. I text Akira: *What are you wearing to dinner?* She doesn't reply and comes straight to my room instead.

"Let me see what you brought," she says, starting to pull things out.

"How many pairs of jeans did you bring?" She's counting them.

"I told you, I have nothing to wear."

"Wait here," she says, walking out the door.

"Please bring something... simple!" I yell after at her. I'm taller than Akira, yet we wear similar sizes.

"Two options," she says when she returns, carrying a couple of tops. "This shirt"—she lifts a purple long-sleeve shirt with a lion illustration on the front—"or this one." She holds up a tight-fitting black sweater. It's not really a choice.

"It smells amazing," I say, coming downstairs and finding the table already set for six. Even with the nice china, it looks casual, to my relief.

"What kind of drink can I get you?" Hoyt asks as he places the bread on the table. He's wearing a navy-blue shirt that hugs every muscle.

"I'll take a glass of wine," says Akira.

"Wine sounds good. Can I help you? I feel bad, you're doing all the work."

"I'm the host. Go pick a bottle," he says, pointing to a door.

I open it to find a storage room. Chef-quality ingredients fill the shelves, including truffle oils, jars of sun-dried tomatoes, capers, and other similar items. I can tell already that Hoyt takes his hobby seriously. On the other side, I find racks of wine bottles. I pick one with a nice label. On the way out, I pass a collection of local whiskey. I tell myself to take it easy with the drinking. I need to keep myself... controlled.

We're sipping our wine when his guests arrive.

Broc says hello while taking off his coat and hat. He's carrying a pack of beer. His brother looks a lot like him, except with longer hair and sadder eyes. Much sadder.

"This is Sawyer," Broc introduces us.

"How do you do?" he replies. Akira seems to stir something in him—like her presence is... bothering him. I look at her, trying to figure out why. She could almost pass as someone local with her plaid flannel.

"Did you... borrow this shirt from the closet?" I pull her aside.

"I don't own any flannels, and it looked comfortable."

"Akira!"

"What?! They're probably from an—" She stops herself when she sees me fidget.

Hoyt walks back from the kitchen, carrying a large covered pan that smells divine. "I should have asked. Any food allergies?" He looks at both of us.

We shake our heads.

"Then let's eat."

"Nice shirt," Hoyt says to Akira when we finally all sit down at the table.

"Are you expecting... someone else?" I ask him, eyeing the empty chair.

"I thought you said Maeve was home," Hoyt asks Sawyer.

"She is. She should be here any minute. You know how she is."

The door opens less than five minutes later.

"You guys couldn't wait?" she asks, taking off her coat.

"Like you weren't trying to make an entrance," Broc says, taking a piece of bread.

"You know where the wine is," Hoyt says without even lifting his gaze.

I study the food when she sits down.

"Hi, I'm Iris," I say to the long brown-haired girl.

"Maeve."

I can't help but notice the similarities.

"Are you guys...?"

"Yes, siblings. Unfortunately," she smiles at Broc and Sawyer.

"It's a pleasure to have you around too, sis," Broc says.

"I'm Akira."

"Now that we all know each other, can we eat? I'm starving," Sawyer asks.

"Always so... pleasant," Maeve says to her brother.

They all act like siblings—Hoyt is just as comfortable with them as they are with each other. I can tell they've grown up together. Including the beautiful sister, with whom Hoyt avoids making eye contact as much as possible. I'm not sure I want to know the reason behind it.

Sawyer keeps glancing at Akira. By the third time, she

demands, "Just say it!" She looks right at him. I freeze, feeling the tension.

"Where did you get that shirt?" Sawyer asks.

"From the closet," Akira replies.

"Well, it's not yours."

"And?"

I watch them, feeling very uncomfortable with their tone. I knew she shouldn't have.

"It's my sister's," Hoyt says. "And you're welcome to anything in there; she wouldn't care. She... left them here."

I look at all of them as the mention of a sister, whom I've never even seen a photo of, is brought up.

"Now, please, Sawyer. Some manners, they're my guests."

"This is delicious," I say, trying to break the awkwardness. Hoyt smiles at me, picking up on my gesture.

Hoyt sits to my right, at the head of the table, while Akira sits to my left. I work hard to make sure no parts of my body are within touching distance of his.

"It really is," Broc says.

"And what exactly am I eating?" Sawyer asks.

"Braised pork," Hoyt answers.

"The sauce?" Akira asks.

"Calvados and heavy cream. French-style." None of us knows what that is, but we all clear our plates.

"How do you both know Hoyt?" Maeve asks, helping us clear the table.

"We met at... an event... a party... in Boston," I reply.

"You guys live there?" she asks.

"They're Harvard professors," Hoyt says, returning with dessert.

The girl looks surprised by his answer. The comment seems to tone down her... aggressiveness.

"Where did you learn to cook like this?" I ask him, taking a serving of the mousse.

"Self-taught. Books and cooking shows."

"Remember the first things he made?" Sawyer asks Broc.

"That garlicky chicken? Inedible," Broc says with a face, and they all laugh.

"I needed a... distraction after Dad left me with all this," Hoyt explains. "It was either cooking or drinking."

"I'm glad you picked cooking," Maeve says from the other side.

Hoyt nods at her.

* * *

"You cooked, let me at least do the dishes," I say to Hoyt in the kitchen.

"See this thing here?" He points at the large dishwasher. "It's my best friend."

I help him load it.

"So you have a sister?" I ask him while placing another plate in the machine.

"Johanna. I haven't seen her since... three years."

"Younger?"

"She's five years younger than me."

"They seem... nice, your friends." I change the subject, sensing he doesn't want to talk about Johanna.

"They are, if you can pass their bullshit first."

"Does Maeve live in the... west house too?"

"No, she just comes by sometimes."

Akira brings the rest of the plates, and we finish loading everything.

* * *

"No bets during the first rounds," Hoyt says, dealing the cards.

"Bets?" I ask him, taking a sip from my drink. I wasn't planning on having whiskey, but I couldn't resist when all of them got a glass, the bottle sitting in the center of the table.

"It's all about the cash with those two," Broc says, gesturing to Hoyt and Sawyer.

"And not with you?" Akira asks.

"I play for the... fun," Broc answers.

Hoyt fakes a cough.

The three men take turns explaining the rules of poker to us.

"So that's a straight flush," Broc says.

"This is complicated," Akira says.

"Says the astrophysics Harvard professor," I comment, and they all laugh.

I have no idea how to play, yet I do anyway. We all joke around, and I feel content. It's nice to feel at ease around people, even with Maeve's judgmental eyes on me the entire evening. Akira and I watch a few rounds while the boys and Maeve move on to betting money.

"You pull this shit every time," Sawyer says, standing up.

"And you're always a sore loser," Broc says.

"I'm out of here. Thanks for dinner, boss," he says to Hoyt. "Are you coming, Maeve?"

"Yes," she says, even though I can feel she wants to stay.

"Nice meeting you both. See you around, Hoyt." She exits with her brother.

"What's the deal with him?" I hear Akira ask Broc.

"Walk out with me?" Hoyt asks me, opening the back door.

Sixteen

"For me, painting is a way to forget life. It
is a cry in the night, a strangled laugh."
– Georges Rouault

"Here," he says, handing me the blanket he's carrying.

"Thanks, it's still pretty cold for spring," I say, wrapping myself in it.

"Are we talking about the weather now?" he jokes, using my words from before.

"I could sense... something between you and Maeve. Did you guys... date before?"

"Something like that."

I swallow.

Hoyt looks back at the house, and we see Akira and Broc laughing.

"They seem to get along," he says, studying our friends.

"They really do. Is Broc single?"

"As far as I know."

"Are you?" It was the whiskey asking.

"Yes, I thought it was obvious."

"Well, with the things I heard... I wasn't sure."

"There is no one."

"What about all the... women at the parties Lara mentioned?"

"It's expected for me to show up with somebody at those things."

"So they are not dates?"

"A couple were, but mostly just models—they want to be in that kind of environment."

I look up at the sky.

"You know, you never told me why you wanted to see me at the awards, upstairs." He takes another sip of his glass.

I sigh. "I didn't have something specific to tell you, I only wanted to... meet you."

"Why?"

I take a sip from my liquid courage. *He deserves to know.*

"The first time I met you... it wasn't at the balcony."

"What do you mean?"

"I saw you... before."

"Where? Another gala?"

"No, here."

"What do you mean, here?"

"Here, this house."

He's looking at me, light reflecting in his eyes. "How?"

"The prism. Does yours do that?"

"Do what?"

"Transport you?"

"I don't understand."

I explain how it all happened.

"I thought I was losing my mind when I saw... the light. Like my... brother."

I can see how he would think that.

"It was me, or... it..." I'm turning my pendant around.

"If I didn't have a cursed prism of my own, I wouldn't believe a word you're saying."

"You think... they are... cursed?"

"What else?"

"So yours doesn't do that?"

"No, I mean, I never tried on purpose... still, I've been around fire enough."

"You have?"

"Well, lighters, fireplaces, occasional bonfires."

"Hmm... does yours do anything else?"

"No, only the light and..."

"What?"

"My senses... are a little... different because of it."

"What do you mean?"

"It's hard to explain... I'm still learning, getting used to it, even after all these years. I... feel more than everyone else."

"Like you can hear, see better?"

"No, more like I can feel things others can't."

"Like a sixth sense?"

"Something like that."

"Do you think that's why when we touch..."

"Maybe."

My body wants nothing more than to get closer to him.

"I should probably go to bed... The drinks..." *I need to get ahold of my feelings.*

"I want to show you something first," he tells me.

We walk upstairs, passing by Akira and Broc comfortably on the couch watching a movie.

Hoyt's bedroom is bigger than mine, with an entire glass wall overlooking the water. The slanted ceiling with its wooden beams makes the room look very tall. A thick rug frames the floor underneath a giant and comfortable-looking bed.

"Here," Hoyt gestures for me to sit next to him. He hands me a small wooden box.

"Your brother's prism," I say as I look inside. "Should I... Can I?"

"I think so, I never feel anything when I touch it. It's like it... died with my brother. Never saw a light in it again, even after I put it on, wetted it... nothing."

"You tried wetting it?"

"I was angry that it did that to my brother, I wanted to understand."

The rectangular prism is held by a silver chain. I slide the bracelet on my arm, and like Hoyt, *I feel nothing.*

"I'm sorry about your brother, it's horrible... what happened to him."

"I wish I had reached for his prism instead of this one," he says, holding his necklace.

I want to hold him, kiss him, take away his pain. However, all I can say is, "Maybe one day we will get answers."

I close the box and go to sleep, *in my own room.*

* * *

I wake up to see a text from Hoyt: *Coffee is fresh, I'm at the gym, come say hi.*

I text him after pouring myself a cup. *There's a gym here?*

Back door, left after the downstairs bathroom.

I open the door to find Hoyt and Broc lifting weights, *shirtless.*

"Good morning." I startle as Akira's voice comes from the other side; she's on the treadmill.

"Hey! What are you doing here?"

"Mostly drooling. How did you sleep?" she asks me, slowing down her pace.

"Good, you?" I take another sip of my coffee, trying not to stare at the strong, half-naked men in front of me. I understand now why they look the way they do.

"Great." She takes a sip of her water bottle.

I watch her. She's in a great mood.

"Did something...?" I ask.

"Nope," she says, speeding up again.

Broc is in his own world, doing push-ups in a corner, sweat dripping off his face.

"Good morning," says Hoyt, taking off his headphones.

I smile at him. "Nice gym."

"It's handy to have a place to let out some... steam."

I know what he means. It was hard to walk away from each other last night—from his bedroom, *his bed*.

Akira asks, huffing and puffing, "What's on the agenda for today?"

"I have some business crap to deal with this afternoon. Do you guys want me to drop you off downtown? I'm going that way anyway."

We say yes.

* * *

Whitefish is a picturesque town. The main street is lined with artisan shops, cozy restaurants, bars, and coffee shops. On one end of the street, I can see the mountains and a sign for the main resort. I'm sure it's a great place to go skiing. The equipment stores are calling my name.

"So... what happened last night?" Akira asks, eyeing a couple of vases from *Wildflower Ceramics*, a local pottery shop.

"Nothing happened," I tell her.

"I saw you guys going upstairs together." She's checking the price tags.

"Can I help you?" asks a middle-aged woman wearing an apron.

"Did you make all these?" Akira asks.

"Yes, all except those." She points to a row of glass vases. "My daughter works with glass."

"They're beautiful," I say.

"Thank you. Feel free to look around, and let me know if I can help with anything."

"Nothing happened, and nothing could have happened, even if I wasn't engaged," I say, continuing our conversation.

"And why not?"

"We can't even touch each other."

Akira stops walking.

"Because of the burning thing?" she asks.

"Yeah."

"Can't you guys just take the necklaces off? For a little bit?"

"No, it doesn't work like that. They feel... part of our bodies. It's unbearable to take them off."

"Why didn't you tell me that before?"

"Because I didn't want you to freak out. Anyway, did something happen between you and Broc? I saw you two having a good time when I went to bed."

"No. He wanted to, but no."

"You didn't want to?" I ask as we walk out the door, bags in hand.

"We live too far apart. It would be... stupid."

I pull out my phone to look for a place for us to eat lunch. There's a text from Aaron.

I know why you're there. With whom.

What? How does he know? He can't know.

I quickly reply: *I'm here with Akira, Aaron.*

I show Akira my phone.

"He can't know. He's trying to bait you."

"I'm not hungry anymore," I say as we sit down at *Fisherman's Cove*.

"Get an appetizer," she suggests.

"Do you think Aaron is just being... jealous?" I ask her.

"For sure. How could he know?"

I sip my iced tea and nibble on the artichoke dip when my phone lights up.

Tell me Iris, do you think about me when you lick Locklear's dick?

* * *

"Thanks, but you didn't have to come back. We could've taken a cab," Akira tells Hoyt when he arrives to pick us up.

"Of course not," he says, opening the door for me.

We drive in silence.

I'm almost done packing when Hoyt knocks on my door. I quickly wipe away my tears.

"Iris, please tell me what happened."

I sit down on the bed. "Aaron knows."

"Knows what?"

"About us."

"About us?"

"That I'm here, with you."

"How?"

"I don't know." I'm trying to control my emotions, but I'm failing.

"Nothing happened, Iris, between us."

"I don't think he's going to believe that."

"That's his problem."

"No, it's mine. Ours. I shouldn't have come."

"I thought you were breaking up with him anyway."

"I was, I am... still, this is wrong. It's all wrong." My tears fall freely now. I'm angry, sad, but mostly ashamed.

"I can't bear to see you cry because of him," he says, taking a step back after taking two forward.

"And I can't bear hurting him."

Hoyt drops us off at the airport, and I barely glance at him when I say goodbye. The flight home is as painful as Aaron's last words.

* * *

I drop my bags at my place and head straight to Aaron's apartment. Akira calms me down on the flight, but everything rushes back when I open his door with my keys. I'm not even sure if he's home.

The door feels heavy as I push against something to open it all the way.

"Aaron?" I call as I lift a fallen chair.

The apartment is completely trashed.

I'm being careful as I step over broken glass when he walks into the living room. There are bags under his eyes. My heart sinks even deeper.

"What happened here?" I ask, taking in the wreckage; everything is broken or disheveled.

"You came back early," he says, his voice slow and tired.

"We need to talk," I tell him.

"There's nothing you can say."

"Aaron, nothing happened."

"Really? You expect me to believe that?"

"It's the truth."

"So you're telling me you went all the way to fucking Montana, and nothing happened?"

"Yes."

"You lied to me."

"I'm sorry, I—"

"We're engaged, Iris."

"Aaron, I'm sorry, I should have—"

"The worst part is that my mother was right all along." He's holding a picture.

I notice other photos on the coffee table. I walk closer and see that they're of... *me and Hoyt.*

"What is this?" I pick one up.

"Proof."

"You had me followed?" There are pictures of the airport in Montana, of Hoyt and me at the gala together, pictures of us at the museum...

"My mother did."

I don't have words.

"I thought I knew you. I defended you to her... for years. And she was right this entire time."

"Aaron, no. She wasn't."

"How long?"

I don't answer. I'm still staring at the photos of myself.

"How long have you been cheating on me?" he asks.

"I wasn't, Aaron. I'm not."

"You're going to keep lying? You owe me the truth, at least."

"Aaron, we just talked. That's it."

"You just talked? You just came back from his fucking house."

"I know, I shouldn't have gone."

"You think?" He picks up a glass from the table.

"I'm sorry. I should've talked to you. I've been meaning to."

"Talk to me about what?"

"The wedding, us... I can't do this."

I see tears streaming down his face.

"What are you saying?"

"I can't do this anymore."

"You're breaking up with me? Because of what? That douchebag you just met?"

"It's not about him."

"Of course it is. We've been together since we were kids, Iris. Then you meet a guy, and what? We're done?"

"Aaron, you know you've always been my best friend."

We're both crying now.

"I can... we can... work things out," he says, stepping closer.

I back away. "Please don't."

"Iris, it's me."

"I can't do this."

"I'm not letting you ruin this. Us."

"It's over, Aaron. I'm really sorry."

His face changes. "I'm going to fucking kill him."

"Aaron, please, you need to... calm down. Hoyt has nothing to do with this."

He lets out a dark laugh. "Out of all the men in the world, you had to pick a client?"

"A client?"

"He didn't even tell you?"

"Tell me what?"

"Your lover's money. I can make it... all go away... with just a few phone calls."

"He invested with you?"

"Why else do you think he was at the parties, Iris?"

"Aaron, please don't do anything stupid."

"I want you to leave."

"Aaron, we need to talk."

"Get the fuck out of my house," he yells, throwing his glass at the wall.

Seventeen

"It is a widely accepted notion among painters that it does not matter what one paints as long as it is well painted. This is the essence of academicism. There is no such thing as good painting about nothing." – Mark Rothko

The sun shines bright on my first day back from spring break, too bright. I haven't left my apartment in days. I can still hear Aaron's words as the glass shattered. The sound is stuck in my head, keeping me up at night, all night. I don't know how to move forward; everything feels harder. Even the simplest things, like showering and eating. Akira came by a few times after I told her what happened. I haven't spoken a word to anyone else—not to Aaron, and especially not to Hoyt. I want to dig a hole and bury myself in it. I'm feeling everything all at once: sadness, fear, anger, relief, and shame.

"Good morning," Akira says from the campus entrance, coffees in hand.

"I don't deserve you," I tell her, taking my first glorious sip.

"I know," she replies with a smile.

I smile back. A faint one, but I do.

"One day at a time, okay?" she says when we part ways.

"One day at a time."

* * *

I'm on my third slide when Jack asks, "Was this influenced by Ancient Egyptian sculptures?"

"Yes, we have a great example of that kind of sculpture here in the MFA in Boston, of the pharaoh Menkaure and his wife. Iconography means exactly that—investigating the visual signs in works of art. Let's take a look at *Melencolia I* by Dürer. It's possible that the winged woman could be the personification of melancholia. Or perhaps she represents creativity, moments before inspiration strikes. There are a few different theories regarding it. We see a rainbow in the sky, and I believe this here... is a planet. This print is known for its hidden curiosities. For example, the radius of the sphere in front of the dog has the same measurement as the distance marked by the compass. Who's heard of the Seven Liberal Arts?"

"Grammar, rhetoric, logic, music, geometry, arithmetic, and astronomy," Flora says proudly.

"Thank you, Flora. Geometry was considered vital to the creation of high art. We see in this engraving many symbols related to it, as well as to alchemy, including the compass, the hourglass, the scale, the sphere, and the polyhedron. Geometry and melancholia are both governed by the planet Saturn, which might be the planet we see in the back."

"My father always says melancholic people are the most likely to succumb to insanity," Jack says. "He's a psychologist."

"That's an interesting idea, Jack. Melancholy was associated with genius and creativity in the Renaissance. I can see how these rare gifts could be linked to madness, especially when one is striving for perfection. There are three realms of genius: imagination is the first, followed by reason and spirit. Perhaps the number one in the title refers to the first realm."

I'm happy to teach, to talk about art, and answer all the questions. It's almost dark when I leave campus. Work has always helped me during troubled times, and today is no different. I dove into writing a paper between classes merely to keep my brain busy. It's time I focus on my career again.

I'm looking for a book in one of my half-packed boxes when my phone buzzes. Hoyt is calling me. I ignore it. *Again.* I read until my eyes are too heavy to stay open.

* * *

"Who do you think she is?" I ask my students the next day.

"The goddess Venus, as the title says," Alec says, chewing gum.

"Isn't she a young bride?" Stella asks.

"She's nobody, just an idealized female," says Mila with distaste.

"You're all correct. Historians can't agree. There have been enough theories about this woman, including the ones you brought up, as well as that she could be a courtesan or a mistress. Titian combined many of those identities in this painting, which makes it hard to know for sure who she was meant to be. No mention of who she really was has been found. This is a seductive painting; the red pillows signal her passion. Painters looked to poetry for inspiration about love, beauty, and lust. And with Venus being the goddess of love, sexuality, fertility, and beauty, the title makes sense."

* * *

I'm putting my things away when Stella comes to see me.

"Can I help you with anything, Stella?"

She looks so young in her hooded sweatshirt. *Or am I just getting older?*

"I was wondering... if you had... any advice for me."

"With regard to what?"

"I'm torn between art history and actual art classes."

"What kind of art do you make?" I ask, pointing to the canvas in her bag.

"Oil."

"And do you love it? Painting?"

"I really do. I can't live without it. It's my escape."

"I don't think it needs to be either-or for now. Keep going with both for a while longer, until you know for sure."

"I'm... I'm afraid—well, my parents are—that I won't make any money with art."

"I see. I won't lie to you, being an artist is hard. Harder than being a teacher when it comes to a steady income. However, just because something is hard doesn't mean it's impossible."

"Do you think I'd be... giving up or selling out? If I only do my art on the side?"

"I definitely don't. A lot of the painters I talk about here had patrons; most portraits were commissions. And they painted what they wanted on the side, too. Everyone has bills to pay."

"Thank you. I don't want to look back and have regrets."

"Take your time making this decision. I know it feels like you need to choose now, but you don't."

"Thank you, I will... continue with both for now then."

"See you Thursday."

* * *

I meet Akira for lunch.

"Hoyt called me," she says, piling books on the table.

"He did?"

"Yeah, he's worried about you."

I look at her. "I need... time. I can't... I don't want to talk to him right now. I need to figure out my life. He makes things... difficult."

"I get it. Time is good, space is good."

"Did you tell him about what Aaron said, regarding the money?"

"I did. I thought he should be... aware."

"Yeah, I should have told him."

"He already knew. He said he knew since he met you that having his money with Aaron's firm would end up badly."

"And why did he keep it there?"

"I think they're in the middle of deals. He can't back away now."

"He never told me about the money."

"You guys will need to talk about it... and everything else, too."

"One day. What are you working on?" I pick up a book from her pile.

"A theory concerning drivers of galaxy growth and their evolution, from webs of gas that feed them to the formation of stars."

"That sounds... fun," I say, unwrapping my sandwich.

"I don't do anything that isn't fun."

I laugh at her. "I want to be you when I grow up."

* * *

At least tell me where to send the vase you left here, Hoyt's text reads that evening.

I pick up my phone and type: *It was meant to be a thank-you gift. For the hospitality. I forgot about it.*

Thank you. Any suggestions on where I should put it?

I know he's only trying to make conversation now. *Dining table?*

My house does need a... woman's touch.

I don't reply. I put my phone away and take a sip of my wine. I need motivation. It's time I start unpacking.

I'm opening another box, singing along to a cheesy song, when I glance at my phone again. Even though part of me wants to be left alone, it's hard to stop checking for messages.

Is Aaron sick? I read Lara's message.
I don't know. Why?
He hasn't been to work all week.

I stop my music. I've been trying not to let myself wonder about how he's doing. *Can you ask... Ted to check on him? We broke up.*

Sure. I'm sorry to hear, Iris.
Thanks, let me know when he does, please.

I empty my wine glass in the sink. My headache is back.

* * *

I am exhausted from the lack of sleep. I make a mental note to ask for a sleeping pill prescription. At least today, I only have a field trip. I'm looking forward to the change of pace.

I meet the students by the new exhibition, *Visiting Master-pieces: Caravaggio and Connoisseurship.*

"I planned this class because I knew this exhibit was coming to our city. We are very lucky to be in front of four paintings that have never been seen in Boston before," I explain.

"It says here that they don't know if these are real Caravaggios," says Liam.

"Right, this one"—I point toward the painting of a boy having his palm read by a Romani girl—"it's probably a true Caravaggio."

"This one"—I gesture toward the portrait of a member of the Order of Knights of Malta—"it's very possibly his too."

"And these other two?" asks Stella.

"Still debatable."

"What is the Order of Knights of Malta?" asks Christine.

"It's a religious order, considered a sovereign entity under international law. They used to require their members to be of noble lineage, but they've changed things nowadays. I believe their current role is to help with international humanitarian relations."

"Caravaggio is one of my favorites," says Gil.

"Mine too. This exhibition provides us with an opportunity to examine his talented hand and to debate what made him so well-known."

"Caravaggio is his last name, right?" asks Liam.

"Actually, that's his nickname," says Gil.

"Right, his actual name is Michelangelo Merisi. Caravaggio is the name of the town he's from."

"He is a murderer," says Christine.

"He did kill a man and lived in exile because of it," I tell them.

"The best artists have dark shadows," says Gil.

"Of course you would think that," says Christine, stepping away from him toward Liam.

"Why are you taking this class again?" Gil asks her.

"It was the only one that fit with my schedule," she replies.

I try to defuse the argument. "Okay, let's move on to *Saint Francis in Meditation* here."

* * *

The trip to the museum turned out to be a little more intense than I anticipated. Gil and Christine bickered the entire time.

I'm heating up my leftovers when my doorbell rings. I check myself—my Harvard sweatshirt is covering most of my body; it's enough to open the door.

"Hi," says Hoyt from the hallway.

"What... are you doing here?"

"Can I come in?"

I move, opening the door wide. "How did you know... where I live?"

"Akira." His eyes go straight to my bare legs.

"Hoyt, I'm... Give me a second." I walk to my bedroom. I put on a pair of dirty yoga pants. My apartment is a complete disaster. I look at myself in the mirror. I look even worse. I wish I could at least take a shower.

"What are you doing here?" I ask, walking back to the living room, tying up my hair.

"I needed to see you."

"I can't believe you're... here."

"Where are you moving to?" He moves a box out of the way and sits in the chair.

"Nowhere. I'm... unpacking."

"Akira told me what happened."

"Why didn't you tell me... about the money?" I ask.

"It never came up. I thought maybe you knew."

"I didn't. Hoyt, what if Aaron... does something with it?"

He shakes his head. "He won't. Not if he wants to keep his business."

"You should've seen his face... I don't know if—"

"As soon as a couple of deals are closed, I'll transfer everything to another place."

"He... how much money?" I ask. "Can he...?"

"I still have the lands, but... there's a lot invested."

I take a seat on the couch. "I'm sorry. I didn't know."

"Iris, please, it's not your fault. If anything happens with the money, it's not your fault."

I look at him, at his beautiful face. *In my apartment.*

"Until you get your money back, I think it's best if we don't... see each other. Aaron's mom... she had someone following me."

"Akira mentioned it. Do you think they still are? Following you?"

"I keep looking behind me when I'm out. Looking for a stalker... I've never noticed anyone. Not that I did before... I don't know."

"Do you need help? Unpacking?" he says, changing the subject and looking around.

"What? No. I mean, how long are you staying?"

"I've got to go back home tomorrow. I have to deal with a builder issue there."

"Where are you staying?"

"I came here straight from the airport." He points to the duffel bag by the door. I hadn't even noticed he was carrying one.

"Were you planning on—"

"I don't want to put you on the spot. I'll find a hotel. I just needed to see you. I even tried the trick with the fire."

"What? You did?"

"When you stopped replying, I wanted to make sure you were okay. It didn't work, though."

"Nothing?"

"No, it seems like you're the only one with superpowers."

I make a face at him.

"Are you hungry?" I ask as my stomach growls.

* * *

"How's work?" he asks as he serves himself from the Thai take-out container.

"Work is the only right thing in my life right now. Even with the tough crowd I have this year."

"I would love to watch you teach."

"I'm sure you would find it pretty boring."

"Impossible."

I shake my head to distract myself from his tone.

We are both eating on the floor, using boxes as props, even though my table is just fine in the corner.

"Your dad never told you anything else regarding the prisms?" I ask him.

"He never wanted to talk about it. He never wanted to talk about anything that mattered, to be honest. Not the prisms, not my brother, not even my mother. All I ever got from him is the knowledge that our prisms belonged to my mother."

"You never mentioned your mother before."

"She died giving birth to my sister."

"I'm sorry, Hoyt."

"I don't remember her well."

"Sometimes I think I'm forgetting my mom too." I take another bite.

"What's your best memory of her?" he asks me.

"Dancing... we used to dance all the time. She would put music on at night, sometimes classical music, and other times, popular songs."

"My mom used to sing to me every night. I still remember a couple of songs."

He stands up, taking his plate to the kitchen.

"Trash?" he asks, looking around.

"Behind you. Sorry, this place is a hot mess. I'm embarrassed, your place was... very tidy."

"You are moving in."

"Actually, I've lived here for years. I was supposed to move in with Aaron, I just never left."

"Why?"

"I think a part of me knew that things would end between us."

I get up to put my plate in the sink. He takes it from my hands, and our fingers almost brush against each other.

"I need a drink," I say, turning around.

I pour both of us an inch of bourbon on the rocks.

* * *

We are sitting in my bed, talking, both propped up on pillows.

"You can stay here tonight if you want."

"Are you sure? I can stay on the couch."

"You won't fit on the couch, take the bed."

"I'm not kicking you out of your bed, Iris."

"I'm offering. I don't mind. It's my turn to be the host."

He moves out of my bed and takes his pillow to the floor.

"What are you doing?"

"I'm sleeping here."

"On the floor?"

"Yes." He's pushing boxes away.

"I'm not letting you sleep on the floor, Hoyt."

"It's not like you can move me."

"This is insane."

"I won't break."

"Can you at least let me put a few blankets down?"

He helps me put layers of blankets, sheets, and pillows on the floor.

"I won't take offense if you want to go to a hotel," I say, handing him another pillow.

"I don't want to leave."

"I don't want you to leave." I say it without taking my eyes off him.

He takes another sip of his drink.

"Good, 'cause I'm not going anywhere."

We are lying down, me in bed and him on the floor next to me, when I turn off my bedside lamp.

"What are we doing, Hoyt?" I ask the question we are both wondering.

"The more I think about not being able to touch you, the more I want to, Iris." I love how he uses my name.

"What if we can't?"

"Then, like a moth, I will burn every day trying."

Eighteen

"You come to nature with all her theories, and she knocks them all flat." – Pierre-Auguste Renoir

I lay awake, listening to Hoyt sleep. My body aches every time he moves around. We are so close, yet *so far away*.

When I open my eyes again, it's daylight. And he's gone.

I check my phone—no messages. I don't have time to wonder where he went. I have to get ready for work. I'm getting out of the shower when I hear the front door. I didn't think he was coming back. He walks to the bedroom, not realizing that all I'm wearing is a towel.

"I got coffee," he says, putting the cup down on my dresser before looking my way.

"Thank you," I say, standing there, waiting for him to turn around. When he finally does, his eyes lock on mine. My prism glows.

"Sorry," he says, walking away to the living room.

I get dressed and find him reading a book of mine while sipping his coffee.

"I have to go to work, but stay as long as you want. You can leave my keys with the doorman," I tell him while packing my bag.

"I'm going to Aaron's office today," he says.

"What?" I almost spit out my coffee.

156

"I have to."

"No, you don't. Hoyt, you're only going to piss him off even more."

"It's a lot of money, Iris. I need to make sure he's being... professional."

"Would you, if you were him?"

He runs his hand through his hair. A habit, I learn, it's something he does when stressed.

"Fuck, probably not."

"I can talk to Lara. She works with him."

"I don't know... do you think she can... do something about it?"

"If anyone can, it would be her."

"Okay. My flight is at two."

"I won't be back before then."

"Will you pick up when I call?"

"Yes, just please stay out of Aaron's way, for now?"

"Fine. If I'm broke, I'm moving in with you," he says with a smirk while making himself comfortable on the couch.

"Very funny."

"See you later, firecracker."

I close the door of my own place, leaving Hoyt inside. *Things are far from getting easier.*

* * *

Any news from Aaron? I text Lara on my way to work.

Ted took him out yesterday. He said he looked depressed.

I don't have time to think about that now. I have ten minutes before class.

Thank you for checking on him. I'm sorry to put you in this position, but can you... make sure he doesn't... do anything wrong with Hoyt's money? For both of their sakes.

On it.

Thanks, Lara. I can stop by your place tonight to explain things.
Sure, no explanations needed. I'm here as a friend.
Six-thirty okay?
I'll order sushi.

* * *

Hoyt texts me when he leaves my place. I can still feel his eyes on me this morning when my prism glowed, leaving my feelings exposed.

My lectures suffer from my lack of focus, and I leave at six in a haze, only to hit traffic all the way to Lara's place.

"You didn't have to... this is a lot of food," I eye the beautiful spread in front of me and take a couple of rolls from the boat.

"Ted can eat sushi for days. How are you doing?"

"Okay, considering it's all my fault."

"Well, give it time... You guys were together for so long. It's supposed to be hard."

"Right."

"What is she doing here?" Ted asks as he enters the room.

"Ted!" Lara snaps at her husband's snarky attitude.

He walks straight upstairs after a quick glance my way.

"I'm sorry," she says after he shuts the door.

"It's okay. I get it. They are friends."

"We are your friends too."

I nod at her. "I know."

"I checked on Locklear's account. Nothing has been touched lately."

"Oh, thank God!" A weight lifts off my shoulders.

"I don't have direct access to it, but I'll keep an eye on it. Aaron can't do anything without ruining the firm and his reputation."

"I hope he can see things straight."

"Ted said he looked awful. The apartment is completely trashed."

"I saw it. I still need to get my things from there."

"We have a client dinner tomorrow night, at eight. I'll make sure Aaron is there. You can pick up your things then."

"Really? I appreciate it."

"Of course."

I put more food on my plate.

I'm tired and a little cranky when I get home, but the Dutch iris bouquet on my table brings a smile to my face. I pick up the card. *Thanks for letting me crash here.*

* * *

Even though I know Aaron isn't home, I still feel uncomfortable opening the door. I could probably live without my things, except my mother's letter is still on the bedside table. I would do anything to have it back.

I slowly turn the key and remember I need to give it back.

I'm looking around when I hear a noise coming from inside the place.

I move toward it, unsure if I should or not. The place still looks the same as when I last saw it—piles of dishes, trash everywhere, and empty bottles of liquor. My stomach turns as I get closer and hear voices coming from the bedroom. Lara texted me minutes ago saying she was with Aaron.

I open the bedroom door, to find them, in bed. *What the actual fuck?*

I stand in the doorway, watching them, until his eyes meet mine. He pushes Lara away.

"Iris!" he yells.

I turn and head toward the living room. He follows me, stopping only to put on a pair of shorts.

I'm thinking about every encounter I had with Lara. She played me, and she played well. *She wanted me to find them in bed.*

"Your best friend's wife, Aaron? Really?"

"You have no right to judge me," he says defensively.

Lara stays in the room. She's smart. I didn't know hate until this very moment.

"I came for my things. I thought you were away."

"Iris, look at me," he says, walking in my direction.

"Don't you come an inch closer!" I yell, then take a deep, slow breath.

"My mother's letter," I say to him. I need to stay calm until I have it in my hand again.

"What about it?"

"It's in the drawer, on the bedside table. It's all I want."

"Iris, please," he says, walking closer again.

"Will you go in there and get it or will you make me face Lara, naked, in your bed?"

He returns with my envelope minutes later.

I take it from his hands, but he grabs my arm with the other.

"Can we please talk?" he asks.

"I have nothing to say to you." I pull my hand back and walk toward the door, stopping halfway to place my key and engagement ring on the table.

"Iris," he calls after me.

"Goodbye, Aaron," I say, not looking back as I walk away.

* * *

"The fucking bitch," says Akira on the phone when I tell her everything.

"I didn't see it, at all. I ate dinner at her place last night."

"I hope I bump into her."

"Akira!"

"What?"

I shrug. "It doesn't even matter. It's not like I'm still with Aaron. Let them have each other."

"Seriously?"

"I don't get to choose who he sleeps with," I say, shaking my head.

"What about Hoyt's money?"

"Shit. I forgot. We're definitely screwed now. I've gotta call him."

* * *

"That's crazy. I'm sorry, Iris," Hoyt says.

I'm surprised. "You're sorry? It's your money."

"She was your friend."

"Well, I guess she wasn't," I reply.

"I'm sure it hurts... to be... betrayed like that."

"Yeah... What are you going to do?" I ask, changing the subject. "Regarding the money?"

He thinks for a moment. "I think I need to get lawyers involved. I'll probably be seeing you again soon."

"Give me a little heads up this time?"

"But the look on your face when you opened the door, and those bare legs..."

"Hoyt!"

"Alright, heads up. No worries."

"Okay, I've gotta go," I say.

"Iris?"

"Yeah?"

"You didn't deserve what happened today."

My eyes well up at his words. "Thanks. Although, perhaps I did."

* * *

I wake up from a nightmare, soaked in sweat. There was a fire in my apartment, and Darion was there. I was trying to unlock my door when I heard Lara's voice saying I was going to burn like the witches of Salem. I've gotta hand it to my brain—great plot.

There's no way I'm going to fall asleep again. I turn off my alarm and see that Aaron has called a few times. I wish I could go back in time and change things. Change how I handled everything.

* * *

When Hoyt said he would be seeing me soon, I didn't think he meant a couple days later.

Apparently, they had to move fast. He's coming with a team of lawyers, and this time he's booked a hotel. I can't help but feel my heart sink when he mentions where he's staying.

"I get it. My place doesn't even compare to what you're used to," I say over the phone in the morning.

"Iris, I didn't want to impose on you."

"That's okay."

"You don't believe me."

"I'd prefer to stay in a hotel, too."

"I'd sleep on the floor for the rest of my life if it meant being close to you."

I let myself relax at his words. "Liar," I call him out.

He chuckles.

"I have a question for you," I say to him.

"What?"

"Do you like to dance?"

* * *

Akira meets me at the entrance of Spiral, wearing a red shirt that leaves her belly button exposed.

"Where do you shop?" I ask, taking in her entire outfit.

"Online. I can't believe you invited Hoyt."

"Why?"

"I can't picture him in a club."

I laugh. "We're about to see if he can dance." I watch as he gets out of a car.

He looks... different. He's wearing an all-black outfit. His shirt buttons are... unbuttoned. Not all of them—just enough to reveal his muscled chest. The prism is nowhere to be seen.

He walks toward the back of the line, but I tell him, "We don't need to get in line."

He lifts an eyebrow.

"We're... frequent customers," I say, walking straight to the door, passing my fans as they yell nice things. For the first time, I don't care about their words.

The instant I hear the music, my prism pulses. It's hidden in my bra again. I'm wearing a tight, short black dress.

I have to be extra careful walking with Hoyt; there's barely any space between us in the packed club.

"Drink?" I ask him, leading him toward the bar.

"Please," he says, looking me over from head to toe. He lingers for a few extra seconds on my chest.

I welcome the stare. It feels good... to be... bad.

"To us," Akira says, clinking her glass against mine. I repeat the gesture.

She clinks her glass to Hoyt's without saying anything. I avoid getting that close to him.

We move to the dance floor.

I'm dancing, but I feel self-conscious with him around. *I need something stronger.*

Akira stays, but Hoyt follows me to the bar once again.

"I shouldn't. My meeting is early in the morning," he tells me when I offer him another drink.

I flip my shot glass upside down on the counter. The alcohol instantly does its job.

"Dance with me," I invite him.

Then I let loose with the music. I close my eyes and let myself feel it, exactly like I'm used to. I move my body and hands with each beat, fully aware that Hoyt is watching. When I open my eyes, I see the hunger in his. I know he would take me right here if he could. The desire in his eyes... he can't hide it. And I don't want him to. I don't care if others are watching, I only want him to see me—free.

Our distance invites others to approach me. He watches as I dismiss each one.

Akira says goodbye, mentioning she has to wake up early. She's obsessed with her latest theory.

Hoyt dancing is almost irresistible. I have to keep looking away to remind myself why I can't touch him.

"This is killing me," he says, stepping a little closer so I can hear him.

"What is?"

"You, in that dress."

"If only you could take it off." I'm feeling perhaps a little too loose.

"Don't give me ideas..."

"Consider yourself... challenged."

"Fuck. Let's get out of here."

Nineteen

"Art enables us to find ourselves and lose ourselves at the same time." – Thomas Merton

He opens the hotel room door, and I walk straight to the balcony. It's a beautiful night; the moon and stars shine above, while the city lights twinkle below. We haven't said a word since the club. I guess, like me, Hoyt's wondering: *what now?*

"Will you try something with me?" he asks.

"I'm not into drugs," I answer.

He laughs, his voice low. "You're enough to make me high."

He steps back into the room.

"Get your prism," he tells me, returning with a glass of water.

I reach for mine and slip it around my neck.

He pulls his out of his pocket and dips it into the water, then hands me the cup to do the same.

Then he steps closer. We let the prisms touch, and, like before, they attract like magnets.

He lifts his hand, and I mirror him.

"What if it burns?" I ask.

"I'm already hurting," he says, his voice quieter. "Staying away isn't easy either."

I slowly move my hand toward his.

It takes only seconds for him to realize it doesn't hurt and for him to grab my waist and kiss me.

His lips are taking mine like they need each other to survive. I bite his lips with my teeth pulling out slowly and he winces. He progresses to swirl his tongue on the top of my mouth and we can't have enough of each other. His hand starts to move on my body when he pulls back *in pain*.

"Motherfucker!" He shakes his hand, bringing it up to his mouth.

"I'm sorry, Hoyt. Are you okay?"

He looks at me with pain in his eyes.

"Are you in pain?" I ask, my voice soft.

"All worth it," he says slowly.

I watch him, still feeling the warmth of his hands on my skin. I want to throw my prism off the balcony. I'd do anything to feel him again. I look away, unable to hide the ache inside.

"Iris." He steps closer.

"No, Hoyt! I can't hurt you again."

"Will you look at me?"

I turn to face him.

"We'll figure it out," he says, his voice steady.

"What if—"

"Just don't give up on me."

If only he knew that I could never, not before, and especially not now that I know what his touch feels like.

* * *

Hoyt insists I take the bed. We've been simply talking since our kiss. I can tell he's tense about the meeting. I hope Aaron and he can be civilized together. But every time I try closing my eyes, I hear Aaron shattering the glass against his wall. I think about his clenched fists from the night I met Hoyt at the party. I'm also having a hard time forgetting about the way Hoyt kissed me. Every time I think I've calmed down, it all rushes back in. I roll over, trying to find a comfortable position, but the heat between us, even though we're apart, is undeniable. I can't sleep here. It's around three in the morning when I leave the hotel, leaving Hoyt resting on the couch. I text him: *I didn't bring a toothbrush. Meet me after the meeting?*

* * *

It's Sunday, and I let myself stay in bed until mid-morning. I took a shower after coming back from the hotel and I even slept for a bit. But now, I'm awake, with a massive headache and feeling hungover. I wish I could hear what's going on in the meeting. I keep checking my phone. They're about to start any minute.

I'm too restless. *I have to do this now*, before I change my mind.

They're seated in near silence. They're waiting for someone. I tell myself, I'm only staying for a minute. I'm under the table. I wasn't sure it would work, if I could get myself here. I kept thinking about finding Hoyt as I lit the candle. And I begged my prism to stay hidden. *When I opened my eyes, I was here.*

I try to make myself as small as possible; I'm not sure how much space I take up in this form. I'm not even sure they can see me. What if Hoyt was the only one capable of seeing the violet light? I can't risk finding out.

I hear a door open, then close. A chair scrapes across the floor. I recognize Aaron's voice. I wish I could see their faces, but I know better than to move. The lawyers begin. Hoyt's attorneys state their reasons for wanting to get out of the deals. I hear Aaron's representatives fight them. Apparently, they hadn't explicitly named me as the reason for backing out—something to do with timing and location. It's just an excuse. Only Aaron's attorneys know the real reason, and they press it.

"My client hasn't given any reason not to be trusted, no misconduct," an older man says.

"Not yet—a matter of time, perhaps," I hear a younger man's voice.

"You have no right to accuse him of anything," the older man responds.

"We have every right," another voice interrupts.

"You'll need proof. And since you don't have any, I guess we're done here."

I hear papers shuffling. I need to stay longer, but I'm starting to feel tired and dizzy. I focus on my breath, telling myself I can control it. I miss something they said.

People start moving. Someone stands up. Then I hear her voice. I turn around, careful not to touch anyone's feet when I spot the only high heels in the room.

"We are committed to our clients. We will remain so." I want to get closer to her, very close. I'm fantasizing about hearing her scream as I burn her feet when the door opens, and people begin walking out.

"How's my fiancé doing?" Aaron asks, and I know Hoyt is still there.

Please don't take the bait, I beg him in my mind, as if he can hear me.

"She isn't your anything anymore," Hoyt says, his voice calm.

"Because of you," Aaron snaps.

"We both know that's not true," Hoyt replies.

"I can't wait to ruin you," Aaron sneers. "We'll see if she sticks around once I leave you penniless."

"You think very highly of yourself," Hoyt says. "And very lowly of her, apparently."

"No matter how much you think she is in love with you, it has always been me who she runs to, and once this fling gets boring... she will come home, to me."

"Keep telling yourself that if it makes you feel better."

I hear footsteps.

"Aaron, let's go," Lara calls.

Aaron moves, and I hear him say, just before leaving, "Everything she does in bed, I taught her."

The door slams shut with force, and I black out.

* * *

I wake up to find my shirt soaked in blood. At least there's no fire this time. I'd placed my candle in a tray with water, just in case. My head throbs when I try to sit up, and I can barely make it to the couch.

I lie down, my vision still blurry. I'm supposed to meet Hoyt soon—I don't even know where. I want to text him, but my phone's in the bedroom. Too far. I know I can't walk that much yet, so I stay where I am, lying still. How long did I stay there for? Definitely longer than the previous times. It's clear that each session is stretching my abilities, stretching the *prism's abilities*.

I must have fallen asleep because Hoyt's knock at the door jolts me awake. Slowly, I push myself toward it.

"What happened?" He moves closer, almost forgetting he can't help me.

"Careful," I warn, stepping back.

"Iris, what happened?" His voice is full of concern.

"I... needed to know what was going on." I walk back to the couch, my head still spinning.

He glances around and notices the candle on the floor. "Did you?"

"I heard everything—well, most of it."

"You were there?" His gaze sharpens.

I nod, sitting back down on the couch. My head is pounding.

"You don't look well," he says, kneeling by me.

"I think I stayed too long."

"We should get you to a doctor."

"No, I'm okay."

"You're covered in blood," he insists.

"I just need a shower." I stand up, holding onto the couch for support, and slowly walk toward the bathroom.

"Iris," he calls after me.

"I'll be right back," I answer, trying to steady myself.

My vision is still spinning, but I push forward. I turn on the water and let it fall over my face, watching as the blood runs down the drain. *I must look lovely.* I'm rinsing out my shampoo when everything goes dark again.

When I open my eyes, someone's lifting me up. By the time I realize it's Hoyt, he's already placing me gently in bed.

"How are you holding me?" I whisper, feeling completely weak.

"Turns out we just needed more water," he says softly.

I try to sit up, but pain shoots through my arm. "My arm," I tell him, wincing.

"Don't get up. I think you hit your head."

I look at him; he's soaked.

"We're going to the hospital," he says, pulling clothes from my closet.

I'm still too weak to move; he helps me get dressed. I hate that this is how he's seeing me naked for the first time. However, there's no room for modesty. I'm too dizzy, too weak. Maybe I have a broken arm.

"The ambulance is almost here. I can't... bring you downstairs." I can see he's upset.

* * *

The next time I wake up, I'm lying in a hospital bed. Hoyt sits in the nearby chair.

"Hey," I say, and he lifts his head from his phone.

"You're awake."

"Thank you for bringing me here."

"The paramedics did all the work."

"Thank you for calling them."

"How are you feeling?""

I think I'm okay. My head hurts a little." I look down at my wrapped arm. "Is it... broken?"

"No, sprained. You got lucky."

A doctor comes in and talks me through everything they did and gave me.

"When can I go home?" I ask.

"We need you to stay overnight. You hit your head pretty hard," says the nurse.

They bring me food, and I finally realize Hoyt is still wearing the same clothes from earlier.

"You can go," I tell him. "I'll be okay."

"I'm not going anywhere."

"You need to change and eat. I don't know, don't you have places to be?"

"Are you kicking me out?"

"No, of course not. I just hate to be... a burden. I'm fine now."

"I'm staying."

"I'll ask Akira to come babysit."

I look around. I don't have a phone.

"I'll call her," he says.

Akira arrives in half an hour.

"What happened?" she asks, though she's not asking me.

Hoyt explains everything to her.

"You are impossible!" she yells at me.

"I thought I—"

"What?" she demands.

"Improved."

"You can't do this again." This time, it's Hoyt who gives me the order.

"Fine."

Both of them just stand there, staring at me.

"I said fine!"

"Next time you want to spy, just call me. I can put you on speaker," he says before leaving.

"Thank you for everything," I say as he walks away.

"See you soon."

* * *

"Is this really necessary?" I ask Hoyt as he opens my apartment door.

"You shouldn't move your arm."

"I'm right-handed."

"Still."

I look around, noticing the change. "Did you... clean my apartment?"

"I just moved things around. There's food in the fridge."

"What?" I open the refrigerator and find it stocked.

"I didn't have time to make you anything, so I ordered a bunch of stuff."

"Hoyt, this is..."

"It's nothing. All your meds are on the bedside table. You need to take them with food."

"Thank you." I want to hug him, smell his hair... I walk away to my bed and sit down. He follows me.

"I wish I could stay," he says, closing the curtains.

"I'll be fine."

"I know you enough now not to take 'fine' very seriously."

"I promise. Akira said she'll come by later."

He takes a seat on the other side. "Will you keep me updated? On how you're feeling?"

"Sure. You never told me what happened after the meeting. Did you get your money back?"

"Nothing happened. The lawyers are working on it."

"Okay. Well, will you keep me updated on that?"

"I will. You should rest."

* * *

It's dark when I wake up to an empty apartment. I make my way to the kitchen and open the fridge. There's more food than I could possibly eat in a week. I open the first container and find orange chicken. It smells amazing. I find the rice to go with it.

I finish eating and go to grab more water when the doorbell rings. Could it be Hoyt again? He has to be midair by now.

"Hi," Aaron says from the hallway.

"Aaron, what are you doing here? I told you I don't want to see you."

"I heard you were at the hospital. Are you okay?"

"How did you know? Are you still... following me?" I'm furious at the thought.

"What? No. It was my mother who did that."

"So, how did you know?"

"I'm your emergency contact."

"Oh."

"What happened?" He's still standing in the hallway.

"I fell, hit my head."

His eyes go straight to my arm. "Iris, if you're covering for him... Did he...?"

"What? No. He would never." I can see in his eyes that he still loves me. "Aaron, you should go."

"Not until I know you're safe." He walks into my apartment, looking for who knows what.

"Aaron, I'm fine. There's no one here."

"Iris, you know you can tell me... if anything happened. I can protect you."

"I fell, Aaron. That's it."

He looks around; there are still boxes everywhere. "Iris, everything that happened, we can still fix it. Us."

"There is no us, Aaron." I move to open the door.

He walks out. "If I find out that asshole laid one finger on you, I swear to God Iris, I will kill him."

"Aaron, please. I told you, Hoyt would never hurt me." I want to make sure he understands, but he's already in the elevator.

* * *

I take another couple of days off work—the students had submitted reports; I figured it was easier than asking someone to cover my absence. I'm busy reading the papers when Akira shows up.

"You weren't kidding," she says, opening the fridge.

"I told you, there's plenty of food."

She picks a lasagna tray and puts it in the oven.

"How's your... theory going?" I ask, taking a seat.

"Let's talk about anything but that." She'd mentioned before that she's having trouble with it.

"Hoyt invited me to a gala," I tell her.

"Seriously?"

"And I'm pretty sure Aaron will be there too."

"What? Why would he do that? You're not going, right?"

"He said his lawyers advised him to be seen in public with me. It would help make their case... that Aaron could act... in bad faith."

"Interesting. What did you say?"

"I said I'll go. Anything to help him get his money back and be done with this drama."

"Right. There's been enough of that."

"Will you help me get something to wear? All my formal dresses stayed at Aaron's. I still have so much stuff over there."

"Do you want to go to the store we went to last year?"

"I was hoping to wear something... different. I need a change. I almost chopped my hair off yesterday."

"I know a place."

"Are you free tomorrow afternoon? The party is on Friday."

"Yeah, I'll text you the address."

I go to pass her the phone when I glance at one of her texts.

"Is that from Broc?"

"Yeah."

"I didn't know you guys kept in touch."

She's typing.

"What are you saying?"

"A dirty joke."

"What? Are you serious?"

"Yeah, why? Don't look at me like that. It's harmless."

"Is it?"

The oven beeps.

* * *

"We're covering Velazquez next week. Please familiarize yourselves with his work," I say at the end of the lecture. It's tricky to teach with only one arm, but a couple of students are kind enough to help. I leave in a hurry to meet Akira, hoping I can still grab lunch before I have to be back on campus for my next lecture.

"For someone who hates parties, you seem to go quite frequently," Akira says, walking around the store.

"Don't you think I know that?"

"How about this one?" She lifts up a leopard print dress. I simply look at her. "Kidding."

The store she picked is a world away from what I'm used to.

But so am I. I'm looking at myself in the mirror... I feel much different from just a year ago.

"You look hot!" she tells me when I come out of the dressing room.

"It's not too... much?"

"Aaron will definitely make a scene."

"That's what we're hoping for."

"Remind me to always stay on your good side."

I laugh. "Welcome to my dark one."

TWENTY

"I INVENT NOTHING, I REDISCOVER." – AUGUSTE
RODIN

I stare at myself in the mirror, at my bright red lips. My arm is still recovering, but luckily, I was able to take off my bandage. The gold dress I picked is borderline inappropriate—too much skin showing. I remind myself that it's all part of the game: make Aaron jealous, get Hoyt's money back, restore my peace of mind.

I'm outside. I read Hoyt's message. I glance at my reflection one last time. Once again, I'm wearing my prism for all to see. I thought about hiding it, only I'm not wearing enough cloth to do so. I'm as vulnerable as I can be.

Hoyt opens the car door for me. I'm a sucker for gentlemanly gestures. Even with the warmer day, I can't skip the coat. I need... coverage.

"You look beautiful," he says.

"So do you," I tell him as I get in. And he really does. There's something about his edginess paired with the tailored tux, I can't keep my eyes off him.

"Thank you for... doing this. I know it's not your thing," he says.

"I'm happy to help. It's kind of my fault you're in this situation anyway."

I glance out the window at the beautiful night sky. Perhaps "happy" is a stretch.

"Iris, if you're not comfortable doing this, I can turn the car around. We can find another way," Hoyt offers.

"I know what I signed up for." I'm to play a dark role... I tell myself it's for the greater good.

* * *

The party is mostly outdoors. Lights illuminate the garden, and waiters move around the gorgeous pool. I hand off my coat at the entrance.

"Wow. You look... irresistible," Hoyt says, staring at my almost-bare body.

"Shall we... play?" I ask, passing by beautiful flower arrangements.

Hoyt grabs a couple of glasses from a tray, and we begin our search for Aaron.

"It's a little chilly for you to be wearing... that," Hoyt says, eyeing me again.

It's colder than I expected, and I'm sure he can see my hard nipples through the thin fabric. *All part of the plan*, I remind myself. And to my surprise, I'm actually... enjoying it.

I haven't stopped to think until now that, after being with Aaron for so long and knowing how jealous he gets, I've always stayed in the shadows, afraid to draw attention to myself. *No more.* Tonight, I will steal stares, invite lust and madness. Tonight, the more jealous he becomes, the better.

We've done two laps around the place with no sign of him. I'm starting to doubt he'll even show. But the Aaron I know would never skip an event like this.

A violinist plays beautifully, and I watch as she moves her arm, precise and intense.

I'm nearly finished with my second drink when I spot them. I can't believe it—are they together? In public?

"Are you okay?" Hoyt asks.

"Yes, I... didn't know they were... together, like this."

"That bothers you?"

"It's not because of him. I simply... can't stomach her, after all she did."

Lara is wearing a pretty pink dress, classy as usual. Aaron looks like the perfect match—a prince and his princess. A part of me wants to flee, but the new part, *the vicious part*, wants to put on a show. I steady my breath.

"If only you could kiss me right in front of him. We could be going home much sooner," I tell Hoyt.

"I could... throw you in the pool," he says with a grin.

I laugh at the idea. "Perhaps we can find our own pool... after."

His eyes change, and my body heats up with the thought.

"Let's get this over with," I say, walking toward Aaron and Lara.

Aaron watches me as I move, heads turning in my direction. He stares at me with predator eyes, ready to pounce. Slowly, his gaze shifts to my right, to Hoyt. Even though we can't touch, we make sure to look like we're together.

Hoyt steps closer and whispers, "Let him think I have you."

"I don't have to pretend that."

"I thought it was below you to rub it in my face," Aaron says when I reach them.

"And I thought it was below you to fuck trash." I look at Lara standing there.

"Look who finally grew up," Lara replies, taking in my outfit.

Poker face, I remind myself. *Play it well, and it'll be over soon enough.*

"Tell me, Aaron, what did Ted say, when he found out you were screwing his wife?" I ask him.

I feel him tense. I'm sure it didn't go well. I actually feel sorry for Ted, but I don't let them read my emotions.

"Why don't you mind your own business?" Lara answers for him.

"We'd love nothing more than to do that. Are you done playing with my money?" Hoyt says in a low, devious voice.

"I'll be done when there's nothing left," Aaron replies, staring at him.

"Aaron!" Lara snaps, reminding him to shut up.

"We both know you can't do that, not without ruining your own business too," I tell him.

"Do you think I care about that? I'd give it all up just to see both of you begging on your knees."

"Looks like you're the one who needs to grow up," Hoyt says.

"Fuck you!" Aaron says back.

"We're done here. I thought you could be reasoned with." I look at Aaron and see the hurt beneath his anger. I still know him well.

"And I thought you loved me." His words hit me harder than I want to admit.

"Looks like we were both wrong then." I know he doesn't deserve my words, but I need this to end. I start to walk away.

"By the way, all those lessons you said you gave her... thanks."

I hear what Hoyt says and look back just in time to see Aaron lose it.

He pushes Hoyt, wanting to start a fight. But Hoyt just backs away and laughs.

Game over.

Thank God.

* * *

I put my coat back on and ask Hoyt, "Will you walk with me?"

"I'm sorry you had to be there for that," he says as we cross the street.

"I'm just glad it's over. I think enough people saw him pushing you."

"Yeah, I think so. Let's hope it's enough."

People walk around us, yet it feels like we're the only ones in the world. We reach the park, and the quiet night stirs up a lot of feelings inside me.

We walk in silence for a while, both of us lost in our own thoughts. Then, the rain starts to fall, catching us both by surprise.

"Got to love April showers," I say, glancing at myself.

It shifts from a light sprinkle to a heavy downpour in minutes.

The second the water hits our skin, we both know what it means—what we can do, feel. We stop walking.

This time, Hoyt kisses me slowly. He takes his time placing one hand behind my head and the other behind my waist. He pulls me closer and I can feel his prism against my chest. I know our lights are glowing, even with my eyes closed. He moves his lips on mine, taking bit by bit until his tongue reaches mine. He teases me with his teeth and I let my body arch against his hands. We are both soaked but we don't dare move away.

I move my hand to his wet hair. I'd fantasized about doing it since the first time I saw him. His strong, hard body is pushing against mine. He pulls back just enough to say, "I don't think I can ever have enough of you."

He kisses me like I have never been kissed before. He tastes like bourbon and I want every drop. *I need more.* I know we are still in the middle of the park; I don't care. Until I do. At that moment a lot of things come rushing to my head as I let myself feel all of it. Aaron's words, all I have gone through these past months, how much I have changed, how much of myself I'm still discovering. I pull away and look him in the eye.

"I don't think I'm ready for this," I say.

He takes a step back.

I'm confused. My body aches for his touch, but my mind isn't ready.

"I'm sorry," I continue.

"You have nothing to be sorry for."

"I think tonight... I realized I've never been by myself. I'm not ready to jump into... something else."

"I understand."

I step closer and take his hand. "It doesn't mean I don't want this... us."

He kisses me on the forehead and says, "I will wait."

I move closer, letting him wrap his arms around me. I rest my head on his chest, allowing myself fully to feel him—for the first time. I know I'm making the right call, even if this is where my heart belongs.

"Let's take things slow," I say, looking up into his green eyes. "I have to figure out who I am when I'm not someone's plus one."

"You know where to find me."

We walk back to the street, holding hands.

He puts me in a cab, and I watch him disappear into the rain while my driver takes me home.

* * *

I want to scream into my pillow. It took all my strength to walk away, to not ask him to take me right there—in the rain, in the hotel pool, in his shower—wherever and whenever he could.

I take off my dress and put on the comfiest sweats I own. I crawl under the covers and cry. Too many feelings need to get out. But I owe it to myself to get my life together, to not lose myself in another role. I can't be someone's anything—not until I figure out who I am when I stand alone. I know I have a journey ahead of me, and it's time to learn who I truly am when let *free*.

* * *

I don't even stop to eat breakfast. I wake up with a kind of energy I haven't had in a long time. I need to unpack. The mantra comes to mind: *messy house, messy mind.*

I start by putting my books back on the shelves. First, I pull out the novels, separating the unread ones into a different pile. I have a habit of buying books and forgetting about them, only to buy more the next time I *I* pass a bookstore.

I open another box with my art history books; surprisingly, I've gone through all of them.

I rediscover my passion for decorating. I experiment with the placement of my antique objects, including my marble statue of Cupid and Psyche—one of my favorite classical myths. Cupid, son of the goddess Venus, falls in love with Psyche, a mortal, disobeying his mother's orders. They go through a series of dramatic events, culminating in the gods turning Psyche into an immortal and uniting her with Cupid. The story proves that love cannot exist without trust.

Hours later, I'm happy to see a pile of broken-down boxes by my front door.

I move on to my bedroom, change my sheets, arrange my jewelry boxes, and proceed to take everything out of my closet.

Maybe I should've broken the tasks into smaller chunks. I'm exhausted, but I can't stop now. Half the clothes I own no longer fit my style. *I've changed in more ways than I realized.*

By the end of the weekend, my apartment is put together. It still needs a deep clean, and a few new furniture pieces will be arriving soon, but it feels amazing to see the progress. I can't believe I waited this long. It's been almost a year since my place looked this nice. I stand there for a while, admiring the outcome, proud of what I've done.

* * *

"Can you believe we only have two more weeks left this semester?" I ask Akira, waiting in line for coffee.

"I know. You never told me if you decided to teach that summer class."

"I'm taking the summer off."

"Nice. It'll be good for you."

"When's your seminar again?"

"Beginning of June."

"Have you been to NASA before?"

"Yeah, a couple of times. I received an offer from them before."

"Why didn't you take it?"

"I've always known, since my lessons with Ms. Turner, that I wanted to be a teacher. What she ignited in me, I wanted to pass on to my students."

* * *

"Professor De Loughery?" Stella calls from the hallway.

"Yes?" I turn around to face her.

"I just wanted to let you know, in person, that I've decided to... focus on my art instead."

"Oh. I'm glad you figured it out."

"I wanted to thank you."

"Why? It doesn't seem like my classes helped much. You're not exactly following in my... footsteps," I say with a smile, half kidding.

"No, they did help. It's exactly because of your classes that I know I'm meant to be an artist. The way you talk about the painters—their passion, their hard work—I know I'd regret not giving it a chance."

"Well, then I'm happy to have helped."

"I'll see you tomorrow for the final."

"See you then."

* * *

I pass by an almost closed door and recognize George's voice. He sounds upset. I'm about to keep walking when I hear him mention Darion's name. I pull out my phone, pretending not to listen.

"You can't possibly believe Morris!" he says to someone.

"George, it's out of my hands. It's everywhere."

"It's a fucking lie."

"You know how these things work. It's not about... the truth sometimes."

"I have a reputation here."

"And I'm sure you'll find another great place to work. This is Harvard; doors will open for you."

"Not after this, they won't."

"I'm sorry, George. I really am."

A class ends, and people begin leaving from a nearby room. I start walking toward my own class.

I pull out my phone and search George's name. The news is everywhere. I quickly read the headline: *Professor George Wilson is damning Harvard's reputation with widespread allegations of sexual harassment and misconduct. It's unknown whether Darion Morris, the plaintiff, will continue his studies at the campus.*

TWENTY-ONE

"I FOUND I COULD SAY THINGS WITH COLOR
AND SHAPES THAT I COULDN'T SAY ANY OTHER
WAY—THINGS I HAD NO WORDS FOR." –
GEORGIA O'KEEFFE

Sweat still drips down my face as I head home from yoga. The new instructor really wanted to make an impression. I rarely have to hold positions for that long, but it felt good to let it all out on the mat. I have two more days of work, and then I'm free until fall. I've never taken the entire summer off before, and I'm not even sure what I'll do with all that time. Perhaps it's finally time to book that Europe trip I've always dreamed of.

I stop by a smoothie shop and order a protein shake. Getting in the best shape of my life is part of my goal for the summer. "It's the new me. You won't recognize me in the fall," I told Akira yesterday after ordering a salad for lunch. She cracked up, though she didn't discourage me. I'm motivated to become the best version of myself—even if I have no idea what that looks like yet.

I enter my apartment, arms full of my online orders. I open each package like it's a gift. I can't quite remember everything I bought—between the clothes, shoes, books, and even furniture, I've lost track. I wanted new things to mark this new phase in my life, but *I might've gone a little overboard.*

I'm trying on a pair of shoes when my phone rings.

"Hey," I say, grunting as I struggle with the shoe.

"What are you doing?" Hoyt asks.

"Trying on a new shoe."

"It sounds like you're wrestling it."

I laugh. "What are you doing?"

"Cooking."

"What are you making?"

"Littleneck clams."

"It's times like this I wish you lived closer."

"It smells amazing here. And I'm always wishing you lived closer too."

"I'm thinking of going to Paris this summer," I say.

"Really? By yourself?"

"Yeah. Have you ever been?"

"No, only Italy and Germany."

"I have the entire summer off," I continue. "I don't think I can stay put without work for three months."

"You could come here."

"Hoyt."

"I know, I know. I promise I'll give you space. You can take your old room."

"My old room?"

"And you can read, maybe visit the resort nearby. There's a lot to do around here, and it's fucking beautiful in the summer."

"I don't know. I was planning on... working on myself."

"I have a gym, and... I can cook you anything you want."

"I'll think about it."

"Okay, I gotta go. I'm eating my amazing dinner outside, looking at the stars."

I chuckle. "You are mean."

"You wouldn't change me if you could."

"Oh... you're good at this."

He laughs. "Good night, firecracker."

* * *

I hand each of my students their final paper, along with their grades. I'm officially done for the summer. I didn't realize how badly I needed a break. A real vacation—when was the last time I took one? I haven't figured out where I'm going yet, just that I'm going.

* * *

"It's only been a couple of weeks," Akira says from the bar stool next to me.

"I'm telling you, I'm already going crazy. My apartment has never been this clean. The only place I have to be is the yoga studio. I think I should ask if they still need anyone to teach."

"You could go to... Montana."

"I can't. I told you, I'm working on myself. I can't do that with Hoyt down the hall."

"You need to get out of the city. You've lived here your whole life—go see something different. What happened to your trip to Paris?"

"I didn't realize how expensive it was."

"You're a Harvard professor. You have money."

"I know, it's just... it's kind of sad to go to Paris alone."

"Then go somewhere else." She finishes her glass.

"I don't know. Do you want another one?"

"I'm leaving early tomorrow. I can't wait to squeeze Chiyo."

"He must be so big now."

"Look at this photo my sister sent me last week." She turns her phone toward me.

"Oh my god! He's so cute... look at those legs!"

"I know. I can't wait."

You go ahead, I'm going to stay a bit longer."

"Are you sure?" she asks.

"Yeah, I've got my book."

"Okay. Plan a trip, Iris. Seriously. You deserve to go on an adventure. Forget the responsibilities. It will do you good."

"I promise I'll think about it."

I'm sipping my wine, reading my book, when I pull out my phone to search for tickets again. I know it's not the money holding me back from clicking "buy." It's Hoyt's invitation. I can't help it—I do want to spend my summer with him, under that beautiful sky. I just need to make sure that, if I do go, I carve out time for myself too.

You could make me anything I want? Anything? I text Hoyt.

Anything. If I don't know how, I'll learn.

Consider your place booked for the summer then, I reply.

Are you serious?

If you'll still have me.

His reply is immediate: *There's nothing that would make me happier.*

Is tomorrow too soon?

See you tomorrow, firecracker.

* * *

"Good thing I have a big truck," Hoyt says, pushing a cart loaded with my bags. His stubble looks a little thicker than the last time I saw him.

"It's mostly books," I reply, wondering how I'm going to stay away from him for an entire season. The past five minutes have been hard enough.

"Books? Haven't you heard of an e-reader?"

"The kinds of books I like to read aren't online."

"And what kind of books are those?"

"Smut."

He coughs, and I laugh.

"I'm old-fashioned. I like to hold real books."

"Feel free to borrow anything from my sister's room."

"She left books too?"

"She left everything."

I want to know more, however I know now isn't the right time to ask.

* * *

"What kind of music do you listen to?" he asks, closing his door behind him.

"A bit of everything. You?"

"Here, pick something." He hands me his phone.

I scroll through his long playlist. "Okay, this is literally... everything."

He smiles.

I click on a dark grunge rock song I like, but my mood quickly shifts. I change it to a country song I know.

"So, what's your dinner request?" he asks, singing along.

"You said anything?"

"Anything."

"Pancakes."

He laughs. "Pancakes? That's your wish?"

"It's my favorite food. Breakfast is my favorite meal of the day."

"Pancakes it is. Any special kind?"

"Surprise me," I say, smiling back.

* * *

Hoyt is sweating by the time he comes downstairs after bringing my bags to my room.

"Thank you for the bags—and for... letting me stay here," I tell him.

"You're welcome," he says, stepping closer. "I want you to feel comfortable here, to do whatever you want. You're not my guest this time; treat it like it's your home."

"Thank you, Hoyt. Really. It feels great to be out of the city's craziness. Especially during the summer heat."

He walks over to the couch and turns on the TV. The casualness of us, together, moves me.

"I'm going to go unpack," I tell him, heading upstairs.

"Remember, like it's your home."

I leave smiling.

* * *

I've brought way too many books and not enough clothes, I realize, looking around. I'll need to make a trip to a local store at some point.

After putting my things away, I sit on the bed. *"Like it's your home."* His words echo in my mind as I change into something more comfortable. I can't spend the entire summer worrying about how I look. I need to relax, let go.

I tie my hair up and bring a book downstairs with me. Hoyt isn't on the couch anymore. I'm about to look for him when his words come to mind again: "Like it's your home."

I walk out to the back patio and dip my feet into the water. I open my book, and for the first time in a long while, I have nothing to worry about. Not right now. Everything else can wait.

I read for a couple of hours before Hoyt finds me.

"Hi," he says, looking at me.

"How long have you been there?"

"I like to watch you read."

"That's creepy."

He laughs. "You look... calm. Lost in the words."

"There's nothing that brings me more joy."

"Not even art?"

"Well, I'm reading about art."

"I want to take you out tonight."

"What about my pancakes?" I counter.

"Tomorrow. Tonight, I want to take you out—to a proper dinner."

"Okay," I say, getting up. "I'll go change."

"Iris?" he calls as I walk away. "I promised to give you space. And I plan on doing that. If I step out of line or if you want me to leave you alone, just say it. Is dinner too much?"

"No, dinner is perfect."

He nods.

* * *

The sun is setting when we leave. The fresh air fills me with life, and I open Hoyt's windows to let it in.

"You look beautiful," he tells me.

I glance at him. He's wearing a button-down shirt and real shoes. No boots.

"Thank you," I say.

We drive mostly in silence. I know he's holding back because I don't want to rush things. I'm not sure myself how slowly I want things to go.

* * *

A beautiful waitress comes to take our order, and I can't help but compare myself to her. I hate that I do that. I remind myself to add something to my summer goals list: *stop comparing*.

"Have you been in a serious relationship?" I ask him, not sure why I'm going there.

"Yes and no."

"What does that mean?"

"I thought we were, and she didn't."

"When did this happen?"

"Almost two years ago. She didn't even feel the need to hide it. I saw them one day at a bar. She acted like... I don't know. She told me she didn't know we were exclusive. I didn't think I had to clarify."

"I'm sorry, Hoyt."

"Don't be. Everything happens for a reason."

"Do you really believe that?"

"I do." He smiles at me.

I look away, not sure how to respond.

"So... what's Akira doing this summer?" He changes the subject.

"She has plans—family stuff, and NASA."

"NASA?"

"Yeah, she's that smart. She's participating in a seminar."

"Broc asked me if she was coming with you."

"I think they've kept in touch," I say, looking out the glass windows.

"I would give anything to see Broc at NASA," he tells me.

"Space cowboy," I wink, and we both laugh at the thought.

We eat and talk about childhood memories, horses, and work.

I want to split the check, but he refuses. I'm not sure how to handle that; Aaron had been paying for me since we were teens, and I could barely afford anything back then.

"Next time," I tell him, "I want to. Next time's on me."

"Will there be a next time?" he asks, lifting an eyebrow.

TWENTY-TWO

"THE HEART OF MAN IS VERY MUCH LIKE THE
SEA; IT HAS ITS STORMS, IT HAS ITS TIDES, AND
IN ITS DEPTHS, IT HAS ITS PEARLS TOO." –
VINCENT VAN GOGH

I wake up feeling refreshed from an early bedtime. When we got back last night, I struggled with what to do. I could have stayed up; Hoyt and I could've hung out, but I knew what I'd be risking. So, I told him goodnight and walked to my room, making sure to lock the door. I needed a barrier. Not from him—it was myself I didn't trust.

As I walk downstairs, I can already smell the food. What I find is the opposite of what I had in mind when I told Hoyt I wanted pancakes. I thought I was asking for something simple, an easy meal. Instead, in front of me are stacks of round cakes filling the counter, each with a different flavor. An array of fruits, creams, and jams surrounds every plate. I couldn't even choose one if I tried.

Hoyt is casually sipping his coffee, completely dusted in flour.

"Hoyt, did you make all these?" I wonder what time he woke up.

"I couldn't decide, so I made them all."

"Hoyt! You didn't have to."

"I wanted to."

I walk closer to a stack topped with strawberries and cream. I've never smelled anything so good.

"I gotta go, the vet is waiting for me. Enjoy."

He walks away, leaving me alone with all the food. I dip my finger into the cream and taste it. A loud moan escapes me. His cooking is going to be the death of me. *So much for getting in the best shape of my life.* I eat until I can't anymore.

I text him: *If you lose your money, you can always open a diner. Those were the best damn pancakes I've ever had.*

We're still waiting for the lawyers to do their job. It's out of my hands now, I remind myself every time I start to worry.

He sends a smiley face in reply.

* * *

I'm recovering from being extremely full when I decide to take a walk. I need to burn those calories, even though I know only a marathon could do that.

Spring has transformed the ranch since I last saw it. The heat has brought in more wildflowers. I recognize the bee balms, daisies, and lilies—but the rest of them, I don't know the names of. They're lovely, each very different yet belonging together. Wildflowers have a different kind of beauty; it's like they fight to grow, to take their place in the chaos of nature. No gardener's hands planted or pruned them. They came up on their own, and that's how they'll stay.

I sit on the grass, letting myself be surrounded by them. There's something about being connected to the earth that makes me feel different. I take off my sandals and spread my toes, letting the grass fill the spaces between them. I close my eyes, letting my body experience everything—the wind, the sounds, the smell of the earth, the distant hum of life around me. Just like I did in meditation, I sense everything, listening to it all.

I open my eyes and notice there's no one here—only nature.

The spot I chose to sit in is far from the house, the barn, anything man-made. I feel like the butterflies around me—part of the world, nothing more, nothing less.

I lie down, but the sun becomes too bright. I roll onto my side, using my hands as a pillow. My prism pulses when it touches the dirt.

What about the earth below me awakens the necklace my mother gave me? I want to know more. I sit up, and the prism slows its pulsing. I lie back down, and it responds by increasing its presence. I repeat the same motion twice, and again, the prism reacts accordingly, increasing and decreasing depending on how close it is to the earth's soil.

I understand nothing about this occurrence, but at least I have someone to discuss it with. Perhaps his prism does the same thing.

* * *

I haven't seen Hoyt all morning. After my walk, I took a shower and enjoyed a glorious nap. When I wake up, it's almost three in the afternoon. I'm just now getting hungry after my morning feast. I need something light.

I open his fridge and realize I'll be eating his food for months. I need to help somehow—maybe with the groceries, or the bills, something. I know he doesn't need the money, but I can't stay for free. Not for that long. I see Broc outside the kitchen window, pulling something with his truck that I don't recognize.

I walk out to meet him.

"Hey, how are you?" he asks, glancing my way.

"Hi! I'm good. Did Hoyt tell you I'm staying for the summer?"

"Yeah, yeah, he was acting like it's Christmas morning, couldn't stop smiling, even when the vet talked about worms."

I smile at the thought of him smiling because of me.

"I was wondering, is there something I can do around here? Like work?"

"Do you mean teaching?"

"No, no, nothing like that. Something to help around the... ranch?"

Broc looks at me like I have two heads.

I explain, "I need to... feel useful."

"Well... you could help with the horses," he finally says.

"Could I?"

"I think so—brushing, washing, feeding, that kind of stuff. But I think Hoyt won't let you."

"He's not my boss." I realize he's his.

He swallows.

"I'm sorry, I mean, he told me to do whatever I wanted, so... will you show me? What to do?"

"Sure, how about tomorrow at six?"

"Six in the morning?"

"We start early around here."

"Six is great. See you then."

I walk back into the house, realizing what I've just committed to. I need something to do around here besides reading and eating my share—or two—of Hoyt's food. *Horses—I can do that*, I tell myself, grabbing an apple and heading back to my room to read about them on my computer.

* * *

I hear a knock on my door an hour later.

"Come in."

Hoyt walks in, completely covered in mud.

"What happened?"

"Blackwater has a... sense of humor."

I would have loved to see whatever mess he'd gotten into.

"We're having a bonfire tonight by the lake. Want to come?" he asks.

"Who's 'we'?"

"Broc, Sawyer, and I think Sawyer's new girlfriend."

"Sounds... fun."

"Okay, see you in a couple of hours."

He turns to leave.

"Hoyt," I call after him.

He comes back.

"Does your prism do anything when you're close to the grass or dirt?"

"What do you mean?"

"I swear mine responded to it."

"Not that I've noticed. I'm starting to think they're all different."

"Maybe."

"See you later?" he asks.

"Only if you promise to shower first. You smell like horse," I tease him.

I can tell he wants to tease me back, but instead, he just laughs and walks away. I wonder how much he's holding back. The tension between us is different now that we know we can touch each other. The possibility changed everything.

* * *

"Iris, look at me," Hoyt says as we walk toward the fire. "Please, stay far enough from it, okay?"

"I will. It's not like I have anywhere to go, though. You're right here."

"Seriously, will you be careful?"

"Yes, I'll stay far away from the fire." I raise my hand to my forehead, as if to salute his orders.

He rolls his eyes, but I know he's right.

Broc is sitting in a fold-out chair, drinking a beer. He passes me one as I sit down next to him.

Sawyer is on the other side with his girlfriend, sitting on a blanket. He says hello and introduces Hoyt and me to April. Her long braided hair falls to one side of her shoulder. She looks shy; I barely hear her voice when she says hello.

A tall, strong fire burns within a circle of large stones, casting light between us.

Hoyt takes the seat next to me, and I take a sip of my beer. I can't help but make a face.

"Not a beer fan?" Sawyer asks me.

"It's so... light," I reply.

Broc laughs while rummaging through his cooler for something.

"We've got stronger stuff," he says, passing me a flask.

I take a sip. "Wow. What is this?" The liquid burns hotter than anything I've ever had.

"Moonshine," Broc replies proudly, lighting up his blunt.

"I think I'll take it back—beer is fine," I say, passing the flask back.

I hear Hoyt laugh as he walks to his truck.

"Here." Hoyt hands me a bottle of whiskey.

"Do you always carry alcohol in your car?" I ask, watching him take a sip of his beer.

"I brought it for you. I know what you like," he tells me.

"You just want to get me drunk," I tease him.

"Shit," Broc says, laughing at Hoyt.

"Shut up!" Hoyt tells him, laughing too.

The night is perfect for a fire—just chilly enough with a clear sky. I can see more stars here than I've seen in my whole life. Even with the light of the fire, they shine brightly above us.

"So, do you guys do this often?" I ask them all.

"We used to, all the time, growing up. Now... not so much," Sawyer says, smoking a cigarette. April and Hoyt take one from the pack he offers. They motion if I want one; I shake my head no. The whiskey's enough, I tell myself, taking a sip straight from the bottle.

"So, what's the craziest story you guys have? Growing up here, you must have so many," I ask, glancing at the three men.

"You don't want to know," Hoyt says, looking at the fire.

"Broc?" I look away from Hoyt, trying to catch Broc's eye.

"Okay, I've got one. It was Hoyt's fifteenth birthday, and we decided to steal a bottle of liquor from his dad. We were stupid enough to think we could drink and ride horses at the same time. We rode all the way to the east mountain, over there." He points. "We tied the horses up by the trees and sat by the river. It was still daylight when we got there. All four of us were used to riding there all the time. No big deal." He pauses the story to take a sip of his beer. I realize Luke must've been the fourth. "We almost drank the whole bottle. Had no idea how strong it was. Up until then, we'd only had beer. A few hours later, we realized we were stuck there. No way we could ride back."

"When my father found us, we were still puking our guts out," Hoyt says, crushing his can and tossing it to the ground near his truck.

"Next time we stole a bottle, we stayed local," Broc says, winking.

There's music playing from the truck, but it's the crackling of the fire that takes my worries away.

"I've got one," Sawyer says, sitting a little taller. "It was Fourth of July. Broc bought a ton of fireworks—too many. We were lighting them off until we realized something had caught fire. We looked back to see Broc's sweatshirt burning on the ground. He freaked out and dumped his cup on it. But Broc never drank water in his life. The alcohol just made the fire worse. We all had to rush in to put it out while fireworks were popping overhead. Those fireworks almost went off right there. We got lucky that night."

"I almost lost my truck that night. Not my favorite story, Sawyer," Broc says, throwing his can.

"You almost lost a toe," Hoyt retorts. "You guys are making us sound pretty dumb."

I laugh.

Hoyt takes the bottle from my hand, and our fingers barely make it without touching.

"This is very nice," I tell him. "Being outdoors."

"I'm glad you're here," he says, and I have to take a few breaths to slow my racing heartbeat.

I watch them all sing along and joke around as the fire crackles. I realize *I'm feeling happy. Or drunk. Probably both.*

"Do you have any stories for me?" I ask Hoyt, taking another sip.

"One night I was outside, in the back of the house. I'd had another fight with my dad. I was trying to figure out if I should apply for college—I was the only one not doing it. He kept telling me I didn't need to go. That I was needed here. That we were rich enough I could just hire people with degrees. He said I didn't need one myself. I was pissed. I wanted to go, like all my friends, even if it was only for the experience. And then I heard a sound coming from the barn. It sounded like a scream. I ran there. I was almost there when I heard it again. I ran faster, realizing it was my sister screaming. When I got closer, I saw Broc sewing Johanna's hand. She had cut herself on a barbed wire. She'd been out late by the river with them. Broc was already good at patching us up. I'm sure she could've waited to go to the hospital, but I'm still grateful for all the times you guys saved me and my siblings' asses." He lifts his can to them.

I watch Sawyer's gaze lock on the fire. Hoyt had mentioned the history between his friend and Johanna.

"What he's forgetting to tell you," Broc says, "is that there was no scream."

I look at him, confused.

"Jo never screamed. She was in pain, but she didn't want her dad finding out she was out late. I remember that night well—she never made a sound. It was Hoyt's sensory thing that alerted him... that she was hurt."

I turn to Hoyt. "Sensory thing? You mean...?"

"He knew when I got in a car crash, he knew when that guy in the bar had a gun... he even knew when his father died," says Sawyer.

"You never told me that your... sixth sense does this," I say, looking at Hoyt, trying to figure out why he never mentioned it.

"Because it's not something I even understand," he replies. "I don't know how to explain. It's a freaking curse, that's it." He grabs the bottle from the floor next to me and takes a long sip. "That's enough stories for tonight," he says, standing up. "You guys can put it out." He looks at me, silently asking if I'm coming too.

"See you in the morning," I tell Broc on my way out.

"What's in the morning?" Hoyt asks, shutting the car door.

"Nothing."

He looks at me.

"You should've told me about you knowing those things—sensing them," I say.

"Why?" We're both a little tipsy.

"Because I trusted you with all my stuff. All my prism's stuff."

"You knew about the sensing shit. I told you."

"You didn't say you knew things, you didn't give me any... examples," I say, shutting the car door a little too hard when we arrive at the house.

"Iris," he calls after me.

I stop and look back.

"I'm sorry. You're right, I... I don't like talking about it."

"I need honesty, Hoyt. If we have any chance of..." I don't let myself finish the sentence. Instead, I turn and walk away, heading to my bedroom.

I need to be up in a few hours for my first day of work at the ranch. *What the hell did I get myself into?*

Twenty-Three

"THE MOST SEDUCTIVE THING ABOUT ART IS
THE PERSONALITY OF THE ARTIST HIMSELF." –
PAUL CÉZANNE

I regret every sip I had the night before when my alarm rings. I know I'm under no obligation to show up, but I still have my pride. When I said I was going to be there, I meant it—a promise to myself, made many years ago, *not to be like my father*. I will follow through with my responsibilities, no matter what.

Broc is already busy when I arrive, even though it's six sharp.

"Morning," I say to him.

"Coffee?" He hands me a jar, and I pour myself some. There's no cream or sugar, but I drink it anyway.

"You seem unaffected by the alcohol," I tell him, sitting on a bundle of hay.

"Just used to it," he replies.

I look around and ask, "What time do they wake up?"

"Between four and five," he answers.

"Okay... so, what do I do?" I ask, setting my cup down.

"Here." He hands me a brush. "I'll take it easy on you today."

I'm brushing the second horse when Hoyt shows up.

"What are you doing?" He eyes my outfit—I'm wearing my own boots with Johanna's overalls.

"Working," I tell him, brushing Jet in long, even strokes, just like Broc showed me.

"Iris, you don't have to... do this."

"I want to. I need to."

"Iris."

"Like it's my home, remember? I'd have chores if it were my own house."

"I didn't think you'd take it as..."

Broc walks back with water for both of us.

"Broc!" Hoyt says, gesturing to me.

"You're my boss, but she's yours," Broc replies, walking off to check on something else.

Hoyt opens Blackwater's door and leads him outside.

"I'll see you later," Hoyt says. I watch as he rides away.

I know we're both still processing the words from last night.

* * *

I walk away from the barn when my hands start to ache. I don't know how many hours of work I plan on doing each day, but I figure it's enough for today. I head straight to the bathroom. I stink.

When I come back downstairs, Hoyt waits for me in a chair.

"Can we talk?" he asks.

"Sure." I sit down across from him.

"I'm sorry, Iris. I should have told you. All of it."

"When we were at the museum, you said... you could talk to me. I thought you meant it."

"Iris..." He starts to move closer, and when I inch back, he backs off. "I did mean it," he says. "I'm just not used to... I'll do better."

"Okay." My short words aren't convincing. I'm not convinced.

"I will... do better," he says again.

"Okay," I repeat.

I'm hoping he'll invite me to do something together, go somewhere, but he doesn't. Instead, he says he has a meeting with the lawyers. I nod and walk upstairs to read.

* * *

I text him an hour later. *Laundry?*

He tells me where the machines are, though he mentions Rosinda can do it for me.

Rosinda? I ask.

She will be around today and tomorrow to clean and do the laundry. Leave whatever you want washed in the hamper in the closet.

* * *

Rosinda is the absolute nicest person I've ever met. I want to get up and help her, but I know I'd only offend her. Hoyt tells me she's been working for them since he was a kid, that she took it personally to care for him and his siblings when his mother passed. I understand she's more than a housekeeper.

She holds my hands and tells me it's good for Hoyt to have me here. She ends with, "He's lonely."

I call Akira and read some more, only stopping to eat.

Hoyt stays busy all day, but I know he's home. His truck is still outside.

I find him in the study, hunched over papers, *wearing glasses.*

"Can I come in?" I ask.

He looks worried. "Of course."

"Everything okay?"

"Same bullshit—government wanting what's not theirs, lawyers wanting more money, horses needing more care... you know."

"Can I help with anything?"

"You already are." He motions to my red hands. He takes his glasses off and throws me a pair of gloves. "I was going to bring these upstairs for you."

"Thanks." I see they're the perfect fit.

I look around the room. I haven't been here yet. Hoyt's wooden desk is across from the window, where two brown leather chairs sit. Like every room in this house, there's a stone fireplace. I wonder what Montana's winters are like. A large map of the country fills an entire wall. Red pins mark certain locations.

"What's with the pins?" I ask.

"Our lands. My lands. Dad used to teach me where they were with the map."

I eye the pins, taking in the immense amount of territory he owns.

"That's a lot of land," I say to him.

"Yeah. It's a lot of headache too."

"You seem... stressed. Let me help."

He motions for me to sit down. "Iris, you're here to relax, remember?"

"Hoyt, please. I want to help... help you."

He takes another look at me and hands me a stack of papers.

"Fine. Can you read these and let me know if I should sign them or not?"

"What? How would I know?"

"I trust your judgment."

I take the papers from his hand. "Okay." I sit down in the leather chair by the window.

I read the papers while Hoyt works on the computer, stepping in and out of the room to make phone calls.

I realize the extent of his responsibilities as I read the contract in front of me. APL wants his permission to lay pipelines in a certain section of his territory, and if he says yes, the people who live on the edge of it will have to move—people I assume don't have anywhere else to go, people who don't know what rights they

207

have. Nonetheless, the pipeline is supposedly a necessity for the nearby town.

I'm almost halfway done reading when he asks me to take a break for dinner.

I walk to the kitchen when he says, "Let's eat outside. You can show me what the prism does with the dirt."

We take our pasta bowls to the grass by the water behind his house. He spreads out a blanket, and we sit there, eating and talking.

"This is delicious, thank you," I tell him.

"My pleasure. I prefer to cook when I'm not eating alone."

"The pipeline—what do you want to do?" I ask him.

"I don't know. It's not the first time I've had to make this kind of call. Only, I don't know who to trust, who's telling the truth, and who benefits from me saying yes or no."

"You don't have anyone to advise you?"

"I do, but they always push for what makes me money. That's what they did with my dad. I worry they're not considering the human lives. I've made... mistakes before."

"We could go there tomorrow and see it in person, who lives there," I say, twisting my fork.

He chews his food and says, "I'm usually advised to stay away."

"I think it's worth seeing it for yourself."

"You don't mind coming along?"

"Of course not."

"Nine o'clock?"

"Ten. I'm gonna need a shower after... work."

He laughs. "I didn't think I'd hired you when you said you were coming to spend the summer."

"I like to work."

He puts his bowl aside. "Now show me what it does." He gestures to my necklace.

I put my bowl down and awkwardly lean closer to the grass.

The prism spins. I pull up, and it stops. I get closer, and it spins again.

"What does it feel like?" he asks, intrigued.

"Like it does when it's wet. Like it's waking up."

"What do you think it means?"

"I don't know. I wish we knew... someone else who could tell us anything about them."

"I think my mother knew."

I look at him. "Why?" I ask, curious.

"Remember I told you she used to sing to us? Before bed? One of the songs, I'm pretty sure it's about the prisms."

"Let me hear it."

He coughs. "I think I remember something like this."

> *"Little dew drops, come down and wash my fears away*
> *Let it fall, let it dry, let me say goodbye*
> *Little shiny treasure, you hold more than you know*
> *The secret to your power lies in the unknown*
>
> *Seven sparkles separated by men*
> *Always attracting, wondering when*
> *Together, the unforgiven omen*
>
> *Little dew drops, numb the heart*
> *Let it fall, let it dry, let me say goodbye*
> *Little shiny treasure, you hold more than you know*
> *The secret to your power lies in the unknown*
>
> *Six senses, they say*
> *Yet one more is hidden away*
> *A rainbow of colors, they sway*
>
> *Little dew drops, come down and wash my fears away*
> *Let it fall, let it dry, let me say goodbye*

Little shiny treasure, you hold more than you know
The secret to your power lies in the unknown"

"You think 'little shiny treasure' is the prism?"

He shrugs. "I wish she had told us about it—what they were, if we ever found them, to keep away."

"You were only five, Hoyt, and your brother six."

"Still."

I let out a yawn.

"I'm sure you're tired after last night."

"Yeah, and work on the ranch starts early," I say with a wink, taking our bowls inside.

"Night, firecracker."

"Goodnight."

* * *

I'm reaching out for the brush when Broc says, "I need your help with their teeth today."

"Their teeth?"

"We need to check for sores, swellings, or pain around the mouth, throat, or along the jawline."

I watch what he's doing.

"Also, let me know if you smell foul breath or see any discharge from the mouth or nose," he continues.

"Don't they have a vet for this?" I ask, a little grossed out.

"Yes, but it's my job to know when to call for the vet."

I move like him, looking for anything unusual, something that could perhaps be an issue.

"Are you and Akira still talking?" I ask as I check Elmwood, probably the cutest foal there is.

"Kind of, more like me texting her and her ignoring me."

"She can be... tough to get through. Keep trying."

"See this"—he points to Lumberjack—"he's kind of chewing slow, favoring one side of his mouth. I gotta really look in there."

I watch as he expertly opens the horse's mouth.

"I think one of his teeth is longer than the others, come see."

I walk over.

"It happens sometimes—their teeth naturally wear down from chewing rough fibers."

"Does it hurt him?"

"Probably a little; horses are great at hiding pain, though."

We continue checking each horse. Fortunately, it looks like only Lumberjack needs help.

I tell Broc that Hoyt and I are checking on a land issue and I have to go take a shower. I'm enjoying working with him; he's calm, always joking around. And I love being around the animals. Time flies when I'm with the horses.

* * *

"How did your second day go?" Hoyt asks on the drive to Nyak.

"I checked for bad breath and discharge."

He chuckles. "Not what you expected?"

"Surprisingly, I enjoyed it. There's something about being around the horses; sometimes I feel like they can genuinely see through me."

"Yeah, I get it."

"What are we doing when we get there?"

"I'm meeting with a tribal chairman. He's going to show us where the pipeline is supposed to go through."

"I read about the reservation area too. It's near there, isn't it?"

"Yeah, the reservation is significantly smaller than the original lands occupied by the tribes in the 1850s, and yet, they can't seem to find a way to add the pipeline far from the area. It's hard to believe."

We drive through beautiful roads; I'm singing along with the radio while snacking on trail mix when he says, "I gotta tell you something."

I look at him. "What?"

"I told you I would do better... be better... at telling you things."

"Okay." I adjust myself in the seat.

"You know the night we met on the balcony? The night I felt your hand."

"Yes, what about it?"

"I felt you... in distress."

"What?"

"I didn't know... it was you, only I felt a need to go there... out to the balcony, at that time. It was the same thing I felt with my sister when she got hurt. It's like you were screaming, from the inside. I swear I almost heard the words, 'get me out of here.'"

I think about that night, wanting to be outside, away from the people. I was almost begging for someone to take me away.

"I think I was hoping... someone would."

"Every time I feel anything like that... I can't help but think I'm losing my mind, like Luke."

"Thanks for telling me."

"I also need to tell you that... you have seeds in your teeth," he says, pulling down the sun visor mirror.

"Well, that's embarrassing," I say, taking a sip from my water bottle.

He smiles. "Don't be. Here." He reaches for the trail mix bag and eats a mouthful.

I laugh, but it does make me feel better.

* * *

We are visiting a third family when Hoyt asks a woman carrying a young child, "Where do you work?" She's dressed like she does outdoor labor.

"There." She points to a farm a couple of miles away.

Each home looks in desperate need of... everything.

We're walking around when Chairman Brown says, "Do your lawyers know? That you are here, Locklear?"

"If they did, they would be accompanying me right now," Hoyt replies.

"And what changed? I haven't seen a Locklear walking these lands since... since Awena."

Hoyt goes still, and I wonder who the chairman is talking about.

"My... mother came here?"

"She was from here."

I look at them.

"I didn't know," he tells the chairman.

"I'm not surprised your father didn't mention it. He was... tough to deal with. What have you been advised to do?"

"Apparently, the pipeline is going to put a lot of wealth in our tax base. APL is tired of tanking the project."

"You'd be pocketing a good amount of wealth as well."

"I'm here because... I'm done being their puppet. These families, would they have somewhere to go?"

"Some yes, some no. The reason I've been fighting them is water. If the pipeline ever leaks, it could harm it. The water supply is used for drinking and irrigation at the reservation."

"I was told the pipeline doesn't cross the reservation."

"It doesn't—they made sure of that, so the tribes won't be receiving any revenue from it. But the reservation's drinking water source is just downstream from where the pipeline would cross."

"So, it's enough reason to deny it. Why are many of the locals supporting it?"

"It's not that simple. The jobs the project would bring—people need it. A good few also think we are too dependent on oil in this country, that it's just a matter of time until they get their way."

* * *

We're driving home when Hoyt says, "They need to find an alternative. I'm not signing it. Not until they prove the risks are worth it. Which I don't think they can."

"Those families, even if they stay... I can't help but think they're still getting the short end of the stick."

He looks at me. "It's been a long time since I had someone to talk to about these things. Since Johanna."

"Why did she leave?" I ask.

"I don't know. She said it was because of Sawyer. She couldn't stand being close to him after they broke up. I'm not sure she was telling me the truth."

"Do you know where she lives now?"

"I don't. She told me she was going to LA, then Seattle. I don't even know. She made sure not to let me know. She's an equine vet; the city would be the last place she would go."

"Why would she lie to you?"

"We were always fighting. About everything. Especially after Luke died. She took care of my father, and I hated seeing her waste her life doing that. Later, after he died, when it was only the two of us, we fought over every decision. My dad left me the land and left her the horses. I knew it hadn't been fair, the way the money was split. I wanted to give her more of it, but she refused. She had ideals concerning what to do with the lands, how to help people in need. I was too worried about the money, the taxes, and the lawyers to listen to her. She said something about me being just like Dad, and I lost it. Told her he left me the lands because he knew she couldn't handle it. She and Sawyer were fighting a lot. I think she left because of everything. I don't blame her. But I think Sawyer still blames me for not going after her."

"Is that why you put all her pictures away?"

"Oh, I didn't do that. Sawyer put them all in the drawer one night when he had too much to drink. I just forgot to put them back."

"Do you think she's ever coming back?"

"I don't know... I stopped hoping she would. I feel like I lost both of my siblings."

"I'm sorry, Hoyt. I'm sure it's been really hard."

He looks away but nods. He turns on the radio, and I let myself wonder what it would be like to stick around... to make him feel less lonely. I let myself ponder if he could do the same for me.

TWENTY-FOUR

"PASSION IS ONE GREAT FORCE THAT
UNLEASHES CREATIVITY, BECAUSE IF YOU'RE
PASSIONATE ABOUT SOMETHING, THEN YOU'RE
MORE WILLING TO TAKE RISKS." – YO-YO MA

A couple of weeks pass. I stay busy with the horses in the morning, getting more attached to them every day. I'm almost ready to ask for riding lessons.

After my chores, I often walk or do yoga. My body is getting stronger with my new routine, even though I barely make it to the gym.

My afternoons are filled with books and helping Hoyt with paperwork in his study. Things are moving naturally; I'm starting to feel... at home. I even started helping Hoyt with dinner, even though all he lets me do is chop and stir. We can't hide it anymore —we want to be around each other as much as possible.

Living surrounded by nature is also doing wonders for my mental health. I've never felt so calm, so... *in control of my feelings.*

I'm done with Broc and his tasks when I notice how perfectly the blue sky looks. It's the ideal day to bring my mat outside. I quickly change into my yoga clothes and head outdoors for a flow. I unroll my mat on the grass and start moving through my saluta-tions. I'm a little sore, and it feels great to stretch my hamstrings and back muscles.

I begin repeating the routine when I notice Hoyt watching me.

I think about stopping, but something inside me insists I keep going. I make sure to hold certain positions longer, *just for fun*. He doesn't move or say anything. When I finish, I cross my legs and take a sip of water.

"There's a better view of the lake on the other side of the house," I say to him.

"I'm pretty sure this is the best view there is." He starts to walk away but looks back to say, "I didn't know you were that flexible."

"You have no idea how... *flexible* I can be."

I hear him mumble a curse as he walks away.

I enjoy teasing him. I still think about his hands on me, every night, like clockwork. The more we talk about real things, the more I learn about him, the more I know that taking things slow was the right call.

* * *

"Can I take your truck to town today, if you're not using it? I need clothes," I ask Hoyt at breakfast.

"Sure. Do you want me to go with you?"

"Are you offering to come shopping with me?"

"Why not?"

"Because I thought men hate shopping."

"I'm not particularly fond of it. But I am of you."

"Are you free?" I ask.

"There have got to be some positive sides to having this kind of money. Let's go."

"Now?"

"Why not? Aren't you done with the horses?"

"Yeah."

He stands up from the table. He made me pancakes again— this time, only the one kind I mentioned was my favorite from the previous batches.

* * *

"What kind of clothes do you need?" he asks me on the way to Whitefish.

"Ranch clothes," I reply.

He chuckles.

"And underwear," I add.

He swallows, hard.

I fuss with the radio until I find a good country song I know. I'm starting to get into the genre.

"I would love to take you to a country concert sometime," Hoyt says, singing word by word.

"I don't think I know enough songs."

"We have time," he says, turning up the volume while opening the windows. I smile. I poke my head outside and let the wind blow through my hair. *I could get used to this.*

* * *

I look around, completely lost at what kind of gear I actually need. There are too many options. Rows and rows of boots, hats, belts... I just want to start wearing my own things instead of borrowing Johanna's.

I'm holding a ridiculous amount of clothes to try on when he says, "Can you model them for me?" He takes a seat outside the fitting rooms.

"I don't think you'll like the sight of me in these clothes. They're... comfortable." I open the door for him to see what I've tried on.

He smiles. I'm wearing a plaid button-down and jeans. I've also put on a new pair of boots—I need another option to switch with the pair I already have.

He's still looking at me, grinning.

"What?" I ask.

"Nothing. I... I never thought I'd see you in these clothes."

"Don't get too used to it. It's just for the summer."

"Right." Something changes in his eyes. My own words make me a little sad too. This thing we've got going is ending soon.

"I think I have everything I need," I say, piling my things on the counter.

"I think you're forgetting..." He leans closer and whispers in my ear, "Underwear."

I smile. I was joking when I mentioned it. But now, I would love to see his face when I browse for some.

"They don't sell the kind I need here."

* * *

I think Hoyt would be uncomfortable when I enter the lingerie store. Turns out, I'm the one who blushes. I remind myself to have fun, to let go a bit.

"Should I model them for you again?" I say, picking a black lacy pair.

"It's pretty wicked to tell me you want to take things slow, then ask me to come shop with you for... that." His eyes are hungry—turns out, he does get uncomfortable. He moves quickly, hiding what's just happened, what's just hardened.

I smile at him.

"But wicked slow can be... so good," I say, picking up a red piece.

He runs his hands through his hair and walks out, saying he's going to wait for me outside.

I end up buying a couple of things.

* * *

"I can make spaghetti," I say the following evening when Hoyt comes back from an equine auction.

"Yes, you can. It's delicious, thank you," he says, putting his feet up on the coffee table and swirling his noodles with a fork.

I close my book and ask, "How did it go?"

"Good, great. Picked a couple. Sawyer did good; I was about to offer more money, but he held me back. How was your day?"

"Nice, I needed a lazy day."

"Really? Are you bored here?"

"No! Of course not, I love it here. Why? Are you tired of me?"

"Iris, I'm serious. Don't feel obligated to stay."

"I'm serious too. You can kick me out if—"

"I would love nothing more than for you to move in."

"Right," I say, looking at him.

"I'm serious."

"I'm serious too. I love it here."

He pulls out his phone. "Let's have fun tonight."

"What?"

"It's Friday. Let's go out."

"Where?"

"It's live music night at a bar downtown."

"Aren't you tired?"

"Let's roll," he says, getting up.

"Okay, give me a few minutes to change."

"It's nothing fancy. You can go like this."

I look at my jeans and shirt. "I don't know..."

"You look good... trust me. Reaaaally good."

"Okay," I say, getting a little embarrassed by the way he's looking at me. At least he seems just as casual with his baseball cap.

* * *

The bar is much busier than I expected. Hoyt has introduced me to a few people, and I realize we're in a small town where everyone seems to know everyone. I take a sip of my margarita and look at the stage where a man is playing guitar. I watch as a couple dances, and I wish for a moment that Hoyt could take me out there too.

"I'm sorry, I wish we could..." he says, gesturing to the dancing couples.

"Oh... it's okay," I say, realizing he's upset.

"Jessie!" He calls over a man wearing a cowboy hat. "Why don't you show my lady what a good dancer you are? You know, I have two left feet," he tells his friend, and I'm about to protest when the man comes over.

"Hey, darling, how are you doing? I'm sorry you're stuck here with this one."

Jessie's wife comes over to say hi to Hoyt. They seem to know each other well.

"Hello, I'm Serena, Jessie's wife." She extends her hand to shake mine.

"I'm Iris," I say, realizing Jessie is actually trying to call me over to dance.

"Go ahead, have fun," Serena says, taking my seat.

I'm lost. Things happen too quickly. Before I know it, I'm being led by Jessie.

"I don't know this kind of... dance," I start apologizing.

"Nonsense," he says, pulling me closer and guiding me along.

The singer seems to like the busy dance floor and starts singing a popular song that even I recognize. I look to my right and see Hoyt dancing with Serena. He winks at me and spins her around. He's not as good as Jessie; even without me knowing the steps, we're moving a lot smoother together. Nonetheless, I want nothing more than to switch partners.

I let myself have fun, and by the end of the song, sweat is starting to form on my forehead.

"Let's get another round of margaritas!" Serena says, calling all of us back to the bar.

"You did good," Hoyt says from my side.

"You aren't so bad yourself," I say, smiling.

He bows and almost spills his drink on me.

"Shit! Sorry," he says, laughing. I like seeing him happy, in his natural element.

"So, how do you guys know each other?" I ask him, eyeing Jessie, who is tapping his wife's ass.

"High school," says Jessie, handing each of us a shot glass.

The song changes, and Serena pulls her husband to the dance floor.

Hoyt and I stand watching them when they call us over. I try to copy the steps everyone is doing, but it takes some effort.

"Are you tired?" he asks me when the bar is closing.

"Why?"

"Because I'm not ready for this night to end," he says, looking at me.

"What did you say earlier? Let's roll," I say, ordering a bottle to go, and he laughs.

* * *

Hoyt pulls over by a mountain lookout.

He opens the gate of his truck and says, "I didn't bring pillows or anything, but I have a jacket."

He lays the jacket down, and I take a seat on his truck. He sits next to me, and I look around us, at the show the sky is putting on.

He leaves the headlights and radio on, and we share the bottle I picked up on our way out.

"We're just a few miles from the house, nothing but dirt until there," he says when I ask about him driving home.

"I guess this is what a country date looks like, huh?" I say to him.

"Yeah, sorry, nothing fancy over here."

"I don't want fancy. I like wild and free."

"Never thought you'd be sitting on my truck bed when I spotted you at that gala," he says, taking another sip.

"Truck bed?" I ask.

"It's what this is called." He pats the part we're sitting on.

"Oh, I didn't even know that. Now I'm certain this is what a country date looks like."

He laughs.

"I bet you take a lot of girls on these kinds of dates." *I'm done trying to be strong.*

"Nobody compares to you."

I look at him. "Thanks for inviting me over, to Montana. This sky is something else," I say, taking another glance up.

"We should head back," he says, getting out of the truck bed. I have no choice but to follow him.

"What happened? Why did you want to leave?" I ask when we get back to the house.

"I was about to break the promise I made to you. I told you I'd give you space, respect your wish to take things slow. That was me doing that, before..."

I can't help but feel mad at myself for putting us in this agonizing situation. I want to say, *To hell with slow!* But I steady myself and tell him while walking to my room, "Thank you, I had fun tonight."

"Me too."

TWENTY-FIVE

"DON'T THINK ABOUT MAKING ART, JUST GET IT
DONE. LET EVERYONE ELSE DECIDE IF IT'S GOOD
OR BAD, WHETHER THEY LOVE IT OR HATE IT.
WHILE THEY ARE DECIDING, MAKE EVEN MORE
ART." – ANDY WARHOL

I'm waiting for Akira at the airport when I spot her hair. Her
new hair. Blue. Only the bottom ends, but still, it's really blue.

"Tell me you didn't drive." She's searching for Hoyt.

I jiggle the keys in my hand. She tries to take them.

"Hoyt let you drive his truck?"

"Yep."

"He doesn't know, does he?"

"I don't know what you're talking about."

I recognize her luggage and pull it from the belt.

"Do you have a death wish?" she asks, helping me with the bag.

"I can drive," I tell her as she follows me to the truck.

"Having a driver's license doesn't mean you can drive."

"Actually, that's exactly what it means."

"When was the last time you drove?"

"It doesn't matter."

"I'm driving." She moves to the left side of the truck.

"I made it here, didn't I?"

"I won't push our luck."

She doesn't get in the truck until I move to the passenger seat.

"Fine, suit yourself. It's a long drive from here."

"So tell me... how are things going? You look different... happy," she says, taking a long look at me.

"Everything is great. Does Broc know you're coming?"

"No." She speeds up.

"He likes you."

"Does he?"

I know she doesn't want to talk about him. "How was Chicago?"

She goes on to tell me about her lovely nephew, the arguments with her parents, and the issue with still being single, unmarried, and without children.

"You can't blame them, now that they have a taste for being grandparents."

"It's never enough with them. I'm never enough."

"At least they care."

"I guess." She pauses. "You and Hoyt, still keeping things slow?"

"Yes."

"And how's that going?"

"Good, great. I'm busy with the horses and the paperwork." It's been days since our outing in the truck bed. Hoyt seems to be taking my request for space very seriously.

"I thought you were on vacation."

"I'm on vacation from my professor's life."

Akira brings up NASA and her latest job offer.

"That's a lot of money," I tell her.

"I know, but like I said, I'm not interested in leaving the academic world."

"I'm sure you could still teach on the side."

"I'm not moving to Texas."

"What about your research?" I ask.

"Still working on it."

I look outside my window. "I'm glad you came." We've barely talked these past weeks with her being so busy.

"Me too. Look at this view."

"Yeah, it's beautiful here."

* * *

Hoyt walks out to greet us. I know he wants to help with the bag.

"How was your flight?" he asks Akira after giving her a hug.

"Long." She hands him his keys. "By the way, Iris can't drive."

He looks at me. "What?"

"Ignore her. She's being dramatic. I made it there just fine."

"Ask her when was the last time she drove."

He looks at me with crossed arms.

"When I took my driver's test, at seventeen. And I aced it," I say, walking into the house.

He looks at Akira, and she says, following me, "She's a handful, isn't she?"

* * *

We're walking outside when Broc drives by. I see when his eyes find her. *The surprise.* Akira pretends not to be affected by it, but I know her better.

He pulls over immediately. "I didn't know you were coming," he says to her.

"Last-minute decision." She's too cold. I feel bad for him.

"Your hair, you changed it." His eyes say more than his mouth.

"I sure did."

"How long are you staying?"

"A few days," she tells him.

"I'll see you around," he says, walking away.

I have to give it to Broc; he plays it casual enough. I know him well by now—he's more than excited to see her.

"Iris, wear a jacket tomorrow morning, it's gonna rain and we'll be outside," he tells me before driving off.

I nod.

* * *

We eat dinner indoors; the rain's coming down heavily, and I welcome the coziness. Hoyt's made a delicious savory pie, and we eat while discussing the latest news he's received from the lawyers. Apparently, Aaron's made a few mistakes—not with Hoyt's money—his is mostly frozen—but with other accounts.

"He's losing it. I think I should be able to get my money back soon," he tells us.

I can't help but feel nauseated. I would never wish to see Aaron fail. I'll always be grateful for our past, all he's done for me. I want him happy.

"His mother finally sent an email, saying the wedding is off," Akira says, taking a bite of her side salad.

"She did?" I ask.

"Yeah, she blamed you too."

"Let me see."

She passes me her phone.

We regret to inform that the wedding of Iris and Aaron is cancelled. We kindly request that you do not contact the groom during this difficult time. We extend our sincere apologies for any inconvenience this may have caused.

"It's not like anyone's going to contact me, though. I don't know any of the guests." I try to keep eating. The wedding was supposed to be in just a couple of weeks.

I excuse myself to bed earlier than planned. I'm still feeling bad about Aaron's news. *What's going on with him?* He was the best at what he did. To lose money like that—he's struggling. I hope I'm not the reason. I wish things had ended differently between us. A part of me wants to reach out, but I know there's nothing I can say that would make the situation better. I only want to go back in time and do things differently. The last time I sat in this bed and cried, I was still hopeful that things could be talked through.

* * *

I haven't slept well; even so, I welcome the work Broc gives me. The stalls need cleaning and care, and the horses are moved to the outdoor space surrounded by a wooden fence.

"This couldn't wait until it wasn't raining?" I ask.

"My schedule's tight this week," he says.

I look at him.

"We're getting a new horse tomorrow," he adds.

"We are?"

"Yes, a purebred white."

"White?"

"Yes. As you may know, true white horses are rare. Most people call gray horses white, but pure white is rare."

"How did you guys find one?"

"I have no idea. Hoyt must have spent a fortune on it. I don't even know why he bought it. It's apparently not a racing horse."

I'm exhausted after the lack of sleep and all the work Broc and I did. We struggled with a broken gate for a while. All that matters is that we got the job done. I stayed longer to help him finish.

Akira finds me when I return. "You look..." She eyes me. I'm dirty, wet, tired, and starving.

Hoyt comes downstairs just in time to see me that way.

"Bad day at work?" he asks as I take off my layers.

"You could say that. I'll see you guys later. I've never needed a shower more in my life."

I walk upstairs.

I take my time washing every body part. My hair is knotted, and it takes me ages to brush it through. When I get out of the bathroom, I see a tray with food waiting for me on the bed: a sandwich with a pickle on the side, an iced coffee, and water on the right, with a note on the left. *I'm an expert at washing off mud if you ever need help.* I let myself dream about the idea for a minute. At least he's teasing me again.

Thanks for the food, I text him.

I read a message from Akira: *Went out for lunch with Broc. See you at dinner.*

I don't want to nap, but my body has other plans—I wake up to a knock on the door.

"Come in," I mumble.

"Did I... wake you up?" Hoyt closes the door behind him.

I see worry in his eyes. "Is everything okay?"

"I wanted to talk to you."

I sit up and rub my face. "What's going on?"

"Aaron's firm asked him to step down."

"They what?"

"I guess they agreed he's not himself. It might be a temporary thing, I don't know."

"What about your money?"

He takes a deep breath. "They transferred the care to Lara."

I stand up. "They what? Can they do that?"

"I guess. We made our case against Aaron, but she's free to... take over."

"This is insane."

"What do you know about her?" Hoyt asks. "Do you think she can... I don't know, handle it?"

"Well, luckily, Lara's a money whore. If she can take a commission from the transactions, she'll do anything to..." I stop talking. "What if... this has been her plan all along? Maybe, since, I don't know, taking over Aaron?"

"You think?"

"It explains it. I don't think she's in love with him."

"Do you know her husband well?"

"He does whatever she wants. Who knows? I wouldn't put it

past him to be in on it too. Maybe he even knew about her and Aaron. It could've been their plan all along. I don't know, I just..."

"What?"

"I can't help but feel bad for Aaron. If I'd known..."

"Iris, you need to stop blaming yourself for this. He's a grown man."

"Yeah, sometimes I still see him as the young boy I knew, who would..." I remember him rubbing my back when I needed help. I don't tell Hoyt, though.

"I don't know what to do. If Lara can finish the deals, maybe it's best to... let her."

"What do the lawyers want you to do?"

"Pull out, keep pushing them to release it all, untouched."

"I would suggest doing that. We can't trust Lara."

* * *

"Pizza?" I ask him, eyeing the boxes on the table that evening.

"I'm too stressed to cook." He's drinking a beer.

"You don't have to cook every day, you know? I'm used to heating frozen meals, opening cans, spreading this on bread."

"I like cooking. I'm just taking a break today."

"Is Akira still out with Broc?" I ask, pulling out a slice.

"No, she's back. She said she'll be right down."

"Sometimes I think I'm home, that I really live here," I say, sitting across from him. There's a game on TV, but he isn't paying attention.

"Me too. It's the reason I like cooking for you. I like that you're here, living here, even if it's only for a little bit longer."

Something about our words makes me want to sit on his lap, kiss him, feel him closer. We continue eating until Akira comes down.

She coughs on purpose. "Am I interrupting anything?"

I shake my head. "Pizza?" I gesture to the boxes.

"Sure." She's still trying to figure out what's going on between us.

"How did your day go?" I ask her.

"It was fun. Broc showed me around Crewneck town."

"He took you to Crewneck?" Hoyt asks, surprised.

"Yeah, I told him I'd already seen Whitefish."

"What's in Crewneck?" I ask, wiping my mouth.

"Bars," they both reply at the same time.

I laugh.

"We played pool, won a few drinks," she tells us.

"Broc sucks at pool," Hoyt says, opening another bottle.

"I don't," Akira says.

I chuckle.

Akira goes upstairs with her journal to work on her theory, and I follow Hoyt to the window to watch the rain come down. He's switched to scotch.

"Are you okay?" I ask him. I look him in the eye, not shying away from what his gaze makes me feel.

"Just tired," he tells me, looking out.

"I heard about the new horse," I say, following his gaze.

"Tomorrow's an exciting day for all of us." He turns around and lies down on the lounging chair. He closes his eyes, and I wish I could go over and kiss him. Perhaps, if I could, I would have.

"Can't wait. Good night," I say, walking away.

TWENTY-SIX

"I NEVER PAINT DREAMS OR NIGHTMARES. I
PAINT MY OWN REALITY." – FRIDA KAHLO

I'm brushing Jet when Hoyt shows up at the barn.

"Morning." I lift my gaze to him. He's extremely sweaty, his gym clothes tight against his skin.

"Hi." Before he can say anything else, I hear a truck coming down the road.

I walk out with Hoyt to see if it's the delivery truck. We're all here. Even Akira has woken up early to meet the rare breed.

The large vehicle opens its back door, and my mouth drops. The horse isn't just white; it's radiant. Without a doubt, the most beautiful horse I've ever seen. The animal's blue eyes lock onto mine, and my prism pulses. I move to pet it.

"What do you think?" Hoyt asks, moving his hands through the horse's mane.

"I've never seen anything like it. He doesn't look real."

"It's a she."

"Where did you find her?"

"I know a few breeders."

"Broc said she isn't a racehorse, though."

"No, she's not. I got her as a gift."

I look at him, and he's grinning.

"A gift?"

"For you."

"What?"

"She's yours."

"You bought me a horse?"

"Did you prefer a car?"

"I don't know... what to say. You can't give me a horse."

"Why not? She can live here. That way, you'll have to come by to check on her sometimes."

I move around her, checking every inch—my horse, *my own horse.*

"You need to give her a name."

"Me?"

"She's your horse."

Broc, Sawyer, and Akira are taking turns petting her, too.

"Mona," I blurt out.

"As in... the Mona Lisa?" Hoyt asks.

"Yes, and also because Mona means a lady of nobility."

"Now all you need to do is learn to ride Mona."

I look at him.

"Sawyer will teach you. You can start the lessons tomorrow, after your work with Broc."

"Hoyt." I want to grab his hands. "This is the best gift I've ever received. I love her."

"You're forgetting the gift around your neck."

I laugh.

Nobody does anything productive. We all want to be around Mona. Each man tries to saddle her, but she isn't having it.

"Looks like we'll be using Jet for your lessons for now," Sawyer says.

I don't know what to think regarding him giving me lessons. He's not exactly giving me friend vibes. Maybe Hoyt is paying him well to do it.

"Thanks. I'm looking forward to them," I tell him.

"Sure thing," he says, trying the saddle once more.

"We should keep her out here for now," Sawyer says to Hoyt. "Let her run."

"Out here?" I ask. "Won't she be... cold?"

They look at me.

"It's summer, Iris," Hoyt says.

"You should've told me she was untamed," Sawyer grunts, trying to catch up with Mona again.

"Horses have a great memory," Akira says from my side. "Funny enough, I never forgot that fact. I also remember something about a novice rider and a green horse being a bad combination. There's a good chance one or both of you will be seriously injured."

Hoyt overhears her and comes closer. "Iris will practice on Jet until Mona is ready."

"Will she... be ready?" I wonder, not meaning to say it out loud.

"Sure. Sawyer has a way with wild ones. He can handle it."

I glance at his friend. Mona's giving him a hard time; I can tell she's afraid.

"Are you sure she's all right outside?" I ask Hoyt again on our way back home.

"It's only for the first night. Let her calm down a bit."

"How am I supposed to care for an animal I know nothing about?"

"You aren't. She's yours to ride. But we'll take care of her."

"Hoyt, this was... I don't know, special. I really do love her already. Is that weird?"

"To love at first sight? I don't think so."

I feel his words go through me.

And then I think of Benny, the only other animal I owned. My eyes well up with tears at the thought of him. I'd forgotten Benny had also been a gift. I wonder how Aaron's doing with the news of Lara taking his place.

* * *

Hoyt decides we need to celebrate Mona. He's firing up the grill while Akira and I prep the skewers and salad.

"Do you miss the city?" Broc asks, taking a seat next to me.

"Not at all. Maybe the museums."

"I've never been to Boston," he says, looking at Akira.

"You should come. It's really nice in the fall. You can stay with me," I tell him.

"I don't think Akira feels the same, you know..."

I look at him. He's fallen for my friend, just like I've fallen for his. "I'm sorry, Broc."

"I'm used to... the heartaches." He gets up to help Hoyt.

It's a gorgeous summer night. The smell of the food, the laughter of my friends, the thought of Mona—my life has turned into something I could never have imagined a year ago.

We eat, we drink, and we sing. Broc brought his guitar. I had no idea he could sing and play until he starts. He sings happy and sad country songs, and I let myself enjoy every bit of the night. I'm done holding back on being happy. *I want it all.*

Once Broc and Akira move indoors, I ask Hoyt, "Will you walk with me?"

He puts his plate down and follows me to the edge of the water, the moonlight guiding us. We walk in silence, until I ask, "Any scary creatures in this water?"

He laughs. "Just fish," he answers.

I stop walking. I didn't know I was ready until now. I start to undress.

I take off my boots, and then my jeans. I'm nearly unbuttoning my shirt when Hoyt asks, "Iris?"

"Swim with me," I say.

The water feels cold at first, but I get used to it quickly. Hoyt copies me, undressing right away. He's looking at me intensely; the night is bright with the full moon shining on the water. I can see his face, his beautiful eyes. I need to feel him.

I swim closer. Our bodies respond to the first touch immediately.

This time, *I kiss him*. Slowly and fast, I want it all but I also want to take my time. I move my lips on his, our tongues meet.

And then he kisses me. With the same need as mine. He moves his mouth down my neck, to my collarbone. I have to hold tight on to him when the water pulls me away. I wrap my legs around him and we stay like that for a while, kissing.

"You are beautiful," he says, pulling away just enough for me to see his eyes blink.

"Thank you for being...patient with me," I say, touching his face.

"I would have waited my whole life for this," he tells me, grabbing my hair gently.

He moves his hands over my body, feeling every part of me. He plays with my nipples and I moan at the sensation. He caresses each breast, taking his sweet time.

We are both working hard to do this underneath the water. *Definitely not the easiest thing.*

I move my hand to sense his arms, his chest, every muscle. I continue studying him; I slide my hands lower, to his cock. Hard, *so hard*. He responds to my touch, kissing me almost violently.

His hands move to my center, descending to my entrance. He touches me slow, gentle, increasing with each stroke. I don't know how I have been able to wait this long for him. I'm starting to lose control when he moves his hands away.

"Don't stop," I tell him and he smiles between our kiss.

"I thought you said...wicked slow is"—he kisses my neck, biting my ear—"very good."

"I lied," I say, yearning for him to resume what he started.

He laughs but his hands goes back to rubbing my bundle of nerves.

"More," I whisper in his ears.

He inserts a finger and I struggle to stay connected.

"The water," I say, trying to hold on.

He starts to pull me closer to where our feet can meet the sand. As soon as we get our feet down, he grabs me to him.

He is moving his fingers again, on me, in me.

Ours prisms are connected, shining under the water.

I want all of him, I need him inside me...and when I try, he pulls back and turns me around.

"It's my turn...to take things slow," he whispers while my body leans on his.

"What?" I ask him, arching my body.

"Tonight, it's about you," he says, using both hands.

He adds another finger and I melt. His precise movements are impossible to take. I moan and let my nails dig into his skin, my entire body consumed by my orgasm.

"Hoyt! Iris!" We hear Broc calling our names minutes later.

We freeze. He calls again and we know something is wrong.

"You get out first," I tell him. I don't want to be seen naked by Broc, even if it's dark out.

"What?" Hoyt's voice is rough. He's still trying to catch his own breath.

Broc immediately starts to apologize when he finds us.

"Sorry man, I didn't..." He turns around.

"What the hell is going on?" Hoyt asks while putting on his pants.

"It's Johanna. She's here."

Hoyt looks at me in the water.

"Go," I tell him. "I will be right there."

I wait until they are far enough away to get out of the water and put my clothes back on.

My prism is still a beacon of light, guiding me down the path back to the house.

* * *

Johanna is as beautiful as Hoyt—same eyes, same color hair—perfectly cut in short layers just above her shoulders.

She stands there, looking at me and Hoyt, *both of us soaked.*

"What are you doing here?" he asks her.

"It's nice to see you too," she replies, her tone full of attitude.

"You disappear for three years and then decide to... show up like nothing happened?"

Akira comes down with towels for us.

I look down at the floor; water drips from my hair.

"This is my house too." She glances at me quickly.

We haven't been introduced yet.

"I'll move my stuff from the room," Akira says, walking upstairs with Broc.

"You can stay in mine," I tell Akira, and she nods.

"What the hell is that white purebred doing in the ring?" Johanna asks, her voice sharp.

"None of your business," Hoyt responds, frustrated.

"It's damn right my business—Dad left the horses to me."

"Not that one." Hoyt runs a hand through his hair.

"How much did you pay for it?" Johanna presses.

"Again, none of your business. Why did you come back?"

"Can we have some privacy?" she asks, eyeing me with clear displeasure.

"She stays," Hoyt says firmly.

"It's about—"

My prism's light blinks, and Johanna looks at me.

"Is that a...?"

"Show her," Hoyt tells me.

I pull my prism out from under my shirt.

"Holy shit. There are... more," she says, sitting down, still staring at me.

"I can give you both privacy," I offer, starting to walk away.

"You might as well stay," Johanna tells me.

"Johanna, spill it," Hoyt says, drying his hair.

"Do you want to change first?" Johanna asks, looking at both of us.

"Johanna!" Hoyt says impatiently.

"It's about Mom," she replies.

."Mom?" Hoyt's voice changes, softening.

"She's... alive," Johanna says, and I almost lose my balance.

"How?" I ask, since Hoyt hasn't spoken yet.

She opens her bag and pulls something out. "Here." She hands Hoyt a photo album.

He flips through it, and I lean closer to look. The photos are of who I think is Hoyt and his brother, with their mom and a little baby. He keeps flipping through the pages. The third child, a little girl, is almost one in some of the photos.

"She didn't die during childbirth," Johanna says.

"Where did you get this?" Hoyt asks her.

"In the safe," she replies.

"The safe?" Hoyt is still staring at the photos.

"I know you never wanted to open the damn thing, so I did. One night, when you pissed me off, saying Dad left you the lands because I couldn't handle it. Well, I wanted to find proof—something else to show you that I was capable of handling it. I knew you hadn't touched the safe since Luke, so I opened it. And this was there. Along with other paperwork. I left the rest. When I realized what it meant—that I didn't... kill her—I needed to know more. I wanted to show you, but I didn't want to raise hope. That she might still be... alive."

"Where did you go?" he asks.

"Searching... for her."

"You found her?" His voice is weak, full of disbelief.

She shakes her head. "No, but I know where she is. I want you to come with me."

"To where?"

"Alaska."

* * *

I sit on Hoyt's bed, brushing my hair when he comes in. I've just gotten out of the quickest shower of my life. I left Hoyt and Johanna talking, only to interrupt a serious conversation between Akira and Broc. With nowhere else to go, I found myself here, in his bedroom.

"Will you stay here with me?" he asks, still in his wet clothes.

"How are we going to sleep?"

"My bed's big enough."

"I don't want to hurt you in the middle of the night," I tell him, considering the idea.

"We'll put pillows between us." He winks at me—that same wink from the party, the one that weakens me every time.

I smile. "Okay, we can try."

I text Akira, telling her she can have my room as Hoyt heads into the bathroom.

I'm under the covers, browsing on my phone, when he comes back, a towel wrapped around his waist.

I can't take my eyes off him—his body. I could still feel him on me.

He disappears into his closet, only to return wearing just a pair of black trunks. I haven't seen him like this—not in this light, wearing almost nothing. His body reminds me of the Greek sculptures I know so well. Each muscle is defined.

I haven't let myself really look at him before. Now, I take my time, tracing the scars and tattoos. A horseshoe beneath his right arm, just at his ribs. His brother's prism shape on the back of his shoulder. And above his heart, there's a date: IV_XVII-I_MCMLXIX.

"What's the date for?"

"My mother's birthday."

"Do you think she really is... alive?"

"I don't know. You saw the photos. Why the fuck did everyone lie to us about it?"

"You don't remember her? After your sister was born?"

"I kind of do, but my memories are scrambled. I thought I did. I told myself they had to be memories of her before Johanna. But I'm not sure if I remember them together, or if I just made some of them up. There weren't many pictures of my mom around the house. Dad always said it wasn't their thing—taking pictures. I don't know. I should have pushed him for answers. Looks like we both have parents who ran away."

"When are you leaving for Alaska?"

"Who said I was going?"

"Hoyt, it's your mom."

"And she knows where I live."

He lies down on his side of the bed, on the side of the pillow mountain I made for us.

"It's hard to lay here and still feel so far away," I say, spilling my feelings.

"You have no idea how much I wish I could hold you right now."

"I think you should go... to Alaska."

"Why?"

"If there was any chance that my mom was alive... I would take it."

He takes a deep breath. "I don't know if I can do it," he says, and I can feel him even without our bodies touching.

"Your sister... she deserves to know too," I tell him.

"Will you come with us?"

"Me? I don't know, Hoyt. I think this is something for you and your family to do. It's not my place to... meddle in."

"I need you."

"Are you sure? Johanna didn't seem to want me around."

"I don't want to cut our time short. We only have a few weeks left until you go back to work."

"When would you be leaving?"

"I need a day or two here to get a couple of things in order."

"Let me think on it. Let me see how your sister takes the idea."

Twenty-Seven

"It is the mystery that illuminates knowledge." – René Magritte

Between wanting to see Mona, my duties with Broc, and needing time alone to think things through, I almost jump out of bed when the clock hits five. Hoyt is still sleeping. We talked for a while last night, until we both needed to rest. It was nice, sleeping in the same bed—even with the mountain of pillows between us.

I borrow a shirt from his closet and make my way to the stables, coffee in hand. I find Johanna by the fence.

"Hi," I say, stopping next to her.

"Morning person?" she asks.

"I help with the horses in the morning."

"How long have you and my brother been...?"

"Not long. We met last year, in Boston."

"Boston?"

"Yeah, I teach there. I'm here just for the summer."

Mona neighs loudly.

"I can't believe he bought her. She must have cost a fortune," Johanna says.

"It's my fault."

She turns to look at me.

"She was a gift," I explain.

"He bought you a horse?"

"He did."

"He bought you a white purebred horse?"

"I know, I thought it was crazy too."

She really looks at me, like she's seeing me for the first time. Our conversation is interrupted by Broc.

"Ready, Iris?"

I take another sip from my travel mug. "Ready."

Broc and I are on hooves duty today. We check for wounds, stones wedged in the frog, and excessive growth or wear. Johanna moves along with us, inspecting each horse thoroughly.

"Why are you helping with the horses? You obviously don't know what you're doing. No offense," she says.

"I... wanted to be useful, while staying here."

"Useful? Aren't you my brother's girlfriend?"

"Girlfriend?" Hoyt asks, hearing us. He's wearing a leather hat. I've never seen him in anything but baseball caps. It suits him.

"I didn't..." I look at him.

"Isn't she?" Johanna asks Hoyt.

He walks toward me and asks, "Are you?"

I keep working. I don't know what we are. "It's complicated," I tell his sister.

"You got her a love sigil?" Johanna looks at Hoyt.

He nods.

"A what?" I ask, but he's already moving away to check on Mona.

"In our family, the tradition is... when you find the one, your supposed soulmate, you buy them a horse. My family calls them a love sigil," Johanna explains. "It's ridiculous, but the Locklears have been doing it... well, forever. My dad used to tell us stories about it."

I take in her words.

"I didn't know what it... meant," I tell her.

"I think we've established that you're his girlfriend," she says, following her brother outside.

Hoyt is in the ring, trying to rein in Mona without much luck.

"That horse won't be ridden—mark my words. She's too wild. She's seen too much. Even if she ever trusts someone, it's going to take years," Johanna says from my left.

I look at Mona, my own horse, shining beautifully in the sun, so wild and brave. Then my gaze shifts to Hoyt. *A love sigil?* That's way more than I expected when I decided to come here for the summer.

* * *

I meet Akira inside when I finish with the hooves. She's hunched over her computer in the kitchen.

"Hi," I say, sitting across from her.

"Hey." She closes her laptop.

"I'm sorry, I've barely spoken to you since you got here."

"That's okay. Your hands are full."

"Are you okay? I couldn't help but sense the tension last night between you and Broc."

"Yeah, it's... I don't know. He doesn't get it. We're from different worlds, this would never work. He just... doesn't get it."

"It's not impossible."

"It is, Iris, and you know it. I work at Harvard. I'm an astrophysicist. He's a cowboy."

"Horse trainer."

"We are not you and Hoyt. We don't have to... we don't have a reason to do this."

"What do you mean?"

She points at the prism.

"You think we're together... because of the prisms?"

"Well, it obviously brought you together."

"Yeah, but..."

She shakes her head. "My family... they would never... accept it."

"They want to see you happy, Akira."

"That's not enough, with them. And I am happy, with the way things are. This has been fun, but I think it's time I go home."

"Are you sure?"

"Yeah, is that okay?"

"Of course. I'll be going home soon enough, too."

"Last night... Are you guys together together?"

"I think so."

"I'm happy for you."

I smile at her. "I'm going to get cleaned up."

* * *

I find Akira and Johanna laughing on the couch when I come back downstairs—like they're best friends. *What in the world?* They're sipping wine and snacking on a cheese tray.

"So he didn't tell you whose clothes those were?" I hear Johanna ask.

"Nope. You should've seen Sawyer's face," Akira replies.

I hear the name Sawyer, and I can't help but watch Johanna's reaction. I haven't seen him around. Broc had left me a message: *Sawyer needs to postpone the lessons.*

"Have you guys seen Sawyer?" Johanna asks us. I've taken a seat beside them.

"He was supposed to help me today, with riding lessons. I think he canceled because you showed up," I tell her.

"Things are..." she starts to explain.

"Complicated?" I ask, smiling.

She just smiles back.

"We're used to it," Akira says, taking another sip of her wine.

We move on to other topics. I decide to pour myself a glass and join them. We cover basic subjects, and Johanna goes on to tell us about her family. We're probably on our second bottle when Hoyt walks in.

"Are you guys... drunk? It's barely past noon."

"Like that ever stopped you," Johanna says.

"She's a bad influence," he jokes, sitting down in the chair across from me.

"You don't have to be shy around me," she says, mentioning our lack of... intimacy.

"They can't touch each other," Akira says, snacking on a cracker.

"Akira!" I yell at her.

"What?!" She keeps eating.

"What the heck is that supposed to mean?" Johanna asks, looking back and forth between us.

Hoyt and I don't say anything.

"It's not like it's a secret," Akira adds. "Their prisms, or something."

"You guys can't... touch?"

We shake our heads.

"How the hell do you date someone without... touching?"

I look at her and take another sip. "Complicated, remember?"

She's still trying to figure us out when Akira stands up. "Who's taking me to the airport?"

"You're leaving today?" I ask her.

"Tonight."

"It's not really a question, is it?" Hoyt says, laughing at us.

* * *

I'm left alone with Johanna while Hoyt drives Akira to the airport. We put a chick flick on TV, glancing at it occasionally. We've stopped drinking, but we're both still feeling a little inebriated.

"Akira mentioned you teach in Boston," Johanna says from the couch.

"I thought I mentioned it."

"You didn't mention Harvard."

I shrug.

"And you're an equestrian vet, right?" I ask Hoyt's sister; they really look alike, even have similar mannerisms.

"Was."

"Was?"

"I've been working as a waitress for the past three years. Been moving around a lot.

"How did you... find your mom?"

"It hasn't been easy. People seemed... I don't know. They pretended they didn't know her. Our dad told us very little about her; all I had was a last name—my last name. But I drove around, took odd jobs, asked every person I met, until an old man told me a story. I wasn't even far from here when I found him—just a little above Malta. He said he knew my mother and knew of my father. I pushed him until he told me how they met. My father owned some land near the reservations. My mom lived there."

"The tribal chairman told us she was from there," I say.

"Tribal chairman?"

"We went to see the families there... Long story, continue."

"My mother lived there with her family. There was trouble at some point, and her family was killed. She was left alone. I think she was only nineteen. My dad heard about the conflict and went to check it out. There was talk about things getting bad, and I think he wanted to avoid them crossing his lands. He found her fighting for her life. He brought her here, and I think they got together then."

"You guys don't have any other family around?"

"Dad's family members are either dead or hate us because of him. Or they just want the money. I guess there could be more of my mom's family around, but... who knows? I only recently found out what her maiden name is. We grew up here; our family was our... employees."

"We have more in common than I realized." I tell her. "How do you know she's in Alaska?"

"I met someone who tracked her name. There can't be too many Awena Kalapuya's around the same age."

"She kept her maiden name?"

"Looks like it. When I couldn't find any proof of death, I started searching for her like she was still alive. I'm still getting used to the possibility."

I go on to tell her about my own family.

"And you haven't looked for your father?" she asks.

"No, I don't really care why he left. Not anymore."

She nods. "What do you and Hoyt plan to do?" she asks, crossing her legs.

"What do you mean?"

"You live in Boston. Are you moving here?"

"Oh."

"You had to have thought about it," she presses.

"Not really. Everything's been... crazy. I don't really know where things stand with us."

"Because you can't... touch each other?"

I blush. "We found a... loophole."

She eyes me with a smirk. "Then what's the problem?"

"I'm... not ready to think that far. We've been taking things kind of slow."

"Right. Love sigils aside."

I laugh.

"You should go see Sawyer. His truck's been parked out front for almost twenty minutes."

She looks behind us and walks out.

* * *

Hoyt finds me in his bed, watching TV. I need a distraction. Johanna's words are messing with my head.

"How are you feeling?" he asks, sitting down beside me.

"Fine now. Not drunk anymore."

"Good," he says with a smile.

"Thanks for taking Akira. It should've been me."

"I don't trust you driving, not even sober."

I look at him. I want to explain that I've lived in the city my whole life—who needs a car in the city? Especially when your ex-fiancée moved around with a private chauffeur. Instead, I ask, "When were you going to tell me about the love sigil?"

"Eventually."

"Did you mean it—giving me Mona—that way?"

"I did."

"But Hoyt, we barely know each other."

"I knew it the first time I laid my eyes on you."

"I'm going home soon."

"We'll figure something out."

I need to change the subject. "Have you thought about Alaska?"

"Jo wants to leave tomorrow. Are you coming?"

"Are you sure you want me there?"

"I've always been sure about you." He stands up and starts undressing right in front of me.

I sit up. "What are you...?"

"I'm taking a shower. Care to join?"

I wasn't expecting the invitation. He keeps undressing, walking toward the bathroom completely nude.

Perhaps I'm still... drunk? I ask myself as I follow him.

He's already under the water when I walk into the bathroom.

"Is that music playing?" I ask, looking around.

"I have a speaker in here."

"In the shower?"

"Had it installed when I did the remodel."

"Remodel?"

"I tore down the wall between my old bedroom and my

father's. I wanted more space and decided to extend this bathroom."

I'm still looking around when he opens the shower door and says, "Firecracker?"

I look at him.

"Will you let me... undress you?"

"You mean...?"

"Get in here!"

I walk in the shower, fully clothed. I laugh as I get under the water, soaking myself. Hoyt pins me on the shower wall and starts to kiss me immediately. It's a hungry kiss, his tongue moves with the same intensity as his hands.

I can feel his naked body against mine and I want to feel all of it. My hands are exploring every inch, every indentation of the muscles in his back, his arms...

He lifts my shirt and his mouth finds my neck as soon as it's off. I'm not sure if it's my body or the prism that throbs. His lips feel hot on my skin and I notice that the water is mildly warm. He unhooks my bra and his mouth finds my nipples. My entire body heats as he bites them lightly.

And then he moves to my pants. They don't come off easily. "Fucking yoga pants," he says as he struggles. He kneels to remove them from my ankles and his mouth finds my stomach. I shiver at the feeling. His mouth continues to kiss my body as he pulls my underwear down *with his fucking teeth*.

He's an inch away from licking my sensitive spot when I pull him up.

"It's my turn. To return the...pleasure," I say, lowering myself to him.

He grunts before I even put it in my mouth. I move slow at first, tasting every bit, licking his entire length. I move around doing the same thing on all sides before taking all of him. His hands are in my hair and I continue my movements, adding my hand for pressure. I can feel him losing control and I tease him, gently scraping with my teeth. I move back and forth until he releases himself.

He pulls me up and holds me under the water.

When his hands move down my body I stop him.

"The water," I tell him. "It's too cold now."

"I'm going to kill Johanna," he says, turning it off.

I look at him confused.

"She must have used all the hot water."

I kiss him again, until my lips go numb, until I'm shivering.

"I don't know what I'm going to do when you leave for Boston," he says as we dry ourselves and lie in bed.

"Let's not talk about that yet."

We sleep with the soft mountain between us again.

* * *

I'm packing my bags, and instead of heading to Boston, I'm packing for Alaska. I don't know how long we'll be gone. I'm not even sure I'll be back here before I have to go back to work. I sit down on the bed, and Johanna finds me in the room.

"Hoyt told me you're coming with us," she says, spotting the suitcase.

"Do you mind? Be honest."

"No. I think it'll be good for us, to get to know each other a little more."

"Really?"

"I do."

"In that case, I'm happy to come."

"Don't know what to bring?" She looks at the mess I've made.

"Not really. I also don't know if I'll be coming back here before I..."

"Bring enough for a few days. We can send your stuff back if we end up staying longer."

"Sounds good. Thank you."

CRYSTAL IRIS

She starts to turn around when I ask, "What's the deal with Hoyt and Maeve?"

"I'd tell you, but I think you should ask him. It's..."

"Let me guess, complicated?"

"Right."

"I just... left a serious relationship. I was actually engaged."

She comes back and sits down on the bed. "And you don't want to jump into something else?"

"I don't think I could handle it, in case it didn't work out."

"Him and Maeve are old history. And I can tell he's crazy about you. I mean, I haven't seen my brother this happy—like, ever."

"And you think it's because of me?"

"I know it is. Still, you need to do what's right for you. I'm not the best at relationship advice, though."

"Did you... talk to Sawyer last night?"

"Yeah, he hates me."

"I doubt that."

"He does. He'll never forgive me for leaving like that. I had to lie to him too. I didn't want Hoyt coming after me—not until I figured out if my mother was alive. Luke's death... Hoyt took it personally. I couldn't bring something like this up and—if it turned out she was gone—break his heart again. He likes to take care of everyone, but I know he's the one who needs it."

She gets up and says, "I gotta finish packing too."

"Thank you. For talking to me."

"Of course. I know my brother can be hard to open up to... I'm here if you need to chat."

"Thanks."

* * *

I'm standing by the fence of Mona's ring. She looks scared, but to my surprise, she comes closer.

253

I look into her eyes... and somehow, she looks back at me. Straight into my soul. *How do horses do that?*

I run my hands through her soft mane. "I'm not leaving you," I tell her. "I'll be back soon. You can trust them, you know—they only want to help you." I give her a big hug. "One day," I say, "we'll ride all the way to that mountain over there, just me and you. But for that, we both need some practice."

"She doesn't even let us get this close. I think she likes you," Hoyt says, walking toward me.

"The feeling's mutual. But she did let you touch her when she arrived."

"She was still drugged."

"Are you guys ready to go?" I ask him.

"Jo is in the truck waiting."

Twenty-Eight

"CREATIVITY IS MORE THAN JUST BEING
DIFFERENT. ANYBODY CAN PLAN WEIRD; THAT'S
EASY. WHAT'S HARD IS TO BE AS SIMPLE AS
BACH. MAKING THE SIMPLE, AWESOMELY
SIMPLE, THAT'S CREATIVITY." – CHARLES
MINGUS

The flight to Alaska is long with the connecting flight, and I welcome the rest. Johanna sits next to me, while Hoyt sits behind us.

"What's the plan, Johanna?" Hoyt asks when we land.

"We eat and we sleep. It's too late to... go there now," she answers.

"Right, too late to say hello to our own mother." I can hear the agitation in his tone.

"Hoyt, please," Johanna pleads.

"Fine, I told you we're doing it your way," he says.

"Thank you," she replies, and I can see they both look worried.

* * *

"Thank you for coming, Iris," Hoyt says, passing me my dinner in our room.

"I'm happy to spend time with you and Johanna. I like her."

"I think she likes you too. She told me to do things right, with you."

I grin. "She did?"

"Yeah."

"What are you going to do if you find your mom?"

"I'm more worried about what happens if we don't. What it'll do to Johanna. Her hopes are high. Too high."

"I think she's worried about you, too," I admit.

"She always is. Sometimes, I think I'm the younger sibling."

We eat and watch a movie. I must have fallen asleep because I wake up in the middle of the night, still in my travel clothes. I change into my pajamas in the bathroom and realize Hoyt barely fits on the couch. The bed is too small for our mountain of pillows. I lie back down, but my brain is wide awake.

* * *

The hotel is nicer than I expect. Not because of the luxuries, it's the view. If Montana is beautiful, Alaska is something else. I'm looking outside when Hoyt brings me coffee.

"Did you even sleep?" he asks.

"Kind of. I slept yesterday on the plane, and my body is still... on ranch time. Did you? The couch looks extremely uncomfortable. Maybe we should get another room?"

"Nonsense. You aren't getting rid of me that easily," he grins.

"I never thought about leaving the city, but these views... I'm going to miss it," I say, trying to control my feelings. He looks hot in his sweatpants and messy hair.

"Do you think you could? Move away from the city?" he asks.

"I don't know. Maybe."

* * *

Hoyt drives, and I sit in the back seat. We've passed the populated tourist areas, and I note we're driving miles away from everything I consider safe.

"The GPS is pointless by now. It keeps recalculating," I say, opening and closing the app on my phone.

"Are you sure it's this way, Johanna?" Hoyt asks.

"You heard what that man said in the bar—follow the water, it's the only house with a red door. How hard can it be?"

We drive for another half hour. Hoyt's right. Johanna's excited, but my heart aches for them. The thought of seeing their mother... I know Hoyt's holding back.

"There!" Johanna points at the extremely old home.

"Nobody can live there," Hoyt says. "There's nothing here."

"Someone obviously does," Johanna replies, opening her window. We drive in the direction of the house.

"You guys go ahead, I'll stay in the car," I tell them as we park.

"No way, you're coming with us," Johanna says. "I need backup with Hoyt."

I nod at her, knowing it's her nerves talking.

We knock, but the immensity of the mountains and land swallows the sound.

"Maybe she can't hear us," I say when no one answers.

Hoyt knocks harder, and the door gives way.

"Hello? Anyone here?" he calls from the doorway.

"I'm going in," Johanna says, stepping past us.

"Johanna!" Hoyt calls after her, but she doesn't look back.

We follow her inside.

As expected, the home is simple—just the absolute basics... and even some of those are broken. There's no one inside.

"Over here!" Johanna calls from the doorway leading to another room.

We walk over.

A woman lies on a bed. She looks ill. I can't tell if it's their mom. The pictures I've seen are from a long time ago. From the looks on their faces, they don't know either.

"Get out or I will start shooting!" A man yells from the living room.

I look back to see he's holding a shotgun.

"Hold there, we're family," says Hoyt to the guy.

"Family? We have no family!" says the bone-thin man.

"Is the woman in the bed Awena?" I ask, surprising myself at my calm voice.

"I said get out!" He gestures again with his gun pointing at us.

"Please, I think she's our mother," pleads Johanna, although Hoyt is already motioning for us to leave.

"The hell she is! She's my mother!" he says, holding his gun tight.

Hoyt and Johanna look at each other.

"We are looking for a woman named Awena Kalapuya, she lived in Montana around twenty-five years ago," I say.

The woman starts to move.

"Please, I've never met her," Johanna says desperately.

"We have money, we can pay you," Hoyt adds.

"We don't need your money," the man replies.

"Is she sick?" I ask him as he lowers his gun a little.

I look at the woman behind me. She's sitting up, reaching out her hand. She seems awake, except... her eyes are still closed.

"What's wrong with her?" I ask.

"She's sick. Her..." The man looks at us, trying to make up his mind. "You need to leave!" He lifts the gun again.

I'm walking toward the door when she starts to sing. The three of us recognize the lyrics immediately. The young man seems taken by surprise.

"She hasn't spoken... in years," he says, walking to the bedroom.

The woman continues.

"Little dew drops, come down and wash my fears away
Let it fall, let it dry, let me say goodbye
Little shiny treasure, you hold more than you know

The secret to your power lies in the unknown

Seven sparkles separated by men
Always attracting, wondering when
Together, the unforgiven omen

Little dew drops, come down and wash my fears away
Let it fall, let it dry, let me say goodbye
Little shiny treasure, you hold more than you know
The secret to your power lies in the unknown

Heart you must give, heart's blood
Brave the mist, don't fear the flood
Heart you must give, heart's blood"

She stops singing and starts shaking, convulsing. The man runs to the room and gives her some sort of shot, bringing her back to lie down. We stare at him, and he yells, "I said get out!" then shoots through the ceiling.

This time, we listen.

Hoyt drives while Johanna cries, and I wish there's something I can do or say.

When we arrive at the hotel, I order them water and food, but they don't touch it.

"We can't leave her there!" I hear Johanna saying when I come back inside.

"Johanna, he had a gun," Hoyt says.

"Then we go to the police," she replies.

"And say what? She's our mother who abandoned us thirty years ago?" He takes a seat next to her.

"Do you think he's her son? Our brother?" she asks him.

"Who knows." Hoyt gets up to look out the window.

"The lullaby," I ask him, "Was it the same one?"

He nods.

"When you sang it to me, when we were little, you skipped the blood part," Johanna says to him.

Awena's raspy voice replays in my head.

"There's no blood part. Maybe she changed it, I don't know—she obviously doesn't seem well," he tells us.

"She should be in a hospital," Johanna says, trying to calm herself down.

"He doesn't want our help," Hoyt says, running his hands through his hair.

"We need to go back. Talk to him, Hoyt," Johanna is almost begging.

"We are not going back there. I'm not risking our lives," he tells her.

"He's right, Johanna. It's too dangerous," I say, stepping closer.

"What if it was your mother, Iris?" she asks.

I know it, like she does: Nothing would stop me.

"Let's ask for the police's help," I tell her.

Hoyt's on the phone and I take a seat next to Johanna.

"We'll get her help, Johanna," I tell her.

"I can't believe it's her." Her tears fall uncontrollably.

I try to lift her spirits. "You did this. You found her."

"What if we're too late?" She seems inconsolable.

Hoyt returns with news: The police will come tomorrow to talk to us. There's no urgency in the situation; we'll have to wait until morning.

"They can't make us wait until tomorrow," Johanna says, wiping her tears.

"Things are different here, Johanna. They have their hands full in Alaska."

None of us sleep well. We simply close our eyes for short stretches of time, taking turns with the nightmares. Hoyt and Johanna share the bed, and I make myself comfortable on the couch. Johanna had fallen asleep, and we didn't want to leave her alone.

* * *

The police arrive mid-morning.

Hoyt and Johanna show them photos and tell them what they know. Still, the officer's manner is clear: This isn't going to be easy. The song tells them nothing, proves nothing. Too many years have passed, and the photos aren't enough. And if the man inside is truly her son, we're at a loss. He has the right to kick us out.

"She needs to be in a hospital," I tell them. "Shouldn't that be enough to check on her situation?"

"Perhaps. We'll see what we can do," says the officer on his way out.

They leave us without much hope.

I persuade Hoyt and Johanna to eat a little.

"We're doing this my way now, Johanna," Hoyt says when she asks him to go there again, to try to reason with their supposed half-brother.

"Iris, talk to him," she asks me.

I'm torn between both of them. I know Hoyt is right, even so, I also understand Johanna's heart.

"Look," Hoyt says, "I'll hire someone, okay? Someone who can maybe... take the guy."

"Take the guy? What does that mean?" I ask.

"Just take him away for a bit, so we can get a doctor in there to check on her."

"Can you do that?" Johanna asks.

"He could be your brother, Hoyt. You can't—" I'm trying to clarify things.

"I'll make sure he doesn't get hurt," he says tiredly.

We agree on the plan.

Hoyt is still looking for someone when Johanna moves to her

room at night. She's still upset, though I think she'll sleep tonight. At least we have a plan.

* * *

We lie down, the past few days weighing heavy on us. I stick with sleeping on the couch. Hoyt falls asleep almost instantly. I follow him minutes after.

I'm having another nightmare when I hear him scream.

I jump up, my heart racing.

I look at him, trying to figure out what happened. I don't understand what's going on. He's hunched over the side of the bed.

"Hoyt, what happened?"

I walk closer and see the strain, the sweat on his face—*he's in pain.* His right hand grips his prism, the indigo light shining between his fingers.

"Hoyt, should I call 911?"

I'm walking away to grab my phone when he says, "No."

I look back at him.

"Something's wrong," he says, standing up.

"What is?"

"I don't know. I need to check on Johanna."

"I'll go," I tell him.

Johanna isn't responding to my knock on her door. I call her name. I call her phone. Nothing. Hoyt is at my side, almost breaking down the door with his heavy knocks.

I call the lobby, asking them to send someone, and they tell me Johanna left the hotel.

"She's gone, Hoyt. She left the hotel," I say.

He moves fast, putting on shoes, racing out the door. I follow him, almost running to catch up.

"We don't have a car," I realize as we run outside. It's a windy night; I can barely keep my hair out of my face.

I'm still trying to figure out what happened when he comes back with keys.

"Whose car?" I ask.

"Filthy rich, remember?"

We drive as fast as the roads allow.

"What did you feel?" I ask him, reprimanding myself for my lack of experience driving. Hoyt insists he's okay enough to do it, but we both know he isn't. The heavy wind gusts aren't helping.

"Turn here," he says. "This was different—it was real pain, not like before, when she cut her hand."

"They said she left just an hour ago. She's probably still driving." I try to calm both of us with my words.

"If something happened to her..."

His face—I wish I could at least hold his hand.

"Don't go there, Hoyt." I step on the gas, relieved the roads are mostly clear.

My heart skips a beat when I spot the familiar car by the red door.

"You stay here. Don't come out, Iris. Please."

"But Hoyt—"

"You wait here for the cops."

"Okay."

He moves, slowly disappearing into the dark. I look at my shaking hands. My body and mind are consumed with worry. I shouldn't have let him go in.

I hear a gunshot, and my heart almost jumps out of my chest. I look around. There's no one here to help.

I get out of the car, my heartbeat loud in my ears. I'm glad to be concealed by the night. I know I can't do anything against a gun, but I can't stay in the car when both of them are inside. It's not bravery or a lack of caution; it's something stronger—than desire to help them that moves me closer. My prism pulses, pulling me toward Hoyt.

I walk, letting my senses guide me. I quiet my mind the best way I know how—by breathing. Between my nerves, the wind, and the humidity in the air, it's almost impossible to keep my violet light hidden.

I stand outside the house, near the window, trying to peek through the closed curtains. I can't distinguish the shadows inside.

The rational part of me tells me to go back to the car, but I know it isn't up to my brain right now. I close my eyes again, asking my prism and my body's intuition to show me what to do. I keep moving around the place until I find a cracked window. The voices inside are muffled by the wind.

I hear Hoyt say, "Let me get her out, please. I just want to get her out."

"I can't let you do that. They will come for me," the man replies.

"They won't. I won't tell them. She needs a doctor," Hoyt begs.

And then I hear it again—*Awena's lullaby.*

I'm considering going inside when I hear another gunshot, and my entire body freezes. At that moment, my prism does something I've never seen it do. It blinks an indigo light. *Hoyt's light.* Pulsing with my heartbeat.

I feel pain in my head, my hands, my chest. My body is tearing itself apart. I can't help but let out a scream. I beg my prism to stop whatever it's doing.

I hear Hoyt call my name, and then I see him—walking out, carrying someone. *Johanna.* He's carrying Johanna.

As my eyes lock on him, the prism's light fades, taking the pain with it. I run to them, toward the car, and help him put Johanna inside.

"Drive, Iris. Drive," he says, throwing the gun into the front passenger seat.

I don't know where the closest hospital is. I drive while my other bloody hand types on the phone. The directions finally appear once we hit the main road. I watch the police car pass us, heading in the opposite direction. *Too fucking late.*

TWENTY-NINE

"ART IS A LINE AROUND YOUR THOUGHTS." –
GUSTAV KLIMT

I don't know what questions to ask or what to do as I watch Hoyt ache for his sister. The doctors took Johanna almost two hours ago. She's been shot, maybe more than once. Hoyt's body is still covered in her blood. We're waiting for news when the police show up.

"Awena is... here?" I ask them. Hoyt can barely pay attention.

"There was nobody else inside the house. She's being examined now," says the officer, glancing at Hoyt's bloody clothes.

"You have to find him," Hoyt growls, his voice tight with desperation.

A doctor interrupts us. Johanna is stable, alive.

"Can I see her?" Hoyt asks.

"Come with me. She hasn't woken up yet," the doctor replies, leading us to her room.

Johanna is sleeping, her head wrapped in a bandage.

"I didn't know she had hurt her head," I say aloud, not meaning to.

The doctor explains that her right ear was injured.

"The bullet must have passed very close," he tells us. "We haven't found any other wounds."

"Will she be okay?" Hoyt asks.

"We did everything we could. Unfortunately, her right ear is permanently damaged. I'm really sorry. We'll know more when she wakes up."

I take a seat across from Hoyt, each of us holding one of Johanna's hands.

"She's alive," Hoyt says, looking at me, tears falling down his face.

"You both are," I reply, my own tears starting to fall.

He nods. We take turns holding her hand.

She wakes up a few hours later, but only for a moment before falling back into a deeper sleep. She seems to be in too much pain.

"Hey there," Hoyt says softly when she opens her eyes that evening.

Her hand goes straight to her head.

"Easy," says a nurse, stepping in.

I walk out of the room to give them space.

I'm looking for coffee when I find myself wandering down a different hallway.

I find Awena in a hospital bed. Though she seems almost frozen, unable to move, I know she isn't sleeping—her eyes are open.

I'm about to call for a nurse when she looks at me. *At my neck.*

She opens her mouth and speaks in her raspy, weak voice.

"You spilled blood."

I barely have time to process her words when she starts to move.

"You spilled blood," she repeats. And again. And again. Her eyes never leave my prism. She's almost out of the bed when a nurse enters.

"What's wrong with her?" I ask, startled.

"Nothing," the nurse replies.

"Nothing?" I ask, shocked.

"She's healthy... besides... her mind," the nurse explains.

Awena is getting more and more agitated. The nurse administers something to her IV. She finally stops repeating the words.

"Are you family?" the nurse asks.

"She... was gone for a long time," I reply.

"We need to move her, we need signatures," the nurse says.

I nod. "I'll get her son," I tell her, leaving the room.

I find Hoyt talking to a doctor; Johanna is resting again. I tell him about Awena, but I don't mention the words she repeated.

"I'll sign whatever they want. I can't... deal with her right now." His voice sounds defeated, exhausted.

"I'll stay with Johanna. Go sign the papers, go back to the hotel... get changed." I motion to his clothes. "I'll call you when she wakes up again."

He fights me on it but agrees in the end.

* * *

Johanna sleeps for hours. Hoyt comes back with a change of clothes for me.

I close the bathroom door behind me, and he says from the chair, "You got out. Of the car."

"Sorry, I..." I don't even know how to explain what I felt.

"You saved us," he says.

"What?" I don't understand what he means.

"Your scream. When he looked away, I moved on him."

I don't know what to say. I want to tell him about what happened with the prism, but Johanna is stirring now.

Hoyt moves to her left side; we still don't know the extent of her hearing loss.

"Doctor said you're doing great," he tells Johanna.

"I'm sorry, Hoyt," she says slowly.

"Sorry? You're the one in a hospital bed."

"I thought I could—""

I know. Don't worry about that right now," he says, taking her hand.

"My head," she says, lifting her hand to it.

"I'll get a doctor," he says, moving out of the room.

"Are you guys okay?" Johanna asks me.

I nod. I stand by her until the doctor arrives.

* * *

"Awena is being moved to a place in Montana. It's not very close to the ranch, but it's the best place I could find there," Hoyt tells me in the hallway an hour later.

"When did they say Johanna can go home?"

"A week, maybe. They want to monitor her. We'll have to take it day by day."

"I still can't believe he shot her. Did you see it?"

"No. When I got there, she was already on the floor, bleeding."

"I heard two gunshots."

"He was trying to scare me. He pointed the gun away."

"I'm so sorry, Hoyt. I'm sorry I can't even give you a hug."

"I'm sorry this is how you are spending your summer break."

"I'm glad I came. I want to be here, with you, with Johanna."

"Thank you for coming, for saving our lives."

"I didn't do anything, Hoyt."

"You, the prism... I told you I don't believe in coincidences."

"The scream, my scream, I think I felt what you did."

"What do you mean?"

"My prism lit up like yours, your color."

"You felt pain?"

"I did, like my body was splitting."

"How, why? I don't understand."

"I don't know," I say. "When I heard the gunshot, I think my body, the prism— I don't know... Maybe... maybe Awena has answers?"

"The doctor told me that she's healthy, but her mind..."

"They told me that too. She kept saying, 'You spilled blood,' over and over again when I found her in the room."

"Don't read into it, Iris. Her mind is gone."

I nod.

* * *

Hoyt and I are taking turns being with Johanna during the day. He insists on sleeping in the hospital at night. We extended our stay twice, as the doctors aren't ready to release Johanna until they're sure she's well enough. I have to go back to Boston tonight. I'm somehow supposed to return to work on Monday. I haven't even prepped any lessons. Luckily, they're all the same as the previous year. My life in Massachusetts feels so far away now.

Hoyt has left, and I'm walking to Johanna's room when I hear the voice. That guy's voice. I'm already calling for help when he sees me and starts to run away.

"Are you okay?" I ask Johanna, seeing that she's awake.

"He..."

"What?"

"He said he came to check on me, and our mother."

"What? He's the one who shot you, Johanna."

"I don't think he was trying to hurt me."

"He shouldn't be here, Johanna. He's dangerous. The police are looking for him."

"I don't want to press charges."

"What?"

"He took care of our mother, maybe all those years, I don't know. What if he really is... my brother? I can't send him to jail, not because of me."

"What if he comes looking for you, or Hoyt?"

"He won't. He doesn't have the means. You saw where they lived."

"I don't think we can trust him, Johanna."

"You sound like my brother."

"Hoyt was... terrified. He thought he lost you."

"I know, I never meant... to cause him... any pain."

"Please talk to Hoyt about—"

"Kai, he said his name is Kai."

The nurse comes to inform me they've caught Kai, and I instantly relax with relief. Even if Johanna isn't planning on pressing charges, I feel better knowing the police have him. Maybe Hoyt can change her mind.

* * *

Hoyt comes back as soon as he hears what happened.

"I'm sorry, Johanna, but that's not an option," he says when she explains how she feels about Kai.

"Hoyt, what if he is our brother?" she asks him.

"So what? He shot you. I don't give a fuck who he is."

"Hoyt, he wasn't trying to hurt me."

"He did. Your ear... it's all because of him."

"I can hear fine. I still have one good side."

"Johanna, this is not up for discussion. We are going home. We're putting all this behind us."

I know both of them well enough to know this is far from over.

* * *

"Will you let me know when you get home?" Hoyt asks as I pack my bag. We ended up staying way too long at the lodge. My stuff is everywhere.

"Yes." I'm already missing him.

He walks closer.

"Thank you for everything you did these weeks, these months. I've really enjoyed having you by my side."

"Thanks for having me at your home. I've enjoyed it too. I never knew how much I could like the countryside."

"Let me get Jo settled, and I'll visit you soon."

"Do you think she's... okay enough to go home?"

"I think so. I'll hire a nurse to change her bandages or take care of anything if necessary, but she should be okay to be driven to and from the hospital for those visits now."

"She doesn't even seem too upset by the hearing loss."

"She's tough like her horses."

I smile at the thought, Mona coming to mind. "Mona... I really don't have words. She's amazing."

"She'll be waiting for you, hopefully tamed by the holidays," he says.

"I'm looking forward to my next break already."

"Me too," he says, kissing his fingers and gesturing to put them on my lips.

I could feel my body warm to the gesture, even without the physical touch.

"You know how you say everything happens for a reason?" I ask him, zipping my luggage.

"Yeah?"

"What do you think is the reason we can't touch?"

"I'll be damned if I know. Probably because if we could, I wouldn't be able to pull myself away."

"And it doesn't bother you?" I ask him.

"I'm thinking we move to the Bahamas, get a beach shack, and live our days in the water, like fish."

I smile. "I could do that."

He smiles back, taking my bag to the car waiting for me outside.

THIRTY

"FOR ME, ART HISTORY IS LIKE A FEATHER BED
—YOU FALL INTO IT AND IT CATCHES YOU." –
DAVID SALLE

I feel like a ballerina inside a music box. *How did I ever live in a place so small?* I almost feel claustrophobic now, after being in Hoyt's enormous house and spending time in the open fields. The view from my windows is gray—tall buildings everywhere I look. And below, traffic. Even with my choice of street, just a few blocks from the river, I already miss the nature, the mountains... *him.*

I text Hoyt before leaving the house: *I'm pretty sure my apartment shrunk.*

* * *

I might not enjoy the view from my place, but the beautiful campus welcomes me with open arms.

"Good morning," I say to Akira, handing her a cup of coffee.

"Hey, thank you!" She gives me a hug, taking the cup.

"I missed you. A lot has happened since I last saw you."

"How's Johanna doing?"

"She's good. Hoyt said Sawyer has taken the nurse job personally."

273

"Oh good. Are you ready?" she asks as we walk.

"You know, first days... they suck."

"What are you talking about? I love their scared faces. I wish I could take a photo of them, looking at me, trying to figure me out."

I laugh. "I forgot, you don't do anything that isn't fun."

She winks, or attempts to.

* * *

My classroom for HAA 233G – The Body and Embodiment in Greek Art has twenty students awaiting me when I open the door. All of them are on their phones. I can't blame them—I have mine in my hand too. Hoyt had replied to my earlier text: *All you city people living like rats in a lab, no idea how you do it.*

I see what you're doing, I text back, getting an instant smiley face in reply.

I spend the lesson describing the marble sculpture of *Laocoön and His Sons*, one of the most influential ancient artworks in art history.

"Where is it now?" Marissa asks.

"In the Vatican," I answer.

"Are these snakes?" asks a girl whose name I've already forgotten.

"Sea serpents. They're killing him. See the one biting Laocoön on the hip?"

"What's with his eyes?" Nick asks as he writes something down.

"Some say the bites made him blind. The exaggerated realism is similar to the Hellenistic baroque style, popular during the Roman Imperial period."

"Isn't Laocoön part of the Trojan War?" Marissa asks.

"I don't remember him being mentioned in Homer's work," James says. I can't help but notice how handsome he is. Leather jacket draped over the back of the chair, both arms covered in tattoos, he is hot.

I tell myself it's okay to say that, to see that—that's all this is, an observation, even if it feels a little messed up to objectify a student. He had also surprised me with his answer. Even for a Harvard art history major, some books are only read if the professors grade them on it.

"No, he isn't mentioned in the Odyssey or the Iliad. Even so, Laocoön is linked to the fall of Troy. The story says it was Athena and Poseidon, who were favoring the Greeks, who sent the sea serpents to kill him. It was a punishment for alerting the Trojans about the wooden horse."

I'm relieved to have my first day back behind me.

* * *

I've debated going there all summer—not only because of guilt but also because a part of me will always care for him. I'm done weighing the pros and cons. By the time I arrive, I've rehearsed the conversation enough times to feel confident it could go well.

"Iris?" Aaron says, surprised, when he opens the door. He looks better than I expected, though still not close to the Aaron I knew. The apartment seems to have been cleaned up.

"Can I come in?" I ask, and he steps aside.

"You look well," he says, looking at me.

"So do you." Only I regret saying it right away; he knows I'm lying.

"Can I get you a drink?" he asks.

"I'm all right, thank you."

He pours me one anyway. I hesitate before taking a sip.

"For fuck's sake, Iris, it's not poisoned."

I let the whiskey calm my nerves; *maybe I do need it.*

"Did you come for your things? They're all packed. I tried

sending them a month ago, but nobody was home," he says, taking a sip of his own glass.

I don't say where I've been.

"I heard about... your firm," I tell him.

"Of course you did. So you're here because of your lover's money."

"I'm here because... I was worried about you."

He looks at me and laughs. "A little late for that, sweetheart."

"Aaron, I never meant to..."

"Hurt me?"

"Yes." Of course he's hurt—I know that—but I'm hoping he'll hear me out. "We met so young. You were all I had. Without my mom, and with Dad gone, I never knew life without you. I... thought it was love—and maybe it was, maybe it was dependency, fear of being alone."

"So you're saying you never loved me?"

"I did love you—a part of me always will—but it's not the kind of love you deserve. You were always my best friend. I loved... what we had."

"I love you," he says, walking closer.

I take a step back. "I didn't come here to..."

"To what?" He stops moving. "What did you come here for?"

"I told you, I was worried."

"I'm fine. You can clear your conscience."

"Aaron, you deserve to be happy. Don't ruin your life because of me."

"Because of you? Because of the woman I love and have loved since I was a teenager? Because of the woman I fought my parents my whole life for? Nothing else matters now, Iris."

"Aaron, don't say that. You'll meet someone else. Your firm—you built that. Don't let them take it from you."

"I don't give a shit about it. They can have it all." He finishes his drink in one gulp.

"Aaron, please, I can't see you like this. You have to move on."

"Move on?"

"Yes. Talk to Lara, give Hoyt's money back, fire her, prove you can handle your deals. Figure things out. Move on."

"What would I get in return?"

"What?"

"If I make them give his money back?"

"What do you want?" *I did not see that coming.*

"A night with me." He gives me a lazy smile.

"What?! No! I'm not sleeping with you."

"Who said anything about sleeping? Just a date. One last time, you and me, for old times' sake. I need... closure."

"I'm not sleeping with you, Aaron!"

"I told you, it's not the sex I'm after. I just want to...have my friend back, for one last night."

"I don't know, Aaron."

"Your cowboy doesn't need to know. You're so good with secrets, I doubt he'd ever suspect."

"Fuck you."

"Fine, tell him. Iris, please? We owe each other that, don't you think? A proper adult conversation, over dinner?"

I leave his place without giving him an answer.

* * *

Akira comes back holding two giant salads."

Are you going?" she asks me at lunch.

"I don't know. If he does give Hoyt's money back, one dinner might be worth it."

"Are you going to tell Hoyt?"

"Not yet. He's in this mess because of me. And now he's dealing with Johanna, his mom, Kai... and he's been spending a lot of money. Who knows how much Mona cost. I'd feel better if I got his money back."

"Are you sure Aaron isn't just doing this to sleep with you? Or try to get you back?"

"I don't know, maybe."

"Whatever you do, make sure it's worth it."

I nod. "Perhaps I need closure too."

* * *

I'm returning a few books to the library when I see James looking at me.

"Hi, James," I say as I walk by.

"Iris." The directness catches me off guard. I don't correct him. I never mind students calling me by my first name. I glance at what he's holding: Machiavelli, Tolstoy, and one of my favorites, *One Hundred Years of Solitude* by Gabriel García Márquez.

"Nice selection you have there," I say. "History fan?"

"I was born in the wrong century."

I often think the same thing. "I don't meet many students who read those books for..."

"Pleasure?"

Something about his tone makes me uncomfortable. I look around. Nobody seems to be paying attention.

"Yes. It's a shame, really."

"I agree."

"I'll see you in class, James." I walk away.

* * *

I have no food at home; I close the fridge door for the third time.

I'm browsing through dinner options, reminded of how many choices the city offers. I settle on Thai when Aaron texts me: *Saturday night?*

I stare at the message. I have no idea what to do about him. I want him to be happy, to move on. I would have done anything to avoid the mess I've created.

Fine, only dinner. Tell me where and when.

I'll pick you up, Saturday at seven.

* * *

I'm showing the class *The Hunters in the Snow* by Pieter Bruegel when James enters the room. I didn't know he was taking this class too. I check the student list.

"You're not on the list, James."

"I switched classes. You impressed me yesterday."

I don't know how to respond to his tone. "Well, I'm glad to see you. Take a seat."

"This painting of such a mundane activity—hunting. Why did Pieter bother to paint it?" I ask.

Nobody answers.

"This wasn't a good day for the men in the painting. The hunt was unsuccessful. See this one?" I point to the man looking down. "His defeated pose... Even the dogs seem sad, with their drooping ears."

"How do we know they aren't just tired?" Ray asks.

"See the small fox on this man's back? Looks like it's all they got. And the tracks in the snow suggest other prey had escaped."

"I still don't know why he wasted time on this scene," Luna says, chewing gum.

"Let's look at the tiny people ice skating and playing hockey. Perhaps Bruegel wanted the viewer to focus on that. Maybe the hunters were merely a way to guide our eyes to the center of the painting."

"But the name, it says *The Hunters in the Snow*," Ray says.

"Art historians gave the name—maybe not the best one. That's the exciting part: we're all still learning. This isn't a realistic painting of a specific location. He mixed what he knew with what he imagined. Pieter traveled a lot; we know he saw many landscapes, and he probably saw those mountains. It's argued that Bruegel played with scale on purpose, as a way to depict the human condition itself. We're locked in life's day-to-day while also striving for something bigger, even glory."

I'm on my way out when James stops me.

"Iris?"

I look back, wishing he'd start calling me Professor. "Can I help you?"

"I was wondering if you've read the *Analects*?"

"Confucius's Analects?"

"Yes."

"I can't say that I have. My focus is on European and American art. Why?"

"I'm researching different takes on supernatural beliefs, for my own writing."

"Writing?" I ask.

"Yes, I'm into research."

"Are you writing a paper?"

"No, a nonfiction book," he answers.

"And Confucius had a take on it? On ghosts?"

"Yes, I believe so—something to do with keeping them at a distance. I wanted to know if you've read it, if it's worth it."

"Sorry, you should ask Professor Yang. She's currently teaching Advanced Readings in East Asian Art and Literature." Something tells me he already knows this.

"Good to know. Thanks anyway."

"Good luck," I say, waiting for him to leave first.

* * *

Akira wanted to go to Spiral tonight, but I was looking forward to a night at home. By myself. When was the last time I relaxed at home? *Next week*, I reply to her.

I'm sitting on the couch with a bowl of popcorn, sipping wine, and watching a thriller when I realize I'm finally at peace with myself. Things aren't all figured out, but I'm happy. I like my life, I like the people in it. I'm happy with my career, my health, my apartment. I'm even proud of what I've accomplished. I'm happy in my own skin. Tomorrow, I'll be ending the longest chapter of my life—*Aaron's chapter*—and I'm okay with the unknown. I'm not sure what the future holds, but I'm ready to face it head-on.

THIRTY-ONE

"THE POSITION OF THE ARTIST IS HUMBLE. HE
IS ESSENTIALLY A CHANNEL." – PIET MONDRIAN

"You look beautiful," Aaron says when I come downstairs.

"Thank you." He's seen this dress before, I'm sure of it. I debated what to wear, but I knew I needed to put on a proper outfit, or he wouldn't buy that I was taking this dinner seriously.

"Where are we going?" I ask.

"You'll see."

We drive in silence for a while. I'm not recognizing the way the driver is going.

"Aaron, where are you taking me?"

"Do you not trust me anymore?"

Twenty minutes later, we arrive at the marina.

"What is this?" I ask as he motions for me to get on the boat.

"Dinner."

"On a boat?"

"Yes. I wanted our last night to be... special."

I hesitate. If this were anyone else, I would have walked away. But it's Aaron. I do trust him. He helps me onto the boat.

"This is..." I look around as the boat drifts into the water.

"I should have done more when we were together. I should have done this before," he tells me affectionately.

I know better than to say anything.

There's a table set up on the deck of the boat, beautifully lit with candles. He pulls my chair out, and I can't help but stare at him. The man I almost said yes to spending my life with. He looks handsome in his crisp white shirt and navy blazer.

"This is beautiful," I tell him.

He pours us wine.

"To the one who got away." He raises his glass.

"To the last fifteen years," I say.

A waiter brings our entrée. I have no appetite, but even so, the few bites I take are delicious.

Aaron doesn't seem interested in the food either.

I look around us, and then he stands up. "You owe me a dance."

"What?"

He pulls out his phone, presses something, and slips it into his pocket. I recognize the song—the very one we had chosen for our wedding dance.

His eyes beg me. I stand up and take his hand.

He holds me close, moving with the song. I let myself enjoy this moment with him, *our last moment*. There's nothing around us now, the city lights far away. We dance, and tears form in my eyes. He looks at me and wipes them away with his thumb. There's so much history between us—so many memories, all muddied by my cowardice, my dishonesty. We deserved to part ways differently.

His lips brush mine, and for a moment, I let myself feel him, feel us. Before the kiss can intensify, I pull back.

"I can't, Aaron."

"Because of him?"

I nod yes.

He follows me to the edge of the boat.

"What's the plan? Are you moving to Montana, or is he coming here?"

I hold tight to the railing.

"Aaron... I don't want to—"

"You don't know. I can tell. I still know you better than anyone."

"We're figuring things out."

"Are you going to abandon your career, everything you've worked so hard for? Give up art? For what? To live in a barn?"

"Aaron."

His words... I don't want to think about his words. *Was he right?* Would I be abandoning my career?

"Iris, I will always love you. I'll always wonder what I did wrong, but I would really hate to see you give up everything for him. Giving yourself up. I know how you feel when you're in front of those paintings; I know how much you breathe history. Please don't forget who you are. Even if it's not with me, I want you to have everything you've ever wanted. It's what I've always wanted for you, since that day you sat next to me in the cafeteria."

My tears fall, and I don't know what to do. He comes closer and holds my hand. We continue looking out at the water. *So much for being ready for the unknown.*

* * *

My headache is back. It's been back since Aaron dropped me off days ago. My insomnia hitchhiked.

I walk for hours, eyeing each painting like it's the first time. I tell myself I'll stay until I feel better; consequently, I remain—and my uneasy feelings do too.

I'm sitting in Monet's gallery when a hand touches my shoulder.

"Hello." James takes a seat next to me. *Very close.*

"Hi, how's your research going?" I ask.

"Great. I'm currently on an Icelandic rabbit hole."

"What interests you about the subject?" I didn't realize I needed the distraction.

"Throughout history, featured not only in religious contexts but in folklore as well, the supernatural comes up again and again. Maybe the laws of nature we know aren't everything that's out there."

I've learned this very lesson this past year. "Have you seen the Japanese print of a female ghost we have here?"

"I have not. I'm embarrassed to say, this is my first time here."

"Where are you from?" I ask as I walk us to the artwork.

"New York. Long Island."

"How do you like Boston?"

"It's great. I feel like I'm around like-minded people here."

"That's what I love about this city. I feel understood."

We stand in front of the woodblock print by Kitagawa Utamaro. "Here it is." I pause, then ask, "How much have you written so far?"

"Of my book? Not much. I'm obsessed with the research. Sometimes I forget it's for a book. I wish I could get a job just doing that—learning."

"I found being a teacher comes pretty close to it."

"I've thought about it, being a professor. I don't know if I have the patience."

"Not a lot of professors do. But it grows on you—the more you help, the more your patience grows too. Let me show you something else."

We walk to another corridor, and I say, "This is a Mayan ritual vessel from around 740 AD."

"Is that a baby?"

"A deity baby," I tell him.

"Amazing."

I smile. It's nice having someone to talk about art—someone who doesn't think an ancient serpent umbilical cord surrounded by dragon heads is anything but *amazing*.

"When you have pages ready, let me know. I'd like to read

them," I say before showing him a few more pieces I think he'll enjoy.

Our tour puts me in a better mood, and I finally leave the museum feeling optimistic.

* * *

"Are you home?" Hoyt asks later that night over the phone.

"No, I'm on my way back from yoga."

"The lawyers called. Aaron's firm wants to meet. They're apparently settling the case."

"What does that mean?"

"They're releasing the money—giving it all back."

"Really?"

He laughs. "I know, it's crazy. Maybe they just came to their senses."

"Yeah, maybe."

"I'm leaving tonight. I was wondering... should I get a hotel?"

"Oh... you can stay at my place... if you want. It's not luxurious, as you know, but I cleaned it up. I don't know if we'll fit in the bed with a mountain of pillows, though."

"I don't care about that. I'll sleep on the floor. Are you sure? You hesitated."

"Of course, you just caught me off guard."

"Okay, I gotta run. I'll see you tomorrow."

* * *

I'm planning to meet Hoyt after my morning lecture. I've left my keys for him with the doorman.

"What are you doing here?" I ask, almost dropping my books.

"I wanted to see you, at work," Hoyt says.

"I have to stop at my office really quick, and then we can go."

"Not even a tour?" he asks.

"A tour?"

"It's my first time."

I laugh. "At Harvard?"

"At college."

I smile. "That building over there is the library. This one, the history of art department. And that one, over on the other side, is where the real smart ones work—like Akira."

We're walking to my office when James comes over. "Iris?"

I turn around.

"I wanted to thank you. I had a great time yesterday."

Hoyt is standing next to me. I don't know if I should introduce him. *I don't even know how to introduce him*, I realize.

"Oh, sure. See you tomorrow, James."

"Your students seem to really enjoy your... classes," Hoyt says as he watches James walk away.

"He meant the museum. I showed him around."

"You did?"

"Yeah, he's taking a couple of my classes. I was there, and we were talking—next thing I know, I was..."

"Giving him a private tour?"

"Are you... jealous?"

"Of him?" He brushes it off, but I notice the signs. I know the tells.

"James is... interested. He's doing research. History nerd, like me."

"Okay."

* * *

Hoyt is quiet on our way to Aaron's office. I hope it's only because of the meeting.

"I'll be at the coffee shop across the street. Meet me there when you're done?" I ask him.

"If I get my money back, coffee's on me." He gives me a lazy smirk.

"Good luck." I hope Aaron follows through with his words.

I'm lost in my book when Hoyt comes back.

"And?" I ask apprehensively.

"Looks like Aaron finally grew some balls."

"You got your money back?"

"Yes."

"All of it?"

"And some. The prick actually turned me a profit."

"I can't believe it. That's amazing."

"Can we go?" Hoyt asks, his tone sharper now. He's mad about something.

* * *

"Were you not going to tell me that you went to him?" he asks before I even close the door.

"Hoyt, it was only dinner."

"Right."

"You don't believe me?"

"Of course I believe you. I trust you. Look, I'm not a jealous person. I just... need..."

"Honesty?"

"Yeah."

"I'm sorry. I feel like it was yesterday when I was the one asking for that."

"How did you... convince him?" he asks me.

"We talked."

"He told me you kissed."

"He kissed me, but it's over. Really over."

"I thought it had been over between you two for a long time now."

"It has. Only... I think he finally understood."

"You know what he said? After he told me you two danced and kissed on a boat? He said, 'Good luck.' He said that after a couple years in the country, your soul will die, that you'll blame me for it. That the art world you love can't be bought."

I let the words sink in.

"Iris, is he right?"

"I don't know. Maybe. We have... no plans, Hoyt. I don't know. Do you want me to move to Montana?"

"Iris! Of course I want you to move to Montana. I live there. I own horses and land. I'm... not a businessman like Aaron, or a history buff like James. I'm a fucking nobody. I've never even been to college."

"Hoyt, I don't care about any of that. I fell for you because of who you are."

He looks away from me. I hate that I can't turn him around, can't grab his hand.

"Hoyt, I mean it. Aaron doesn't understand because... this part of me, he never met."

He turns to me. "What part?"

"The part that loves the countryside, the smell of grass, the taste of hot coffee in the cold mountain air, the part that loves the feel of a horse's soft hair, the part that can't wait to spend nights by the fire. It's all new to me, too. I don't know if I can leave the city, my job, the museums. I honestly don't know. But I'm willing to try. For us."

"I don't want to be the reason you're away from what you love."

I look him in the eye. "You are the reason I'm in love—with more than just art."

He walks closer. "You...?"

"Yes, I think I knew it was love since my prism took me to you."

He comes as close as he possibly can. "How am I supposed to not kiss you right now?"

"I don't think we'll fit in my shower," I smile, but I'm honestly considering trying.

"Let's get out of here."

"And go where?"

"Pack a bag."

Thirty-Two

"Surrealism is destructive, but it destroys only what it considers to be shackles limiting our vision." – Salvador Dalí

The elevator door opens to the rooftop room, and my eyes can't take in the entire place with one look. It's enormous, luxurious, beautifully designed, and most importantly, *ours for the night*. I walk straight outdoors, passing the bar, the indoor jacuzzi, the giant bed. I look up at the pool—so blue. The water features are turned on, including a little cascade on the right side, all perfectly lit. Just like the city in front of us. No stars above, the lonely crescent moon stealing the night.

"This place is incredible," I say as Hoyt joins me.

I can almost feel his heartbeat.

"I was close to buying us tickets to the Bahamas, but I didn't think I could wait for the flight."

He looks me in the eyes.

We both understand what this night means.

"Wicked slow?" I ask, and he nods.

The bar wall has everything one could want. Rows of bottles lined up in front of me. I pick a favorite.

I take a sip from my glass, letting the caramel burn as it goes down. Just how I like it. And then I hear jazz—my kind of jazz, smooth like bourbon. Hoyt must have found a way to connect his phone. I look around and find him staring at me from the other side of the room. He makes his way toward me and is about to pour himself a glass when I shake my head no.

He lifts a brow.

I take the bottle outside. I know he's right behind me.

I walk to the outdoor chairs and motion for him to sit.

"Give me your phone," I say.

He pulls it from his pocket and hands it to me.

I change the music. My plans call for something different.

I take another sip straight from the bottle and increase the volume of the speakers. The beat hits my body, flows through me, straight to my head.

I glance at Hoyt one more time, then turn away to face the moon.

I let my body move however it wants. No control, no hesitation. Tonight, *I am free.*

My prism pulses, my blood runs hot. I dance and dance. I look at Hoyt; his eyes are glued to every move of my hips, my hands.

I take off my boots slowly, bending low, letting him take in the view. I keep dancing barefoot. I'm high on the music, the alcohol, and the lust. My hands move over my body, through my hair, and it unsettles him. I watch as he adjusts his pants, making room for himself.

I continue to sway and tease him. I take off my shirt and throw it at him. He laughs. I don't. I'm enjoying the role-playing. I change the song to something sexier. It calls for less dancing and more stripping, so I obey. I pull off my pants while staring at him, and his eyes grow hungrier.

I dance in my underwear for a while, until I can't wait any longer. I walk closer to him, keeping eye contact, and unhook my bra. I quickly turn around, and pull down my panties while facing away. He lets out a grunt.

I dance completely naked, fully aware how I look in his eyes. He stands up and says, "I want to touch you."

I walk away, taking the bottle with me... into the pool.

Hoyt starts to take his shirt off, but I stop him. I tell him it's my turn to undress him. He kicks off his shoes and dives in fully clothed.

I stand on the shallow edge, the water only covering my bottom half. He swims closer until he's only an inch away, watching me. I take a step forward.

"You are beautiful," he whispers in my ear.

I begin to undo his shirt, button by button, my fingers brushing his chest slowly.

I let myself feel his bare torso, the promise in each muscle that he could take me however he wants. Then I move to his pants. I take my time unzipping carefully.

I leave him only with his tight trunks, but not for long, I pull them down from behind, feeling his ass on the way.

He looks like a god under the night sky, his indigo light shining in agreement.

I take a sip of the whiskey and kiss him. He moans to my taste, and I know he wants more. *A real sip.* His hands pull my hair gently as his mouth kisses mine, like we have all the time in the world. I suck his tongue slowly and find myself mad for his touch.

I pick up the bottle again, this time I pour it on my breasts. He licks every drop, his tongue swirling on my hard nipples, biting, sucking. He drags his tongue up, slowly, to the middle of my throat, up to my neck. He bites my ears and whispers, "I want to taste you."

I let myself go under the water. He props me up on the edge of the pool and uses his strong, tough hands to spread my legs apart. His lips find my thighs and I'm at a loss. I steady my breath, and tell my body to hold on. My prism's light reflecting on his face. He makes his way in, biting, licking, teasing, until his tongue finds my center. He doesn't hesitate; his tongue strokes me lightly, then harder, until my hands finds his hair. I didn't know it was possible to want someone this badly.

He continues moving his tongue on me, and then in me. He slides his tongue as far as he can until I can't take anymore. I want all of him. *I need all of him.*

I make sure to go underwater again.

"A reward," I say as I pour whiskey in his mouth.

He kisses me hard and my hand finds his cock. I want all his length in me. He turns me around to kiss my neck as his fingers stroke my clit. I arch my body to him. He licks my back and moves a finger inside me. He can feel me pulsing, and right when I don't think I can hold anymore, he adds a second. I'm too close.

"I want you, all of you, now," I say.

He bends me over the edge of the pool and pushes his cock inside me. Inch by inch. And there are lots of them. More than I have ever experienced. When he's done stretching me, when he is fully inside, he pulls out. My entire body trembles. It's his turn to tease me; I'm almost begging when he slides it in me again. This time in one slow smooth move. He reaches to rub my clit and I let myself move on him. We find a pace in which both of us lose control completely. His hands are holding tight on my hips, both of us getting closer to climax with each thrust. I had no idea sex could feel this good. I want to scream when I finally let myself orgasm along with him.

He turns me around, his lips finding mine, his tongue telling me he wants more.

I let our prisms connect and watch as their lights disperse in opposite directions.

"Iris?"

I look up into his gorgeous green eyes.

"I love you," he says between kisses.

"I know," I say, kissing him back. "I love you too."

He lifts me up, and my legs wrap around him.

He kisses me hard and moments later I feel he's ready again.

"That was quick," I tease him as I stroke him with my hand.

"I told you before, I don't think I can ever have enough of you."

"I want to try the indoor tub now," I say, stepping out of the pool.

He follows me like a puppy.

I change the music back to jazz and let myself relax as the jets do their thing. The hot water feels soothing after the pool. Hoyt pulls me onto his lap, and our prisms find each other before our lips do.

I move my hands through his hair and let myself really look into his eyes. I kiss him slowly. *I don't want this night to end.*

He makes his way inside me again; this time I sit on him, feeling him for a few minutes. We fit perfectly. "I understand the appeal of tantric sex now," I say, and he laughs.

"I'm available for practice," he tells me.

"I'm too impatient," I say, moving on him.

"You feel so good," he murmurs, closing his eyes.

"I think it feels different when they are... connected," I say. "Or maybe I drank more than I realized."

He pulls his prism away, and we both immediately feel the difference.

We both let out a moan when we allow our necklaces to link again.

He lifts me up and down while I touch myself. Every time I want him deeper and deeper; *it was me who could never have enough of him.*

As we both climax, our prisms do something wicked of their own. They cast gold sparkles on the water, on the walls, all around us. Hoyt's face is covered with them, and I assume mine is, too. It only lasts for a few seconds, but in that moment, I understand the true meaning of the word *magic.*

We both watch as the golden speckles fade away, leaving the prisms to shine their respective colors again.

"I didn't think it was possible to like this... curse," he says as we hug and kiss.

"I didn't think it was possible to feel this... happy."

He smiles at my words.

"Are you happy?" he asks softly.

"Very." I touch his face lightly. "If I could sleep in the water, I would," I say, realizing we'll have to get out eventually.

"I don't want to stop touching you, kissing you. I just want to... cuddle you in bed." He kisses me softly.

I hug him tight. We stay like that for a while, until we both know it's time.

"My skin is peeling off," I say, looking at my hands as I dry myself off.

"Do you really have to go to work tomorrow?"

"Yes, and I thought you had a flight to catch."

"I don't want to go anywhere, or do anything else," he tells me.

"What about Jo's surgery?"

"I guess I should be there for that."

"Hoyt?"

He looks at me.

"We'll figure it out." I know he understands what I mean.

"I'm starving," I say, putting on a soft robe.

"Let's order the entire menu," he jokes, handing me the piece of paper.

"Everything does look amazing, especially the desserts."

* * *

We sit on the bed, waiting for the food, when I ask him, "Have you gone to see your mom again?"

"No, but Jo has."

"Do you think your mother's lullaby could hold some truth?"

"I used to think so, that maybe there were seven prisms, like it says, seven sparkles."

"And now you don't?"

"After seeing her, I think it could just be random words put together."

"It does say that they attract each other. And also mentions... the sixth sense."

"I know, I've gone mad going over those words growing up. Even if it's the truth, it also tells us nothing that matters."

We hear a buzz, and Hoyt goes to open the elevator door.

"Oh my god! You did order the entire menu!" I say, eying all the food.

"Only the dessert section. I got your sandwich and—"

"My fries," I say, taking a bite of one. I let out a sound of pleasure, and Hoyt looks at me.

"You're going to be my undoing," he says.

I laugh, taking my food to bed.

"Wow, this is really good," he says, taking a bite of his burger.

I get up and go to the food cart again to bring the ice cream sundae to bed. I dip my fries in it, and he looks at me. At my lips. I know I have ice cream on them. I lick it.

"Fucking hot," he says, and I laugh.

"What? Me eating ice cream and fries?"

"You, doing anything."

"Want some?"

"Of you or the food?"

I smile. "Here." I feed him the combo.

"Wow. I think we should scrap the beach shack plan and move in here." He licks his finger.

"Definitely," I say, taking another bite, and we both laugh.

* * *

I'm putting another pillow between us when he says, "I meant what I said earlier. I understand if you... can't see yourself in Montana."

"Let me finish this semester. I can take some leave. I meant it too, that we'll figure it out."

"I could move... here," he says, surprising me.

"What? No, you can't. Your horses, your sister."

"Broc can take care of the horses, and Sawyer can look after Johanna."

"Hoyt, what would you do in Boston?"

"What will you do in Montana?"

"I'm too tired right now, but I'm sure I can think of something."

He pulls himself up, propping his elbows on our mountain of pillows, and says, "I love you, firecracker."

I smile. "Stop looking at me like that! Go to sleep." I push a pillow over him. He smiles, turning away.

* * *

"Iris, you're going to be late," Hoyt says, nudging me with a pillow.

"Shit! What time is it?" I ask, looking at my phone. "Did I turn off my alarm?"

"You have thirty minutes to be in the classroom."

I'm brushing my teeth, putting my hair in a ponytail when he walks into the bathroom.

"I still think you should call in sick. It's a shame we never made it to this amazing shower."

I look at it; it does look amazing.

"I can't do that today. I'm being... reviewed."

"What?"

"Yeah, they do that sometimes. Have someone sit in on the class, evaluating."

"Why are you only telling me this now?"

"I'm not worried."

"I can see that."

"I don't mind it, really." I finish putting my shoes on.

"I just got you a car. The driver's waiting. Get out of here," he says, handing me my bag.

"Have a safe flight, call me after the surgery," I say, pressing the elevator button.

"By the way—last night, best night of my life," he tells me, and I look at him.

"I love you," I say as the elevator opens.

"Seriously, get out of here before I throw you in the pool."

I bring my index finger to my lips, then gesture it to his, just like he did before, and leave.

THIRTY-THREE

"THE AIM OF ART IS TO REPRESENT NOT THE
OUTWARD APPEARANCE OF THINGS, BUT THEIR
INWARD SIGNIFICANCE." – ARISTOTLE

I make it to the classroom just in time; luckily, the hotel was only fifteen minutes away. Flynn is the last one to enter the room, and I wait for him to sit before beginning. I've chosen the controversial painting *The Ugly Duchess* by the Flemish artist Quentin Matsys (1513) for the lecture. I know I'm taking a risk, but I doubt Walter Flynn wants to hear about da Vinci again.

There's something about having my lessons reviewed that reminds me of being a student myself. And yet, I don't mind it at all. If I'm being honest, I welcome it with open arms. I'm not entirely sure why. However, after last night, I learned something about myself: I like the attention—not exactly on my body, but on me in general. Especially when it comes to my work. I'm proud of what I know, how I think, how I feel about the arts. I don't mind being evaluated because I want recognition.

I don't mention Flynn to the students; I want them to ask their questions, participate like any other day—even if the one being judged is me and not them. The auditorium is packed. They probably don't even notice the stocky old man in the back.

"The painting looks brighter in person," says Mary. Some

students roll their eyes. Mary has a way of always mentioning her travels.

"There are a few different theories about who is being portrayed in this oil painting. Anyone want to share what they know?" I ask.

"Wasn't she the ugliest woman in history?" says a tall blonde girl. I've forgotten her name.

"This woman was mistakenly identified as Margaret Maultash, Duchess of Carinthia and Countess of Tyrol. Enemies called her that," I explain. "Any other guesses?"

"Is this a satirical portrait?" asks Gil.

"Why do you think that?" I ask him.

"Because of her wrinkled skin, the withered breasts..." he answers.

"Why would Matsys want to make fun of her?" I ask.

"She looks like a man," says Terry.

"Let's take a look at what she's wearing," I say. "The horned head-dress—we know it was out of fashion for the time. Her dress, with its laced corseted front, is outdated as well. We know she must be wealthy from the ornaments and the large gold-and-pearl brooch. If it's a satire, which many believe it is, then perhaps Quentin could be mocking old women who try to inappropriately recreate their youth."

"Is she holding a red flower?" asks Mary.

"Yes, although it's only a bud. Perhaps a symbol of a flower that will never blossom."

"It says here she had Paget's disease," says Terry.

"No phones, Terry. We're learning to describe what we see and think for ourselves. And yes, some say the woman had the disease in which bones become enlarged and deformed. If she is indeed suffering from it, then perhaps Matsys is sympathizing with her instead. He could have even used a live model for this portrait. Any other guesses?"

Silence fills the room.

"What if she isn't a woman after all?" I ask.

Flynn coughs, and I'm not sure if it's on purpose or not.

"It's a new theory; it's currently being discussed that this is actually a cross-dressed man comically playing the role of a sought-after young woman, a carnival tradition," I continue.

"I believe this new theory doesn't have enough proof to be taken seriously, let alone be discussed in the classroom," says Flynn. I'm surprised to hear him speak.

I'm still digesting his words when James says, "You don't think we should be aware if a new theory is being discussed?"

"I think, as historians, we have the responsibility to stick to the accuracy of history. We can't feed into every theory out there," Flynn tells him.

I take a breath and respond, "I believe, as historians, we have an even greater responsibility to find the truth. I encourage discussion in my classroom. I hope each one of you will continue to seek history for the purpose of finding the real stories, not just the ones we're accustomed to."

The rest of the lecture goes by in a blur. I'm very much aware of how my review is going—not well—even if Flynn doesn't say another word. I reassure myself I didn't make it this far in my career by trying to please others. I did it by being myself. I finish the lecture and wait for him to approach me.

"You know I'm going to have to report on this," he says, coming closer.

"I stand by what I said." I acknowledge him with a simple nod.

"You'll hear from us soon." And he walks away.

Perhaps I should've played a little nicer.

"He isn't a student, is he?" asks James. I hadn't noticed he was still there.

"Hi, James. No, he isn't."

"I'm sorry if I said the wrong thing," he apologizes.

"You said the only right thing."

"Is there anything I can do? I could write you a good...review?"

"Thank you, but unfortunately, I think the damage is done. I appreciate your offer, though. How's your research? Anything for me to read yet?"

"Actually, yes. Here." He pulls the papers from his backpack and hands them to me. "It's just a rough draft, though."

"I'll let you know what I think."

* * *

"Are you kidding me?" says Akira by the coffee cart.

"Nope."

"I can't believe Aaron gave all of it back."

"Actually, he did more than that—he apparently turned a profit too, for himself and Hoyt."

"Wow."

"Yeah, it feels good to have that figured out, at least."

"What do you mean?" she says, taking a seat on the bench.

"I was reviewed today."

"You were?"

"Yeah, and I don't think it went very well."

"Why? You're so...loved here. Everybody knows."

"I was too...impulsive."

"It's going to be fine, Iris."

"Yeah...we'll see."

"Is Hoyt still in town?"

"He left this morning; Johanna has surgery tomorrow."

"Surgery? I thought she was doing well."

"She is, it's reconstructive plastic surgery."

"I see."

"How are you doing?" I ask her. At least my coffee is perfect.

"My parents are coming to visit on Sunday."

"That's great."

She looks at me. "It's hard to complain about them when you have none. Still..."

I laugh. "Sorry."

She laughs too.

"Girls' night? Friday?" I ask, and she agrees.

* * *

I'm letting myself soak in worry when Hoyt texts me he's home. I miss him already. I replayed his words all day in my head: *best night of his life.* I think it had been the best of mine too. And then I replay our other conversation: *What am I going to do in Montana?* I need a productive way to clear my head. I'm looking out my window when a runner goes by, completely lost in the act. Maybe it's time I give the sport a chance.

* * *

And maybe I'm wrong. *How in the world do people do this?* I can still see my building, and I'm already out of breath. *Wow. I guess I'll walk most of the way.* I have music blasting in my ears, and it helps with my worries. By the time I reach the riverwalk, I'm a sweaty mess. I walk most of the way, increasing to a run whenever I can. I make it two miles before I turn back. Other runners pass me like I'm the tortoise in the fable. Or at least I hope I am.

* * *

I've just gotten out of the shower and am getting dressed when Hoyt calls.

"How did it go today?" he asks me.

I'm still out of breath. "I think I blew it, actually."

"I'm sorry, Iris."

"Whatever. On a positive note, I just came back from my first run."

"Oh good, I was hoping I hadn't interrupted something...else."

"Very funny."

"How far did you go?"

"Four miles."

"That's good."

"Probably won't be able to walk tomorrow, though."

He laughs. "I miss you already."

"Me too."

"What do you want to do on your birthday?" he asks me.

"Oh... I don't know... I think it falls on a Thursday. I have to work the next day."

"I want to take you out, even if it's just dinner. I know a party isn't really your thing."

"Are you coming here?"

"Of course I'm coming."

"You've been traveling a lot."

"I will be there."

I smile. "Dinner is perfect."

* * *

I've finished my lecture for the day when I receive an email from my department chair. *I'm wanted in the office.* I know it has to be related to my review. I walk toward it with my head high, even though my stomach twists and my heart sinks with each step. I've been too confident, arrogant even. Perhaps I need the lesson. I'll apologize. I love my job; I realize that now, when it could be in jeopardy.

"You wanted to see me, Turner?" I ask, taking a seat across from the woman I have much respect for. She's made a name for herself in the field, and I've always appreciated her advice. I always thought we got along, and I hope this won't change things. She's wearing a classic black dress and her hair is perfectly curled with precision. I'm glad I'm dressed appropriately, in slacks and a sweater.

"As you probably already know, Flynn's report was... interesting."

"I can explain—" I start, but she cuts me off.

"Don't. It's perfect."

"What?"

"You are perfect."

"I don't understand."

"We've been looking for someone like you for years. Someone who can take this up a notch. We need someone like you at Harvard."

"Need me?"

"I want you aboard the Art, Film & Culture Faculty Committee. I want you to expand research. We should be doing more when it comes to art here."

"I don't know what to say. Thank you, Turner... Can I think about it?"

"Think about it?"

"I have a lot going on in my private life right now. I'm very thankful, and I'll give you an answer soon."

"Okay. Iris, opportunities like this don't come often."

"I know, I really am extremely grateful."

"Let me know on Monday."

My head is spinning. I wasn't expecting a promotion. I wasn't even expecting to keep my job. My old self would've jumped at the opportunity.

That had always been the plan—to grow my name, to follow Turner's steps. Yet, as soon as she offered, I hesitated. Was Aaron right? Was I forgetting who I was? Was I giving up my career? Who was I if not a professor? *That's my identity.* If I give that up and move to Montana, who will I be? Thank God it's Friday. I've never needed an escape more than tonight. Tomorrow... all my worries and decisions can wait until tomorrow. I just need to ask Hoyt something first.

I text him: *Call me when you can. We need to talk.*

My phone rings an hour later.

"How's Jo doing?" I ask.

"She's great. Should wake up soon. Everything went well."

"I'm so happy to hear that."

"You said you wanted to talk?"

"I need to know, Hoyt. I just need to know."

"Know what?"

"What happened with you and Maeve? How... serious was it?"

"Oh... I wasn't expecting this... hmm." He pauses.

"That serious?"

"Look, it's complicated."

"Okay."

"She... was my brother's girlfriend."

"She was Luke's girlfriend?"

"Yeah, only for a year, but he loved her. After he died, I was in pretty bad shape. I did stupid things."

"Okay."

"She was a stupid mistake. I should have never..."

"So you..."

"We slept together once. I was drunk, she was there. I was a douchebag. I've never regretted anything more in my life. She didn't deserve it. Broc and Sawyer didn't deserve it. Luke didn't deserve it. Yet I can't change it. I messed up."

"You only slept together once?"

"Yeah, when I was nineteen."

"That's it?"

"It's not that simple. We grew up together. Every time I see her, I realize I hurt her. And her family. I should have known better. I should have been better."

"I understand."

"I'm sorry, Iris. I know I should have told you sooner."

"I just needed to know that... there isn't anyone else. That there wasn't anything else going on between you two."

"No, Iris. I told you, there was, is, no one else. There is only you."

"Thank you for telling me."

"I love you."

"I love you too."

"I fucking hate that we live this far apart."

"Yeah. I wish you could come dance with me tonight."

"Dance?"

"Akira and I are going to Spiral."

"Hmm."

"What?"

"You... dancing..."

I smile.

"Give Jo a hug for me."

"Firecracker?"

"Yeah?"

"Thank you."

"For what?"

"For loving me."

THIRTY-FOUR

"CREATIVITY IS MAGIC. DON'T EXAMINE IT TOO
CLOSELY." – EDWARD ALBEE

The club is packed, as usual, leaving us barely any room to move on the dance floor.

"Maybe it's time we find a new place," I tell Akira as someone bumps into us. "This place is getting too popular."

She lifts her glass to mine, doing our usual cheers. "I love this song!" she says, pulling me to dance. I take a sip of whatever she ordered for me; it tastes artificial and girly. She says it's new. "They were almost giving it away for free."

We dance together for a while until she meets someone. I tell her I'm going to the bathroom to give them some space.

I pass the ridiculously long line and head straight for the sink and mirror. As I'm fixing my hair, my vision blurs for a split second. *Maybe that new drink is out of my league.* I check my phone and see Akira's text: *I'm outside.*

Why is she outside? Is she ready to leave with that guy? We haven't been here long. I head toward the door, looking for her.

I'm almost there when I black out.

* * *

My senses are overloaded; a strong chemical smell wakes me up. My vision is completely blurred. I can't even make out where I am. *What the hell was in that drink?* I hear voices but no music. I don't remember getting out of the club. Did I fall? Pass out? Maybe someone found me.

"Akira?" I call.

My voice is weak, too weak for anyone to hear me. I try again: "Hello?"

"She's awake." I don't recognize the man's voice.

Two big figures move closer. I try to move back, only to find I can't. I'm tied to something. I shake my head. *Where am I?* I beg my brain to wake up, but the fog is too heavy. I try to move my hands— they hurt. They're tied up tight.

I manage a scream. "Help!" My voice echoes. My eyes are still working hard to form faces. Panic sets in.

My breathing gets out of control; my body shakes as I try to free myself from whatever is holding me still.

"Easy, bunny. You're not going anywhere," I hear the man say.

I try moving again; my wrists burn from the motion. I scream again, this time a little louder.

"Nobody can hear you. Save your breath. You're going to need it."

Shit. This is not good. I try to focus on my breathing. I need to think. I need to think. I need to get out of here. Akira! She'll know when I don't show up. She'll call the cops. Someone had to have seen me if I was taken. The club was packed. Someone did. I try to calm myself. *Someone had to.*

"She needs time. She's too high. I'll come back in an hour," I hear another man say. "Do not touch her."

I let the words sink in. *I have one hour.*

I hear a door open and close. It's loud. It has to be a gate. Where am I? How long have I been here?

The drink—if someone put something in my drink, did they put it in Akira's too? I panic for her.

"Easy, bunny. You're so... fresh," the man says, licking my face. I manage to spit on him.

"Feisty... just how I like it," he says, grabbing my face.

My head is killing me. I scan my body. My legs are tied up. My wrists are tied up. My vision still isn't one hundred percent, but I can feel whatever I'm on wearing off. I close my eyes and listen to my surroundings. I can hear cars; I must still be in the city. No other voices—just the man's heavy breathing and footsteps. I need to find a way out of here.

My mouth is dry.

"I need water," I say.

"You don't get to ask for things," the man replies, spitting on the floor.

"Please, he won't be happy to come back and find me like this. Water will help."

"Smart one, aren't you?"

"Please, just a sip."

He brings something to my lips. I drink it. It tastes clean.

He comes closer and takes a whiff of my neck. "You smell so... sweet."

I know better than to fight him off. I need to somehow get him to play along.

"Why am I here?" I ask.

"That's not for me to say."

"Who are you?"

"I'm your hunter, little bunny." He keeps chewing something.

"What do you want from me?"

"I'm just the hunter. I do what I'm paid to do."

"And what were you paid to do?"

"Bring you here."

"And not touch me," I remind him. "My wrists... they hurt."

"I can't untie you."

"It's not like I can go anywhere. My legs are still tied. Please."

"I said no."

"How about some food?" I beg.

"I don't have anything here."

"You could get something. You have an hour."

"I'm not supposed to leave."

I take a deep breath. I need to think. My vision starts to clear; it's dark, but I can see the man in front of me. He's maybe in his forties—an unkempt beard covers most of his face. I try to take in as much information as I can—about him, about where I am, about what happened.

"Where did you find me?"

"You don't remember? That filthy place. The club."

"How did you manage that? You must be... highly skilled, for people not to notice... you taking someone."

"Nah. People looked away. You were passed out, they thought I was helping you."

"What did you put in my drink?"

"Something to tire you out. It should be wearing off soon."

He walks closer, and I say, "Please, I need to use the bathroom."

"Can't do anything about that."

I can see lights outside. This looks like a warehouse. I can't see the walls properly. I look at my feet. The floor is kind of wet—something leaked. Something reeks. And my purse is nowhere to be seen.

I decide to take another shot. I yell for help.

The man comes closer. "I'll shut you up if you scream again."

I yell again.

He's angry, he slaps me in the face. "The next one will hurt," he says, even though I'm pretty sure he's already left a mark on me.

"You are not supposed to hurt me," I remind him.

"He'll understand if you don't cooperate."

I let myself calm down, my face burning where his hands hit me with force.

I don't speak again for a while, I wait until my vision clears.

Whatever they gave me is gone now, and I feel every bit of the pain in my wrists, legs, and face.

I need a plan. Someone will notice I'm gone. Akira will know. I look around—she isn't here. I feel a flicker of relief. Hoyt knows we were at the club. Maybe he called me. No, it's late. He probably hasn't.

"I'll pay you," I tell the man. "Whatever he offered you, I'll double it."

He laughs. "It does sound like a good offer, but he'll find me. He's not the type you mess with."

"They'll know when I'm gone. My boyfriend will know. And he'll have you killed if you don't let me out."

"I don't think anyone's coming for you, little bunny. You were alone in the club, weren't you? If I were your boyfriend, I wouldn't have let you go dance like that—alone."

"He didn't know I was there, but he'll know when I don't come home."

"He didn't, huh? Then maybe you are worth the fun." He comes closer and uses his hand to feel me. He caresses my breasts and I want to vomit.

The man's touch brings something to mind—*Hoyt.* Would he know if I'm hurt? Could he sense it? Is he too far away? I'm not sure how his sixth sense works. I never asked about the distance. Maybe he'd only know if I were really injured. *I need to be in pain.*

I scream again, this time at the top of my lungs. The man lunges at me. He slaps me once, twice, three times. My chair falls back. "Bitch!" I hear the man say. I yell again.

"Do it again and you will regret it," he says, pulling my hair.

My head pounds. I can feel blood in my mouth and running from my nose. That has to be enough.

Whatever's on the ground is now all over me.

I realize: what could Hoyt even do if he knew? He's too far away. Even so, he knows I'm in the club. He'll call the cops. If he can sense me... two thousand miles away... *I'm too far.* I'm close to crying in desperation when I see the gate open.

I recognize him instantly. The red hair gives him away, even from behind. *Darion.*

"I told you not to touch her." He steps closer.

"Darion? Please, help me," I beg.

"What the fuck happened?" He asks the man, not making eye contact with me.

"She screamed. I had to shut her up."

"Fuck," Darion mutters, coming closer.

"Are you still high?" he asks me.

"No. Please, Darion, untie me."

He's looking at me head to toe. He attempts to touch my prism but he pulls back immediately. It burned him.

"Fuck! Make it stop!" he yells.

"What?" I ask.

"I need you to take it off," he demands.

"I'm not taking it off," I tell him.

"The hell you aren't."

"Is that why you brought me here?" I ask.

"You didn't know?"

"Know what?"

"That I was after it."

"What do you mean?"

"Years. We've been after you, after it, for years," he tells me impatiently.

"How... do you... know about it?"

"It's not time for stories. Now take it off!"

"You'll need to untie me first," I say.

"Fine." He pulls out an army knife and cuts the rope. I rub my hands together. "Now, take it off." He points the knife at me.

"I can't," I reply. I need to think—and fast.

"What do you mean you can't?"

"I can't. It doesn't... want to be off."

"Control it."

"I can't. I don't know how."

His eyes darken with anger. He kicks a chair nearby.

"If you think this is a game, you're very mistaken. I'll cut it off if I have to." He's yelling now.

"You know just as well as I do that it won't let you."

"Then tell me how you did it. How you... kindled it?"

"Kindled it?"

"Awakened it."

"I don't understand," I say. *I really don't.*

"Don't play dumb. I don't have time for this."

"I'm not. I don't know what you're talking about." That's the only plan I have—stall. For as long as I can, until someone finds me.

I have no weapons, no phone. All I have is this—this conversation.

"We tried for years. Nothing. You obviously figured it out. Tell me how you did it."

"What do you mean you tried for years?"

"How did you get it?" He's pissed, but he's willing to talk. I'll take it.

"My mother gave it to me." I have to give him some truth— enough to keep this going.

"It wasn't hers to give."

"What are you talking about?" *What is he talking about?!*

"She stole it."

"She would never."

"You have no idea who your mother was, do you?"

"I know she would never steal anything."

"I'm sorry to burst your bubble, but she did steal it."

"From who?"

"From my father."

"What? How do you know that? How do you even know she knew your father?"

"Because my father is her brother."

I let the information sink in.

"You're saying... you're my..."

"Cousin. Now, tell me, Iris, how did you do it?" I look at his red hair. Could he be telling the truth?

I'm still lost, trying to process what he said, when he yells, "Fuck! You really don't know, do you?"

I shake my head.

"You had to fuse yourself with it, otherwise it would've been a... dead diamond."

"I didn't do anything. I just put it on."

"Right. You think I'm stupid?" He pulls out a gun and brings it to my head.

"I swear Darion. I'll help you. Okay? Just put the gun away."

I don't have to fake it. I really am terrified.

I try to take the necklace off. I try to give it to him. But I can't —it's too painful. He sees it.

"You need to... disconnect first, defuse."

"How?"

"Fuck, Iris, you should know. Now, stop fucking around."

"I swear, Darion, I don't know."

"When you first put it on, what happened? Where were you?"

"I was in..." Awena's voice comes to mind. *You spilled blood. You spilled blood. You spilled blood.* When I cut my finger on the broken glass, that's when I saw the light. Maybe... that's what Darion wants to know. I can't tell him. But I have to give him something.

"I was in the bathtub, when... I felt something for the first time."

He grabs a bottle of water and throws it at me. The prism glows.

"Try to take it off now," he tells me, pointing the gun.

I really try. An intense jolt of pain hits me.

"What else, Iris? I know your brain, think."

"There was nothing else..."

"You know what? I'm tired of this. Bring the girl," he orders the man.

Frantically, I glance toward the door. *Please don't, please don't.*

I see Akira's bloody face and I want to kill him. "Let her go!" I yell.

"She'll make you talk..."

Her mouth is covered with tape. Her eyes lock with mine, begging for help.

"Now...where were we?" Darion walks closer to Akira and points the gun at her. "My father told me we needed you alive, but her... I'm free to do as I please."

"Darion, no!" I start yelling. "Fire! Fire! There was a candle." I know that the moment I mention the blood, Akira and I will both be dead.

"Do you have a lighter?" he asks the man behind him.

"In the car," the man replies.

"Go fucking get it," Darion orders him.

I have to think of a way out of this. A way to keep Akira alive.

"Darion, look at me. If you touch her, I swear, I'll die—but I won't tell you anything about this necklace. If you want answers about your father, you leave her out of this."

"I don't think you're in a position to negotiate."

"Do you want to risk it?"

I'm not sure if he buys it, but at least he moves away from her.

The man returns with the lighter.

"Give it to me," I tell him.

"The fuck I will." He brings it closer to my prism, and I brace myself. As soon as the flame gets near, I have to go. I close my eyes and focus on Hoyt—on his face, on him kissing me. I black out.

I find Hoyt in his study. He's on the phone, his hands covering his face. He's in too much pain. Broc is there, too. I have seconds. I make myself visible to both of them. Then I move. I have no idea if this is going to work.

I get closer to the wall, to his father's map, and try to go through it. It burns where I touch. I proceed faster and faster. I focus on being the light—my violet light. I move around the map, burning and forming the words *Darion, HAR*. I black out before I can add VARD.

When I wake up again, I see Darion staring at me. *Is he frightened?* My head hurts. I feel sick. How long was I gone?

"What the fuck happened?" he asks me.

I taste more blood. Akira's eyes are on me, barely blinking. I nod at her. I want her to know that I asked for help. I'm not sure if she picks up on my message.

"I blacked out. It hurt me—the flame, the prism."

Darion's angry and scared. I know he's growing desperate. Is it possible for Hoyt to find me? It's the middle of the night. It would take days to track Darion down. We don't have days. We have minutes. I need to do something else.

"I need to rest. I need a minute," I tell Darion. I feel weak, but luckily, whatever that strong smell on me is keeps me from passing out.

"I don't fucking have time for this," he says, looking away.

"Maybe... if you told me what you know... maybe we can figure this out together. I don't want to die, Darion. I want to give you my prism, I promise."

"Your what?"

"My prism. That's what I call it."

"Huh."

"What do you call it?"

"Amulet."

"What do you know about it?"

"I know that there are more. The prophecy says seven. My family has been looking for them for centuries. This one on your neck has been in their possession for a long time, but nobody could figure out how to fuse it. Your mother stole it and disappeared."

"Why didn't you take it before? You saw it, at the river, months ago."

"My father. He wanted to do this differently. He wanted to gain your trust, tell you about the family. He... wanted you to... join us. Help us. He thought there was a chance you wanted a family, since your mom was dead."

"Help you do what?"

"Use it, of course. And then find the other ones. He found you a couple of years ago, found out your mom was dead. He decided I should go to Harvard, get close to you. We weren't sure you actually even had the amulet—you never wore it. Not until last year. We knew if you did possess it, you hadn't fused with it. Or you would've had to wear it. We thought maybe your mom had passed it on to someone else. We waited. My dad said we had to play the long game. He's wrong. It was a waste of time. I grew tired of waiting."

"How many other... amulets does your family possess?"

"None of your business."

"I'm asking because... have they never... fused any of them?"

"They don't have other ones. They're still... tracking them."

"Why do you want them?"

"Are you kidding me? Why do we want the most powerful things on Earth?"

"What are you going to do with them?"

"Whatever we want."

"All it does is shine a light."

"If that's all you think it does, then you have no idea what's on your neck."

I realize he's right. I don't. "Then tell me."

"I'm done with the history lesson. You're the professor here. You tell me how to fuse this thing, or she's dead." He points the gun back at Akira, and she shakes.

I have one other idea. It's risky, but I have to try it.

"Let me try with the lighter again. Let me hold it this time."

Instead of holding it, I throw it on the floor. The flammable chemical ignites instantly.

This time, I don't think of Hoyt. I think of my light—my violet light only. And then I'm out. I'm out of the chair, out of my body. I'm shining in the air, right in front of them. The men are staring. I take a look at my body in front of me—my eyes are rolled up, white. Blood drips from my nose. I have to be fast.

I set a line of fire, separating the men and my body from Akira. I burn the tape that ties her hands and feet. She runs.

The men try to get around, but whatever chemical is on the ground is also everywhere else. The fire picks up quickly. I hear shots. I'll burn the whole place down if I have to. I keep moving, igniting more and more of the liquid on the ground.

I look at my body. It's surrounded by fire. The men are coughing, trying to reach me. They can't pass. But I can. I move toward my body. I burn the tape around my ankles and set myself free.

And then I open my eyes. I'm back in my body.

I'm too weak to run, but I manage to get up. Somehow, the prism creates a veil around me. I can't burn. I literally walk through the fire, *unbothered*. I hide, watching Darion and the other man try to find a way back into the building, a way back to me. I wait inside. *Hidden in the flames.* I stay there until they leave, until the cops show up. Until Aaron shows up.

THIRTY-FIVE

"FROM MY ROTTING BODY, FLOWERS SHALL
GROW, AND I AM IN THEM, AND THAT IS
ETERNITY." – EDVARD MUNCH

When I open my eyes again, I'm in the hospital. Everything hurts. My entire body is exhausted.

Aaron speaks from my left. "How are you feeling?"

"Akira..."

"She's okay. She's in the next room."

I nod. "How did you...?"

"Hoyt called. He told me to find you, to find Darion. I remembered you mentioning him from Harvard. I told the police. They were running license plates and IDs when we heard about the fire. Darion's family owns this place. We came as fast as we could."

"He..."

"He's gone. They'll find him, Iris. They will."

I know before he even says it. *It doesn't matter.* Even if they do find Darion, his family... They know. They know about my prism. They'll never stop until they have it. And I know I can't be without it. I have no other choice. *I have to run.*

I allow myself to feel scared for two breaths, then I shut it out.

I look at Aaron. "I need your help."

"Whatever you need, Iris."

"My apartment. I need you to go there, pack me some clothes,

321

shoes, my computer, my passport—it's in my bedside table—along with my mother's letter. Don't forget the letter. Bring it here as fast as you can."

"Where are you going?"

"I don't know yet. I can't be here, Aaron."

"Iris, you need the doctors."

"Aaron, please. I'm in danger."

His eyes are on me, scared. In spite of that, he leaves with my keys. I'm glad they found my bag at the club. I must have dropped it there.

The police come by to ask me questions. I give them descriptions. *How long do I have until Darion and his family find me again?*

I ask the nurse to take me to the room next door. I have to talk to her.

Akira's eyes open as I hold her hand.

"Are you okay? The fire? How did you get out?" she asks me.

"The prism—it somehow protected me from the fire."

"Iris, they ran. The police—"

"I know. Look." I grab both her hands. "I'm going away. I don't know for how long, but you can't come looking for me. Nobody can. Or you'll all be at risk."

She sits up higher. "You're not running away alone, Iris."

"I have to. I'm not letting anyone get hurt because of me."

"Iris, please, listen to me. I can go with you."

"Akira, you've done more than enough for me," I say, tears welling up. "Please, I still need one last favor."

"What?"

"I need to break up with Hoyt. I need your help convincing him that I... never loved him. Or he'll come looking for me. Darion doesn't know about him, about his prism; he would've said something if he did. I need to keep it that way. I can't ruin his life, his family. They have a life. You have a life. I don't want anyone to lose that because of me. Will you please help me?"

She nods, crying.

"I need to call him before he gets on a plane," I tell her.

"Iris?" Hoyt's voice is weak; he's been crying.

"I'm okay," I say.

"Oh, it's so good to hear your voice. Aaron told me you were in the hospital. I'm at the airport. I'll be there as soon as I can."

"No, Hoyt, don't."

"Don't what?"

"Don't come, please."

"Why?"

"I... don't want to see you."

"What happened, Iris?"

"Darion, I think he wanted to...rape us... He didn't. We are okay. Akira too."

"I need to see you."

"Hoyt, please. I..."

"What?"

"I can't do this... us."

"What do you mean?"

"I'm sorry, Hoyt. I just can't."

"Are you... breaking up with me? Over the phone?"

"Hoyt... I'm sorry, okay? Aaron is here. I'm not alone; he'll take care of me. I belong here, with him."

"Aaron?"

"It's always been him. I'm sorry, I've gotta go."

I let myself cry until the nurse comes to take me away. I ask her for another minute.

"Akira, please, promise you'll play along. Tell Hoyt you knew Aaron and I were still seeing each other. Please. If Darion or his family finds out about him, I..."

"I promise, Iris. Will you tell me where you're going?"

"I can't. For your own safety. I'll try to... I'll be okay." The nurse starts to move me, insisting that both Akira and I need rest.

323

Aaron arrives a little later. He has two bags instead of one. "I'm going with you," he says.

"No, you're not. Aaron, you can't."

"I'm not letting you go by yourself. You're still hurt."

I know he won't let me leave alone. *I should've thought of that.*

"We need to move now. Sign the papers, sign my release, please." We both do, acknowledging that we know the risks.

"Where do you want to go?" he asks me on the way to the airport.

"Somewhere they speak English."

He's searching on his phone for plane tickets. "London?"

"Sure."

I'm nibbling on some food he ordered for me while we wait to board.

"What happened there, Iris?" he asks.

I think about telling him, but I know it would put his life at risk. He knows so little about the prism. He could live a normal life.

"Nothing. You guys got there before they could do anything. They'd just gotten started."

"I'm so sorry, Iris. About everything. How did Hoyt know?"

"I texted him. I... used Akira's phone when they weren't looking."

"You didn't call the cops?"

"I...tried but I had to be quiet."

I ask the waiter to bring us drinks.

And then I wait.

As soon as Aaron leaves for the bathroom, I run. I buy a ticket for the first flight I can find where a visa isn't required. I'm on a plane minutes later.

I take my seat; luckily, there's no one next to me. I can't wait another second. I rip the edge of the envelope as the plane takes off.

Hi sweetheart,

Happy birthday! You're a woman now. I wish I could have been there —here—to see you grow up. I know you must have a lot of questions for me. I wish I could explain everything in person, but you're too young right now, and I don't have much time left. The doctors gave me weeks.

This necklace—my family called it an amulet—is not a normal piece of jewelry. It's special. It's been in my family for a long time. I took it from them. I knew they wouldn't use it for good, and I couldn't stand by their plans. This amulet contains power—yes, like magic. I know it sounds unbelievable. I remember when I first found out, too.

But take it seriously, Iris. This is not something to mess with. The energy in it is too powerful; it's impossible to control. Protect this amulet with everything you have—if it falls into the wrong hands, life as we know it may not endure. People will get hurt. I know it's a heavy burden to carry, but I believe in you. I always have. You can do hard things. Iris, whatever you do, never put it on. I know you'll be tempted, but fight it. And most importantly, never, ever let your blood touch it. It needs blood to awaken, to fuse with your soul. Once it's fused, the stone becomes crystallized, and you'll be connected to it for life.

Your father will answer your questions. I've told him all I know. Go easy on him. I had to ask him to wait until you were thirty to give this to you. I figured let you live a little first.

I love you so much, my ballerina, more than life.

Mom

A NOTE FROM BLAIR

Dear readers,
Thank you so much for choosing to read Crystal Iris. I poured my heart and soul into writing it, and I truly hope you enjoyed the book. If you did, I'd be incredibly grateful if you could leave a review. Your feedback means the world to me, and it helps new readers discover my series! After all, the best way to take a chance on a new book is when a friend recommends it.
Thank you again!
Until next time,
(*Crystal Iris – Book II* is coming soon).

Acknowledgments

A huge thank you to:
my family, for a lifetime of support and encouragement;
My husband, for being there every step of the way through this
and so many other crazy projects I dragged him into;
my son, for his unconditional love;
my first readers, for their time and enthusiasm;
the inner child in me, who naively pushed me to take the leap.

CONTENT WARNING

abuse/neglect
violence/blood/gore/vomit
death/suicide
drugs/alcohol
fire/guns/weapons
explicit sex

ABOUT THE AUTHOR

BLAIR M. SHADOWS is an old soul with a wild heart. A writer with a weakness for art, history, sweets, and caffeine. A mother who struggles with balancing all. And a wife who is, more often than not, overwhelmed by both love and her never-ending to-do list.
Blair has spent her fair share of years in NYC and LA and now lives in Texas with her husband and son.

ONLINE:
BlairShadows.com
INSTAGRAM: @blair.shadows
TIKTOK: @blairshadows
SPOTIFY Book Playlist: Blair Shadows - *Crystal Iris I*

Made in United States
North Haven, CT
31 December 2024